About

Marian Smith was born in Belfast and raised in Castlewellan, a small town in the north of Ireland. She has two sons. Working as a Spiritual Counsellor for over twenty years, she practises New Age Counselling. She runs a private practice from home, using mediumship, astrology, numerology, past life regression, energy healing, counselling and dream analysis. She also channels messages from the Angelic and Ascended Master Realms during sessions.

This is Marian's first book, encouraged by a desire to reach a bigger audience and deliver spiritual insights into the life of a medium and healer, in the hope it might inspire and inform those seeking such knowledge.

AND SO IT WAS

MARIAN SMITH

AND SO IT WAS

Vanguard Press

A CIP catalogue record for this title is
available from the British Library.

ISBN 978 1 80016 324 9

*Vanguard Press is an imprint of
Pegasus Elliot MacKenzie Publishers Ltd.*
www.pegasuspublishers.com

First Published in 2022

**Vanguard Press
Sheraton House Castle Park
Cambridge England**

Printed & Bound in Great Britain

Dedication

To my amazing sons. Two of the brightest stars to drop onto the Earth.

Acknowledgements

With deepest gratitude to the Ascended Masters, Spirit, Angelic and Enlightened beings who are always by our side. Without their knowledge, this book may never have found a voice.

Special thanks to J.E. Bennett for the front cover illustration and for the many enchanted journeys around the park.

Chapter One
October 2003

Rose McGrath rubbed her ageing hands against the smarting cold blasting in from the Irish Sea. Not one inch of Delaney County Park's two hundred acres of land was shielded from the unsympathetic gusts. Trying to find protection from it was next to impossible.

Lillie Pond did have trees and sturdy bushes surrounding it. Coupled with a wooden bench, sitting there brought the best opportunity for shelter and rest. Besides, Rose surmised, Andrew insisted they waited in this very spot every day they came to the park, until his playmate made an appearance.

'Andrew!' Rose panicked when he walked too close to the water's edge. 'Step back,' she ordered the forty-four-year-old Down's Syndrome man. 'You'll get your feet soaked again.'

Andrew didn't look pleased. Having to give up his pebble skimming in favour of dry feet was a hefty price to pay for his aim to be the best. Practice made perfect, as Ellen told him many times. If anybody knew that, she definitely would. If not for her he'd never have learned about the sport in the first place. She was the best – and only – he'd seen play it.

11

Up the narrow, steep hill and hidden from view, the same Ellen O'Hare puffed and plodded her way towards the pond area. She'd just climbed a vertical mound herself – in her opinion, equivalent to a baby mountain – and was feeling both elated because she'd made it and breathless because, oh boy, that was hard.

She stood at the top of the mount, rewarding herself with a breather. Looking down at the hill she'd just climbed never failed to bring a treat to her senses, regardless of the weather.

The scene was electrifying. Not once, in the many, many trips around this park, had its allure ever failed to delight. Hail, snow, sun or wind, the Irish sea, folding along the edge of the carpeted emerald fields and bushy woodlands, brought pleasure beyond what any material gain could ever achieve.

Miles and miles of pastures, supporting forests and countryside with nature kissed walks, smiled down to the blue current of water below its hills and valleys. The animals residing there enjoyed rich grasses and hedges to feed upon, nourished by the clear, unpolluted crisp air that complemented the salty climate.

Inhaling greedily several times helped her gain a little momentum to continue. Ellen looked around for her companion, searching against the confines of her newly purchased, large collared, rain proof jacket.

'Moby!' She'd found him. Having to shout against the bursts of wind whirling down the hillside took grit.

'Wait for me,' she wheezed, 'and leave that dead crow alone!'

Of course, Moby ignored her, preferring to practice his doggie duties without human interference. He'd picked up the scent of the unfortunate bird's demise from the minute they'd started the climb. Nothing would stop him from investigating.

Ellen hesitated on her walk towards Moby, just long enough to realign her hat down over her ears and her blonde, shoulder length hair that had escaped the scarf's confinement.

'Please don't do that,' she pleaded with Moby beside the corpse. 'You'll catch a flu or something worse and then where will we be, eh?'

Andrew's voice carried up from the pond area encouraging Moby to find him. It saved having to physically drag him away. His ears pricked up, listening. The voice came again. There was no mistaking it this time.

Leaving a spray of dust with his departure, Moby raced ahead. He too was keen to start play time and knew the routine well. They'd been practising the same thing for quite a while now. It was well rehearsed.

By the time Ellen caught up with Rose, Andrew and Moby were in full swing. With a swim out to fetch the stick thrown (Moby), a blast of excited cheers from its thrower (Andrew) and a sneeze and then a smile coming her way from Rose, Ellen took a seat beside her older friend, glad of the rest.

'You look frozen.' She rubbed Rose's upper arms, hoping to warm some cold blood. 'Have you been waiting long?'

'Nearly an hour,' Rose complained. 'Andrew was throwing a hissy fit to get here from seven this morning.' She looked agitated. 'There was no convincing him it was way too early. He's huffing with me now.'

The extensive age difference between the two women was irrelevant in their friendship to them both. With old souls, age played little part in compatibility.

When they'd met in this same country park, in roughly the same space they sat in now, a year ago to the day next week, not only had Rose and Ellen connected, but Andrew and Moby too.

With a simple 'hello' exchanged between them both, and a comment or two on the rainy weather, Moby's reluctance to leave a playful Andrew forced both of them to extend their chat to other topics.

Rose explained Andrew's love for animals and his devastation at their own collie dog passing away the month before.

'I'm not keen on getting another dog,' she explained. 'I'd be left with the biggest part of its care and I'm getting on in years. It's quite a commitment.'

'Let's sit and they can play for a while.' Ellen felt sympathy for Rose. 'Might save you having to defend your new dog decision if play is all Andrew wants.'

From that simple conversation to present day, their friendship evolved. On their many chance meetings, they chatted effortlessly and easily about everything under the sun (and once under the full moon, on a bright November afternoon).

Four or five times weekly, the routine was established between the small group. Two of them played games, while the other two got caught up and explored old and new subjects. It was working out well for all concerned. And so, it was founded.

Of course, Rose was known to a few of Ellen's family members. On occasion, her two sons, Matt and James, would accompany her around the park, school holidays permitting. She'd also met Ellen's mum, Anna. Similar in age, both she and Rose clicked immediately.

Anna, a sun-sign born Gemini personality, brought flightiness and flavour to their giggly chats. Rose and Andrew ended the McGrath name, with no family left behind them. It was a pleasure to be included in both Ellen and Anna's household events.

With Anna's husband, Eddie, in spirit, her time since was filled completely with her three daughters and one son. All of the girls were well settled with partners and children but having a big family gathering from time to time helped Anna feel needed.

'So.' Rose nudged Ellen from her dreamy state into current reality. 'How are the plans going for Maeve's visit?'

'Oh, good gracious.' Anna was expecting her older sister's arrival that very day. 'Mum has us all cleaning and decluttering her house since the weekend. My poor hands are full of welts.' She held them out for examination. 'I'm expecting hard skin any day now.'

'I think its arrived, dear,' Rose teased. 'Those fingers look like sandpaper.'

'Nobody likes a wise ass, Rose.' Ellen returned the banter. 'Rein it in, or I'll toss you in the pond.'

'I'll try my best but it ain't gonna be easy. I'm wise by nature, not choice.'

'Thanks for that.' Ellen nudged Rose's elbow. 'You're a real buck eejit, don't you know.'

'Guilty as charged.'

Ellen and Rose laughed out loud at their repartee. They'd similar styles of humour, also discovered from the get go. It was great to have the superficial gone, with no need for pretence.

Silently though, inside Ellen's core sighed a great big moan. She was concerned – had been for months now – about her marriage to Fergal. They'd rowed that very morning over his lost van keys. The tiniest little details were exploding into lava eruptions between them.

Of course, it didn't help that she'd called him a prat when he blamed her for shifting his van keys from their usual spot. Nor was it a good sign when he'd slammed the front door to an inch of losing its hinges on his way out of it. Things were not great. It did not feel good.

Fergal was a builder. A lot of his work demanded contracts be sought out, most of which were secured overseas. Being apart for weeks at a time was both a blessing and a discomfort. But those kinds of things took their toll.

Ellen was a freedom loving, independent Sagittarian, Fergal a self-sufficient Aries. The gaps between family togetherness suited both parties, mostly, so they made it work (for the biggest part). It was difficult, though, to re-establish momentum when he was home for longer periods. She'd have a routine established that he'd have to adjust to. It was not always an easy ride. Arguments ensued regularly between them, of all sizes and proportions.

Last year's very lucrative contract in England had provided substantial profits; there were advantages to be had. The contract was the main reason for their move to a bigger house, by way of investment.

However, since said move, nothing had felt right between them. Fergal seemed a lot more restless when he did get home. Ellen felt the shift between them in her bones, as the distance grew wider.

The boys enjoyed the added space with the new location: basketball hoop on the driveway; bigger bedrooms for computer stations. Ellen loved the big kitchen, en-suite bathrooms and reception areas, yet never felt it was home.

With a double garage, large back garden with decking and patio area, Fergal had extra room available to store tools and park his Transit van. In their last home, they'd had a simple driveway that held little else but their two vehicles, at a pinch.

Moby enjoyed 'his' bigger garden; pesky birds included. Matt was closer to his school friends and James a stone's throw from the golf club (his second favourite sport).

On paper, everything in their new abode seemed ideal; the stereotypical, successful urban family. In reality, it wasn't so amazing.

Ballygo Town offered most everything a growing family needed. Schools, shops, leisure centre and clubs were all within walking distance. Heck, there was even a cinema being built, breaking ground that very week. All seemed serene yet looks were often deceiving. Time would tell if all would hold together.

Rose McGrath was a wise woman. What she lacked in youth, she far outshone in perception. Her short, permed, white hair was thinning and wiry in places from age. Her deep hazel brown eyes told tales of hardship and strife, never once losing their intensity and vitality for life, regardless of how difficult things hit.

Dark eyebrows, speckled with occasional dots of grey, spoke of once natural beauty, hidden now behind lines and wrinkles, covering her oval face.

A sun-sign born Cancerian, sensitive to more than anyone would ever guess, she came with displays of natural empathy, shown in immeasurable amounts.

Rose's ageing bones had created bumps between the shoulder blades and twists in her fingers and thumbs where none resided before. Her once slim five-foot five stature was now shrunk into a plump physique, taking away a few noticeable inches of height.

A spinster all her seventy-one years, she regretted nothing, at least not in that area anyway. Born into a simple life to modest country parents, Rose was their youngest daughter. She lived where she'd been raised to this very day; in a cottage lacking great luxury, yet practical and down to earth, nonetheless.

Rose knew Ellen was worried. She felt it in her very core. At thirty-six years old, the five-foot six woman with long blonde hair and green eyes had maturity way beyond earthly progressions.

She'd noticed her younger companion's furrowed frowns increasing in their appearance over the past while. She'd heard the odd hidden promptings in her stories about 'Fergal saying this' or 'Fergal doing that' and knew all was not as positive as it could be between them. But, until Ellen sought her counsel, there was little to do but wait.

'What time does Maeve's plane land, then?' Rose enquired, referring to Anna's sister again. 'Are you still doing pick-up?'

'I am.' Ellen was looking forward to her aunt's arrival. She hadn't seen her mum's only sibling in years. Maeve had been living in England since marriage. Now her own husband was a late one, time had afforded her the freedom to visit.

'I'll need to leave soon.' Ellen gave warning, knowing Andrew wouldn't take lightly to his time with Moby being cut short. 'Mum and I should be at the airport for Maeve's three thirty arrival.'

'I'll promise extra television time for him.' Rose already had a plan. She had known instinctively Ellen and Moby wouldn't be hanging around the park today for long. 'I've fresh bananas and his favourite ice-cream for splits later. We'll cope. Don't keep yourself late.'

'You're a star.' Ellen stood to go. 'I'll likely be around tomorrow again if you're here?'

'Should be. We'll play it by ear.'

Andrew was furious. Banging stones into the water, causing quite a splash back, brought no harm to anyone but himself. He pulled faces, punched the air and finally ran behind a tree trunk, hiding from Rose's view.

'Boy's a dear.' She rolled her eyes skywards. 'Andrew... please quit faffing about!' Lack of sleep the night before dictated Rose's degree of patience now. Normally used to Andrew's mood swings, he was pulling at her very last string.

Moby was soaked to his flesh and whiffed a bit, as he and Ellen took their leave amid Rose's shouts of "*Star Wars Trilogy*" and "*creamy dessert promises*," to little avail.

'Oh dear,' Ellen felt bad leaving Rose to sort things out. 'I'm sorry,' she mouthed towards her friend, who smiled the resigned grin of a woman well used to such antics. 'See you soon.'

Time to see what the rest of that day brought their way.

CHAPTER TWO

'Hi, it's me,' Ellen called, entering her mother's home with a trip over the doorstep and a stumble down the hallway, clumsy Sagittarian style. 'I've brought Brad Pitt with me.'

'In here, Ellen,' Anna called from the kitchen. 'Baking up delights and calorie laden treats galore. Our hips will waggle well, in the weeks to come!'

Having deposited Moby back home, with a fresh bone to chew and a cosy bed to snooze on, Ellen felt confident the big dog wouldn't fret until either her or the boys got back. He was dry, tired out and content.

The intense smell of freshly cooked cakes and pastries increased tenfold when Ellen opened the kitchen door. Some of its aroma floated into and around the rest of the house. 'Wow.' She was consumed. 'My mouth's watering.'

Anna looked pleased.

'Excellent,' she approved. 'The exact effect I wanted to create.'

Looking expectantly behind Ellen, she faked a search. 'Where's Brad?' she asked innocently. 'I was looking forward to meeting him.'

'Hidden in the car boot for later,' Ellen joked, biting into one of the freshly iced buns from the cooling rack on the kitchen counter. 'Every girl needs a treat now and again,' She munched happily. 'I'm simply securing mine.'

Anna smiled at the humour. She unconsciously rubbed flour covered hands through naturally streaked, greying hair. Grown to shoulder length, Anna looked livelier than most her age.

'You look like a cotton bud,' Ellen teased. 'Your hair's dotted with white.'

'Away with you,' she scolded, walking towards the hall mirror to check. 'Jane Fonda has nothing on me, sure.' One of her mum's favourite actors to model herself on.

The fresh tomatoes, crusty bread and cheese they ate for lunch were truly scrumptious. Ellen would have loved a third piece. The walk had added appetite. She eyed the biggest chunk of bread lying in the basket. Her mind played havoc, as she battled with desire and the voice in her head.

'Best not.' The voice won hands down. 'I'm on a diet and besides,' she strengthened her reserve, 'no point walking three miles four times a week, if I'm not going to watch what I eat.'

'Diet indeed.' Anna tutted disapprovingly. 'The very notion restricts and punishes the mind,' she lectured. 'If you're hungry, have it for goodness sake.'

'I shouldn't,' Ellen persisted, torn between heeding her mother and honouring the deepest of desires to flatten her tummy. 'I've so many clothes that don't fit.'

'So, buy new ones.' Anna's naturally slim figure knew nothing of Ellen's constant battle of the bulge. Ellen only had to look at food and it showed. Anna always ate what she wanted.

'You know I have Dad's metabolism,' Eddie was no slim Jim. 'Gemma and Conor have yours... lucky buggers.'

'That's true.' Anna's family were divided by both parents' genetics. Ellen and Kate were always heavier than Gemma and Conor, even as kids. Kate seemed to carry the most weight, by all accounts finding it harder each diet, to shift the pounds.

'If we're worried about something, it can cause us to over indulge with all sorts of things.' Anna offered an alternative to food cravings. 'Is all okay with you?'

'Yep,' Ellen answered, a little too quickly with the lie. 'All's grand, thanks.' She'd say no more about that thank you very much, especially to Anna.

Thing was, Anna liked Fergal a lot. She'd voiced her opinion on him many times over the years, sticking up for him when Ellen complained, taking his side even when she didn't. Ellen had no intention of sharing marital concerns. Anna simply wouldn't be neutral. Staying shtum it was.

'So, tell me how goes it with the book?' Ellen changed the subject entirely. 'Do you love astrology as much as me now?'

'Umm.' Anna scoffed down a slice of beefy tomato. 'I'd like to say I do, my dear,' she slurped a sip of tea, 'but I'd be lying. It's really complicated!'

'Ach, Mum.' Ellen didn't hide her obvious disappointment. She had loved planetary shifts and personal horoscope charts from as far back as she could recall. The night stars held such appeal. 'Are you serious?'

'Fraid so, sweet cheeks. It's not my thing.'

'Even the houses and nodes?'

'Even those.'

'Sun sign, moon or ascended traits?'

'Yep.'

'Shocker… I really thought…'

'More tea?'

'Not for me.'

Anna knew Ellen was let down. She wished another answer was possible, but it simply was not. She'd read, re-read and then leafed through the book Ellen left her, but zilch connected. The longer she tried coming to terms with the information in it, the fuzzier her thoughts grew.

Anna also knew her youngest daughter had gifts the rest of her family didn't. From a young age, she'd watched her chat to many imaginary friends, predict future events (global and personal) and intuitively have responses that books, and other teachings didn't.

'The master guides told me,' she'd answer when questioned about her source. 'They know everything. You just need to ask and look and listen for the signs, that's all.'

'You don't think we should have her tested for schizophrenia or the likes, do you?' Eddie would ask Anna occasionally, particularly when freaked out as another of Ellen's predictions came to fruition. 'It's all a bit weird or something.'

'Catch a grip, man, dear,' Anna scolded. 'I was similar when younger. Difference was my folk wouldn't allow it. Our daughter's fine,' she reassured her frightened husband. 'Just encourage confidence and don't make it weird.'

'It's hard not to, especially when she's giving me messages from my brother.' He had passed away the previous year. 'She would never have known about the fort we built when younger or the socks we stuffed apples into after an orchard raid.'

'I know it's hard but just go with the flow.'

Dismissing Eddie's concerns so readily was important for Ellen's gift to grow. Anna knew this, having had her own intuitiveness repressed from as young as five years old by her family.

It was true that generations differed considerably. When Anna was young, religious practices were global and community stronger than the current day. Such things as intuition, meditation, energy healing or yoga were undervalued (and misunderstood) considerably, in favour of doctrines and repressions.

Never in a millennial of Sundays would Anna's parents inspire or motivate their youngest to strengthen her insights. Behaviour that didn't conform was considered sinful, verging on black magic.

'The dead are at peace.' Anna remembered to this day the sternness of her mother's words, when offered a message from her late grandfather. 'Let them be. You're committing a mortal sin with this talk. Away with you and have nothing more about it.'

For years after, Anna kept quiet, trying desperately to repress her natural urges and shut down spiritual insights and messages. It had not been easy one little bit, especially at school and during religious education classes. Her remark that 'The Bible doesn't have all the answers' landed her two days in detention.

When she actively told the head of year there was 'no such thing as hell' and that 'sin was a man-made principle,' he protested so strongly, her parents were called to the school for an urgent meeting. One month later and she was un-grounded, with a set of new rules laid out for 'future acceptable behaviour'.

Down the years, Anna rebelled regardless, often stretching her conduct to an inch within said boundaries. Little would deter her from personal opinions, earning her a reputation of impertinence, with a subsequent nickname of "Motormouth."

With Ellen's birth and later discovery, it seemed a second chance had been rewarded. As far as Anna was concerned, this time around, no gift horse would be looked in its mouth and things would be very different.

With Eddie's untimely passing, Ellen made his loss that bit easier to accept with her messages from him. Having it verified that is was Eddie leaving feathers everywhere and flicking lights at night, was reassuring rather than unsettling.

Of course, not all family members were on board. Gemma and Kate were wary about it all, often leaving the room when talk of spirit (or the likes) came up. Conor was indifferent, listening without comment.

Now, as soon as lunch was finished, the airport trip loomed heavily. Anna had started to show signs of nerves felt earlier, as she tittered on about nothing much – a proven sign she was unhinged – and then visibly started to shake a little. It seemed this visit of Maeve's was causing quite a stir, both emotionally and mentally.

Her home was crisper and cleaner than any hospital or nursing home, sterilised within an inch of its life for fear of judgement, Anna was made all the more apprehensive for the build-up.

'You okay, Mum?' Ellen asked, noticing how pale her mum had gone in the space of minutes. 'You seem on edge.'

'Umm.' Anna hesitated. 'Would it be bad mannered if I stayed home instead?' She asked uncomfortably from a place of fear. 'My stomach's tying knots at the thought of meeting her.'

'Really?'

'Umm.'

'How come?'

'You've no idea what growing up was like for me, Ellen. Maeve was a terrible bully, you know. It's the biggest reason why we're not close.'

'I didn't know.'

'The thought of her coming has me walking on eggshells.'

'Goodness, that bad?'

'Fraid so.'

'Stay.'

'You think I could?'

'I do. Make chamomile tea to help settle the nerves. Here.' Ellen searched deep into her bag. 'Dab this jasmine oil on your wrists a few times. It'll help soothe the mind.'

'Great, thanks.' Phew, off the hook. Funny old fears, running riot all day long, had found a voice and were granted a simple solution. 'I'll call Conor while you're gone.' He always provided grounded reassurance, Virgo style. 'Thanks, Ell.'

'Ask him if he'll be home for Christmas.' Ellen knew her brother was getting it tough in a few key areas of his life. 'It'll be great to see him after so long.'

'I will. Drive safely and put a…'

'White shield around myself and the car,' Ellen finished off, well versed in the routine. 'I have it covered already.'

A real hum-dinger lay ahead.

CHAPTER THREE

Before Anna had a chance to lift the telephone receiver, its shrill pierced the stillness.

Startled by the unexpected explosion into the otherwise quiet house, she clutched her chest with fright.

'Holy Moley!' Her hand gripped the new cashmere sweater, recently purchased for Maeve's benefit. 'Why in the name of Moses am I so on edge?' Was Maeve's visit worth all this added stress? It would need to be.

Conor McDowell's deep, manly voice, sounded excited greeting his mother.

'It's great to hear your voice.' He felt instant connection. 'I'm missing you all so much that it's turning me into a big girl's blouse.'

'Turning?'

'Ha-ha.'

The thirty-year-old man had been finding it difficult to settle in France. In the three months, two weeks, four days, seven hours and thirty-four... no, wait... thirty-five minutes since he'd arrived there, tears, tantrums and haggling were occasional issues.

'It's because you made my life too comfortable when I was at home,' he said. 'I'm not used to roughing it now.'

'You were also taught how to get a grip,' Anna retorted. 'Tough love, baby. Stay focused to achieve your dreams.'

Conor was always so down to earth, practical and independent. It was as much a surprise to him, as to his family, that it was taking longer for him to settle in France than expected.

Hands down, he was in love with the place; who wouldn't be? Dainty French architecture; fluffy, cotton white ocean waves beating off the fine-grained sands; colourful mountain villas that glinted and sparkled when the sun hit the right spots... Nice was nothing if not a true artist's paradise.

Conor knew he was lucky to be here. He saw that having the chance to experience the world in the way he had – Cuba, Mexico, South America, most of Europe and some of Asia, so far – was a gift that many would never know. Grateful to his very backbone for it all, home was home. His Irish roots were hard to beat.

'What's up?' Anna asked. 'Is all okay?'

'Yes,' Conor lied, because he was emotionally struggling. 'Just thought I'd check in.'

'Okay. Very good. You've just missed Ellen. She's off to collect Maeve.'

'You didn't go?'

'Umm, I thought it might be better to have tea and a bite ready instead.'

'Okay. Won't Maeve be expecting you, though?'

'Naw. Shouldn't think she'd mind.'

'Are you sure? From what you've said she's a stickler for tradition.'

'Let it go, Conor.' Enough of the analysing. 'Any more of this and there'll be none of it.'

'Fair enough. You're okay though, right?'

'I'm grand. Handling things my way. Now, what's the craic with you?'

They chatted and joked their way through a conversation. Was everyone well? Mostly. Who'd passed away in Ballygo recently? Anna narrated, while Conor yawned. And how was he getting on with work?

'I managed to get time off at Christmas,' he announced. 'I'll be home for a few days this year. Given his job, it was something close to a miracle. He'd missed the past two.

This lean, six foot three, brown haired, dark eyed man was Anna's youngest and only son. Irish mothers were amongst the most protective of their sons. She was no exception.

When all was said and done, wrapping him in cotton wool had, at times, caused controversy with her daughters.

'It's not that I love Conor more than you,' Anna answered Gemma's (and sometimes Kate's) accusations of favouritism, many times in the past. 'It's that he's the youngest. I still consider him the baby.'

Conor had taken his father's passing exceptionally hard. For months on end, after Eddie had finally succumbed to cancer, Conor stopped speaking altogether. He was twenty at the time, just shy of his twenty first birthday.

Nothing worked. Therapy (herbal, cognitive and counselling), medication (private and National Health Service) and a trip to Wicklow (over two-hundred-mile round journey) to see a man with a cure, failed to reinstate his verbal interaction.

Anna was beside herself with worry. Devastated and nursing her own grief – Eddie and she had been attached at the hip – had to take many backseats, until Conor was sorted. His hair began to fall out in clumps after the third month of silence.

He lost weight, so much so she feared anorexia. His personal hygiene sunk to new lows – bribery worked when body odour appeared – and he hardly slept, wandering the house at all hours of the morning and late night.

Eight months into the dark side, Anna passed Eddie's shaving kit and leather strapped watch to her son. Sitting on his bed, listening to the weirdest music, (if you could call it that), she entered the bedroom and handed them over.

'He'd have loved you to have them.' She extended the items to him lying on the bed. 'Not sure if the watch is your style or not. It'll make a good keepsake nonetheless.'

An hour later, he walked into the living room, where they were all enjoying the sitcom *Will and Grace*, sat down and asked what was for dinner. Anna nearly choked on the biscuit she'd just popped in her mouth. The three girls stared at him like he was an alien. Wearing Eddie's watch did the trick. Obviously, his dad was helping.

'Not sure about that.' Gemma strongly disputed the claim when Anna commented on their dad's intervention. 'Welcome back, weirdo. We thought you'd done a runner there.'

That same guy was now moving mountains. Not only was he travelling the world – well had started too – he'd just secured an apartment in Nice that had come alongside his restaurant job. He sounded well pleased with himself, telling Anna how he'd made new friends and was known widely as the Irish Paddy.

'They mock my broad brogue.' He mimicked the French and Irish drawl for Anna's benefit. 'Think I might settle here for a bit. See how it works out.'

Naturally, things developed into a more serious note when Conor asked about Gemma. He knew she'd been causing semi-sleepless nights for Anna; she'd confided in him in their last phone chat. He wanted to help find a solution.

'Kate and Ellen tell me they think she's hitting the bottle a bit too hard again.' This was not a new problem. 'I wish I knew how to better handle it.'

'Have you spoken to her about your worries?' That was a big request where Gemma was concerned. She was difficult to approach, snappy and snarly like a demented terrier. 'Might help to let her know you know.'

'Oh God.' The very thought brought a cold sweat. 'She'd devour me.'

'Well, Mum,' practical as always, 'nothing more to do than wait until she asks.'

When things ran their natural course, their phone catch up reached its conclusion. Anna promised she'd call in a few days to fill him in on Maeve's visit and Conor told her not to ring on a Monday or Tuesday evening, when he had late shifts. They exchanged endearments of love and hung up.

For a while, the jumping jacks in her solar plexus had taken time out for lunch. Now they were back, this time with a vengeance.

She checked her reflection in the hall mirror for the second time that morning. Picking an imaginary hair off the new peach jumper, Anna walked to the kitchen, coaxing herself into tea with a shot of whiskey. It might help.

It seemed to. Twenty minutes later, as she lay back into what was Eddie's recliner chair, she felt sleepy with the effect of the sizeable measure of whiskey. Closing her eyes brought flashing white and yellow spots temporarily into focus.

Suddenly a rush of cold air leapt across her face, taking her breath away. Although this happened regularly, it never ceased to shock. Eddie McDowell was in the building.

She felt his presence, tall and commanding, standing at her side. The smell of Old Spice aftershave, his favourite, wafted in the atmosphere. He'd called to say hello when Anna's reserves were lowered from the whiskey.

'I miss you here,' she whispered through closed eyes. 'Every single minute of every long day. When my time's up and I join you, you're in for a hiding, leaving me so soon.'

It felt (a little) comforting to know her husband was never far away. Maybe she'd doze for ten minutes. He could join her in dreamland, where nothing was restricted and where they could dance.

One of their most favourite things to do.

CHAPTER FOUR

The shrill of the doorbell wakened her from her slumber. Anna hadn't been fully under but felt annoyance her sleep was so rudely interrupted, nonetheless.

Dizzy on her way out of the chair, she reached to steady herself before continuing. The bell rang again. She tutted at the caller's impatience.

'Hold your horses, frig sake.' The command echoed around the hallway. 'I'm coming.' This better be worth it, mood she was in.

It wasn't. Her next-door neighbour, Ida McCracken's grandson, visiting from Canada, wanted permission to retrieve his football from her back garden. Considering it was his fourth trip there in as many days, without asking, she wondered why the manners now.

'My gran said I mustn't trespass.' The Canadian accent sounded strange standing in Ireland. 'I'm sorry to disturb you.'

Now she was up, sleep time was over. Wide awake and ready for another cuppa, Anna knew she'd be the bathroom's biggest visitor that day. Small bladders were one thing: weak ones a whole new contest altogether.

There was a chunk of time left before Ellen returned. The house didn't need attention by any means. The outdoors was blowing strong winds, some robust enough to knock her over, so gardening was a non-starter. She'd baked all the goodies planned. They were boxed and labelled, residing in the cupboard. She was at a loss.

Eddie had issued few strict rules in his day. A firm, at times unyielding cardinal personality, his Libran desire for balance displayed itself in structure and discipline without control.

One of these policies that stood the test of time was no television before five o'clock, come hail, rain or sun. Since his passing it had stuck and was now an assumed trait, not just in Anna's home, but in all her family's houses too.

Anna was restless and didn't have the constitution to sit and read. The earlier tiredness had worn off, though not the whiskey to calm her, thankfully.

She lifted a magazine. *House and Gardens*, (for Maeve's benefit again, to look posh) and leafed through it. Unimpressed with the content she threw it to the side.

Looking around, she wondered what she should do. Keeping her mind busy was crucial. Any unaccounted-for time to ponder, would surely turn into dread.

And then it struck her. It had been a while, years really, since she'd allowed her little box from the past to surface. Given the visit, there was no better time than the present to let it see daylight again.

Her bedroom wasn't particularly spacious. The queen size bed barely allowed room for the large double wardrobe at the bottom of it. She'd squeezed it in regardless.

Fergal and Donal (Gemma's husband) tried convincing her there just wasn't the room for the big pine cupboard. Donal stained his groin pretty badly fitting it as well. But in it went. Anna was victorious in her determination.

Standing on tip-toes, Anna tunnelled her way through the top shelf which bulged with hats, handbags, belts, scarves and gloves. She finally felt the cardboard box, right at the very back, hidden.

With a free hand, the box was extracted to the front of the shelf, tipping a few items onto the floor with its unveiling. She'd put them back later.

Back in the kitchen, the box sat glaring at her from the glass table. It was tattered and frayed at the sides from years of use, secured with three large elastic bands to keep it tightly closed.

Given it was almost as old as she was herself –well, she'd a good twelve years ahead of it – it was nothing short of a miracle it hadn't collapsed already.

She deliberated its opening. Was she ready to return to memory lane, a place that grew brambles and nettles instead of roses and daisies? Her upbringing hadn't been cruel, more mundane and restrictive. Freedom was scarce, liberation just a word.

Maeve was the eldest and her only sibling. There'd been talk – hushed, of course – down the years of her parents losing a baby boy, born three months prematurely, between the girls' arrivals. A dysfunctional weak heart, the cause. Discussions afterwards were few and far between, as it was in those days. Two daughters completed the family of four.

Maeve despised Anna from the get go. Given the eight years' age difference, this new kid on the block disrupted her life, taking away attention, stealing focus and generally making her life a living misery. As far as Maeve was concerned, Anna was the devil incarnate. She treated her accordingly.

In the past, many tales of jealousy, anger, rejection and envy provided a springboard for Anna to never want anything else to do with her sister.

She'd had a lonely upbringing, playing with her dolls alone, rejected in the schoolyard to stand deserted – Maeve bullied others, saying they weren't to go near her – with nips, bruises and cuts galore, when things turned physical. It was childhood hell, brought on by nothing but sibling bitterness.

Anna sighed. She opened the shoebox and glanced inside. Pictures of her parents wedding day, looking sombre and serious, stared back. A white lace ribbon from her first communion, turned yellow at the edges.

Miniature bits and bobs collected down the years accompanied birthday card collections, starting at age fourteen (with some years missing), lay haphazardly on top of one another, most discoloured and crackled with age.

When the handful of tiny pebbles collected at the box corner came into view, Anna stopped and stared. Immediately transported back to the very day she'd collected them, the locusts jumped into action, poking her ribcage and making her feel sick. The fear was still lodged after all these years.

The family had been visiting her dad's sister's house, one bright, breezy Sunday in August. The countryside, where their large two-storey house overlooked the farm, was at its peak. Grasses were full, trees and bushes sprung wild flowers of all descriptions and there was the forest close by, ideal for two young girls to go off and play in.

'Let's pretend you're my hostage,' Maeve coaxed, playing out a scene from a movie they'd recently watched. 'I'll tie your hands behind your back and shove this in your mouth.'

Desperate to have the approval of her older sister, and biggest enemy, Anna reluctantly agreed. She'd have done a lot of things to win favour.

'Please don't do anything scary.' Her pleading was based on many previous occurrences. 'It frightens me.'

'Don't be silly,' Maeve assured slyly. 'I promise you'll get nothing more than you can handle.'

The blindfold across her eyes, the stinking rag shoved in her mouth, the tight rope gluing her wrists behind her back were painful, but durable. Anna knew if this was as bad as it got, she was brave enough to stand the effect.

Allowing her small body to be guided, Maeve's demands to 'move it' accompanied by the shrugs and thumps to her back and shoulders were painful – her sister's pretend stick gun – yet she successfully held her resilience.

When the final push came, it brought with it two unforgettable memories. The first was the lack of control as her legs left solid ground, falling down the deep hole. The second was the unbelievable pain that struck her head, hitting and then bouncing off a large stone, buried under the soil.

The blackness that resulted from the blow rendered her unconscious. Six hours later, they found her concussed, but still alive. Maeve claimed she'd wandered off with no clue as to where.

Frantic with worry, the police were called, their search soon discovering Anna's unfortunate episode.

Apparently, the hole had been dug to bury animal carcasses ages ago. It was now covered over by tree branches and brambles, making it difficult to find and placed there purposely by Maeve to divert the search.

'You got what you deserved,' Maeve told Anna later. 'Witches are evil,' she accused. 'You belong to Satan.'

It took years for Anna to be able to sleep in the dark afterwards. Even now, a hall lamp was left on, especially since Eddie's passing.

Anna's mum once told her that her great-grandmother was able to read tea-leaves and predict the future with playing cards. It was when she'd caught Anna, age three, talking to her 'imaginary' friend, Tulip Top, a fairy from the bottom of the garden.

Later, at around the age of four, when Anna relayed messages to her parents, from relatives passed into spirit, Maeve made fun of her, making Anna feel peculiar and believing she was odd. From then on, anything Anna felt was kept well away from family ears, especially Maeve's.

This visit of Maeve's today was doing a number on her. All this sudden nostalgia couldn't be good for her mind, never mind her soul. Anna shoved everything into the box again, apart from the pebbles, with the purpose of replacing it into the wardrobe.

Walking past the waste bin, she stopped. Lifting its lid, the peddles hit the rubbish inside, landing on the used kitchen paper without a sound. For the briefest of seconds Anna stared at them. Then, just as quickly, the lid was replaced, and she was off down the hall to the bedroom.

'Enough now,' she commanded. 'Time to put the past where it belongs.'

She'd start moving forward, even if it was a hop, skip and jump, on wobbly legs.

CHAPTER FIVE

Maeve Jenkins disembarked the aeroplane, with a ball of mixed emotions weighing at her lower back travelling like needle points down both legs.

Having spent a lifetime living in, and putting up with, a cocktail of negative thoughts, she'd grown to assume the worst. Her expectations seldom disappointed.

She tapped her left foot impatiently. The young mum in front, struggling to carry one of her children while cautiously guiding the other down the aeroplane's metal steps, annoyed her considerably.

It rained a drizzle. The typical Irish climate irritated Maeve even more. It seemed little had changed from her previous visits many moons ago to this cold, damp and dreary island.

It appeared, she mentally noted, that despite occasionally assuming otherwise, she wasn't missing anything much and certainly nothing of great worth.

'Mother Mary,' she prayed silently through thin lips, 'give me strength. I should have stayed in Kent.' This was a diabolical disaster altogether.

Impulse, driven by anger, Maeve pushed the crying child in front out of her way. She'd reached her limit.

The three-year-old bumped into the handrail and whimpered in surprise and pain. His mother gasped, shocked beyond belief at such rudeness. Maeve escaped, racing in front and to the airport's terminal, deliberately ignoring the 'nasty old woman' comment from the affronted parent.

Maeve was frustrated. '*Self-entitled brats she hummed with mental force. Darn good wallop with a cane across their knuckles would teach respect.*'

Maeve's journey to the arrivals lounge was fraught with physical pain and mental tension. The battered biscuit tin containing her latest offerings, dug deep. Blood spots appeared on her upper arm, challenging her to address its effect. She charged ahead regardless, ignoring it.

Her late husband would regard this situation as a chance for her to grow stronger. She readily agreed with his theory simply because it wasn't worth her efforts not too.

'*What doesn't kill us makes us tougher.*'

George was a hearty man, but she loved him as much as her wifely duties required through each of their forty-three years of marriage.

'Submission is for the weak,' he told her, (pounding a tall scotch and replacing the leather belt) after another of his beatings. 'Toughen up and stop that bloody weeping. Crying makes you fragile. Remember that.'

George was a mine of information. Maeve learnt a lot from the overweight, bald five-foot six sales man. Apparently, she was 'no looker,' had 'smelt badly all the time,' and 'was lucky to have him.' The broken arm, black eyes and misshaped jaws down the years, proved his point. What she didn't learn, was beaten into her.

The fact they'd never been blessed with children wasn't allowed to be his problem either. It was all down to her.

'It's because you were a slut in your last life,' he accused her nastily, after another chance to become a father failed. 'You're making me pay for it in this one.'

Little attention was given to the scientific tests that her ability to conceive was secure while his was not. George may have passed three years ago, yet his legacy lived on in his wife's head.

First to arrive at the baggage claim, it was a relief for Maeve to sit and wait. The offending biscuit tin was given a seat beside her. Its contents were a gift. She trusted Anna would enjoy homecooked treacle and date bread. If she didn't, well, she'd be nothing short of a fool.

Even though she'd entered the bread into the 'Women's Institute Annual Baking Competition' back in Kent, it had failed to win approval in any of the listed categories. The usual people had won. Long-standing members and those affiliated with the institute's management committee.

In Maeve's eyes, it was always a fix based on who knew who and not on individual achievements. Back scratching was a real thing in those kinds of circles she'd concluded, and she was no arse-kisser.

It was a bit of a drag, however. Maeve wanted to be the best. She wanted to come of shinning in front of Anna. It had been years since they'd met. A bit of bragging wouldn't go amiss. Not getting first place for her bake stung hard, setting her plans back considerably.

The more she pondered, the deeper she mentally huffed and puffed. Her mind worked overtime. What could she do to make things better?

Minutes passed, bringing with them the arrival of the young mum and her children from earlier. Maeve avoided looking directly at them. The corner of her eye would do nicely for now.

The Aquarian-born woman detested direct conflict. She wasn't afraid of it mind, but if it was to be avoided, it would be. Best to devise a quick plan B.

The fancy goods store opposite looked appealing. It was time to make a quick getaway. Pulling the pink gloves back onto her long, lean fingers and re-buttoning her heavy, woollen coat, Maeve checked her thick stockings hadn't rolled into clumps around her thin ankles.

Her suitcase arrived. Grabbing it quickly, she raced towards the small shop as fast as her seventy something body allowed.

Hopefully, there'd be a solution to her problem there.

CHAPTER SIX

The plane from Manchester was getting ready to make its descent into Belfast City Airport.

It was raining outside. The drops of water spilt down the plane window, collecting in small puddles, only to be blown back into the air. Grey clouds hung heavy in the sky, suspended on a promise for a rainy afternoon ahead.

Considering she'd just left much the same climate behind in Manchester, Kate McAllister wasn't looking forward to another drenching now.

Mostly frequent flyers, the passengers inside the plane sat with laptops on their knees, glad of the chance to get caught up with overdue work. Others were resting their heads, having an early morning snooze. The plane rattled noisily getting closer to touch down.

Kate relaxed her head against the seat, eyes firmly closed. Far from snoozing, she was having thoughts she didn't quite know how to handle. The broad smile painted on her bright glossy lips, consumed most of her small, round face, giving clear signals of the pleasurable feelings consuming her mind.

Her auburn, wavy hair spanned across the backrest of the plane's seat, while her chunky arms rested on its metal armrest. Although her bulging body wasn't at its most comfortable in the chair's lean confinement, she disregarded this fact, substituting its endurance with a pleasurable imagination.

Adam Malone, the five-foot-five, dark-haired, blue-eyed hunk of a man, gave reason to the delightful madness that entered her mind, body and soul. She was consumed with him on all levels. Their affair had lasted longer than she'd ever hoped for. Dare she venture to assume another month of this bliss? That remained a delicious mystery.

Kate almost groaned out loud as she recalled and replayed every delectable detail of the last four days over and over in her head. It felt amazing. Adam Malone's bedroom behaviour, on their long weekend away, surprised her into a state of dazed incredulity, and at its peak, rendered her breathless.

The delightful and naughty Indian 'Karma Sutra' book, listing hundreds of sexual positions, was by far the most useful tool either of them had brought on their 'sneaky' trip away.

In fact, Kate was sure if it weren't for it, they'd never have enjoyed their weekend so much. It was a godsend, she felt sure, and smiled sneakily now at having been so insightful to have carried it along.

'Clever girl, Kate,' she whispered beneath garlic-infused breath (steaks in sauce, last night's hotel room service, her treat). 'You deserve a medal for foresight.'

However, Kate felt annoyed deep down. She knew, having researched years ago, the same book had originated from sacred scriptures.

It had been subjected to nothing but indecent and crude vulgarity down the years. She felt uncomfortable how those little facts had been over-looked, all in the name of pleasure for their trip.

With her eyes closed gently against any stranger's stares, Kate continued her past few days' re-runs.

'I like this number sixty-nine position, Adam,' she ventured, leafing through the big hard-backed book in the hotel room. 'Pick your favourite.'

Adam smiled shrewdly to himself, while unpacking his fur-lined thong and matching condom box, confident of their extended use in the days ahead. He winked responsively.

'By the time we've experimented with the other sixty-eight positions,' he promised fervently, thrusting his groin in her direction and licking a cold sore on his bottom lip. 'You'll not want to show favouritism to any one position in particular, Hot Pants!'

With the mentioning of her "sex name", the substantial and heartrending guilt Kate was feeling, having left her husband and children behind in Ireland just hours before, vanished with his perfect smile. All was well in fantasy land again. She indulged greedily.

The bump of the aeroplane's wheels on the hard surface below, brought her back into the unpleasantness of her own reality. She sighed, quite annoyed at the return. Opening her eyes and looking around assured her that everyone else seemed interested in their own business and thankfully not in hers.

Kate cleared her blocked throat with a few coughs and smiled an apology to the balding man beside her as he covered his own mouth and nose for fear of catching what Kate was offering.

Adam's work commitments dictated that he stayed an extra day in Manchester. Her own, on the other hand, did not. Kate missed his male presence sitting close and longed now to be able to reach out and hold his reassuring hand regardless that it was generally damp from his sweaty palms.

When she was without Adam, Kate felt very much alone and scared of her own actions. How could she be this person; the unfaithful wife, the mother who lied to her children? Did this render her a bad person?

In her most insecure moments, she felt horrible. In her most delicious times, she was sexy, wanted and desired. Surely, she could somehow achieve an acceptable balance.

Shame and remorse battled with self-reproach in her head. Adam was always so good at dispelling these negative emotions, finding practicality and logic behind their affair's intent.

'My wife stopped putting out years ago,' he'd reassure her. 'You're not even in love with John. You deserve to have your needs met. Screw the lot of them!'

Maybe it was because he was absent, or maybe because she knew deep down her actions belonged to no one only herself, but Kate felt pretty rotten at that moment. To add insult to injury she had a whopper of a cold sore developing on her bottom lip. Its throb was considerable and would take days to clear.

'I couldn't feel worse even if I tried.' Such a contrast to her thoughts just minutes before.

Her self-imposed offences forced her towards the novelty store inside the terminal as soon as the flight disembarked. Buying gifts often dampened her inner turmoil. She was an expert in the knowledge of shame. Part of her loathed that she should be educated with it in the first place.

Entering the book and fancy goods store, some thirty minutes later, Kate's awareness was immediately drawn to the elderly woman in the corner of it.

The pull towards her was magnetic, as though they shared common ground. Strange as it seemed, Kate felt drawn to the older woman. Her aura caught and held her attention. She frowned, captivated by such eccentricity.

Heavily engrossed with a box of soft novelty bears, the mature hands lifted and threw the objects from one to the other and then quite violently chucked them back into the box.

Then she picked them up again and began the process over. Her rumbling mumbles were spat out rather angrily, yet Kate knew she was oblivious to the noise she was making.

Her expression told she was lost in a world of her own. Kate excused herself to pass. As she did, the older woman yanked the "1st Prize" rosette away from the toy's front and stuffed it into her coat pocket. She threw the bear back into its box and hurriedly left the area.

Kate gasped. Not only had she witnessed a crime, but realisation finally dawned. This woman, the thief, was her mother's sister, Maeve! She had to be. Family photographs didn't lie. The pull she felt towards her earlier was not a coincidence, Kate felt sure.

'Goodness!' she jested. 'I thought I was the criminal in the family.'

In one way, Kate pondered, it was great that life rarely failed to surprise. In another, she frowned its truth, there were times it was all right to live a mundane, routine-driven existence. At least that offered a degree of safety.

Kate wasn't sure if she should smile, gasp or chase after her aunt and threaten to reveal everything. As she waited, deciding, she was sure of one thing. It would appear the week ahead was going to be eventful if what she just witnessed was anything to go by.

Let the games begin.

CHAPTER SEVEN

Ellen rushed towards the arrivals department, red-faced, panting and sweaty. The new roll-on deodorant she'd been trying out, (by way of playing her part in helping the ozone layer) was not working as effectively as she would have liked.

The green t-shirt she wore had noticeable stains under the armpits and she had a light band of sweat under her boobs. Normally a healthy timekeeper as well as a conscientious hygienist, aggravation was causing a fluster she didn't like to feel.

Ellen was practising meditation every day for the past two months and knew how beneficial this was for calming and focusing the mind. She was therefore really cross at herself now for how easily she'd allowed the slow tractor, the elderly sightseeing couple (driving at a snail's pace) and the roadworks on the way here, to disrupt her newfound calm. She apparently needed extra practice.

Lifting the sheet of paper from her bag with the name *'Maeve Jenkins'* sprawled across it in thick black ink, she allowed it to unfold. Holding it up for all to see (feeling somewhat foolish), she began pacing around in the hope of finding her aunt.

Tripping across a baby's pram wheels as she walked, Ellen managed to wake the sleeping child inside. She was rewarded with a foul look from the infant's mother. It had taken a lifetime to get the teething baby settled in the first place.

'So sorry.'

'Umm hum. Dead on.' The mum was not pleased.

Forcing herself around the seated area for a second lap of the lounge, paper in tow, resignation and mortification eventually forced Ellen to sit. She knew Maeve's flight was on time and had landed. Waiting it out now, seemed the best and least awkward thing to do.

As she sat, Ellen enjoyed a spot of people watching. Often a favourite game she played as a child, she was delighted at making up stories about those analysed now.

She decided the woman with the baby was actually a drugs smuggler who had hidden the million-pound stash in the child's nappy.

The man sitting opposite her was really a mountain climber, returning from the North Pole after months away. He'd managed to lose one of his feet to frostbite. The frozen foot was kept chilled in the bag beside him awaiting surgery.

The elderly gentleman beside him was his grandfather. Later they would discover he was actually his own father and the father of his infant daughter. Although it looked like the older man could barely stand straight, it would transpire that he had fathered more than twenty children with another one on its way in mid-spring. A proper Casanova!

Ellen giggled at her own humour. This was fun. The chunky, middle-aged woman sitting close by glanced her way, smiled responsively and then continued to read the newspaper.

Ellen knew it would be little hardship to sit in the airport all day playing games but a quick glance at her watch told her time was running on and she was hardly jogging alongside it.

It was time to bring the focus back to the intended task sooner than later. Reluctantly she did just that. Realising her aunt had yet to appear, Ellen decided something different was needed.

'Time to call in the Big Guns.' Divine help was required.

For as long as she could remember, Ellen's belief in Angels and Ascended Masters, (those Beings of extreme wisdom and kindness), had taken her out of many scrapes, worries and predicaments.

From childhood into adulthood (and somewhere in between) right up into present day she had known countless instances of their help.

It was simply a matter of asking. Then, by keeping an open mind (in order to recognise the help offered) and of course if it didn't influence free will, the request was answered.

Ellen scratched her head and searched her brain, turning heaven ward for insight. She wondered what pure energy would have the best impact in the current dilemma. Archangel Raphael immediately came to mind. It was time to put the heavenly being to work.

With a silent request for Raphael to help find (and then deliver) Maeve her way, she finished with a 'thank you.' All that was needed now was patience, faith and trust. Those attributes were growing stronger every day.

The smell of freshly brewed coffee coming from the café opposite tempted a trip inside its doors. The aromatic scents were alluring. Ellen longed to indulge her taste buds.

Considering the huge slice of carrot cake that was practically calling out to be eaten, Ellen's resistance and willpower were under serious threat. Terrorist gangs named "comfort", "reassurance", and "go ahead", battled in her head.

She resisted the pull with every ounce of determination mustered. She'd only regret it later. Battling bulges was hard work.

Keeping a close eye on the scene around her, (and more importantly, averted from the café and its temptations), Ellen first noticed the large peacock feather prodding from the older woman's hat.

As further details arrived, the yellow coat screamed attention, while the baby blue earmuffs and purple neck scarf practically hid self-consciously around her neck and ears.

Ellen could have sworn she heard giggles and gasps in her background. She ignored them in favour of not indulging sensitivities.

Having just left the restrooms where she'd decided to hide after her recent theft incident, Maeve's impatience to leave the whole airport behind was vital. She walked with the speed of a tree-climbing squirrel. Her eyes pierced the crowd with a vulture-like glare, searching out prey.

The very second Ellen looked Maeve's way, she knew she'd found her aunt. The similarity to Anna was uncanny. The same piercing blue eyes, and square jawline marked the resemblance.

Okay so Maeve was leaner and taller by inches. Her nose was sharper (and a little crooked) but still the similarity was undeniable.

'Hi there,' Ellen introduced herself with a touch of Maeve's arm. 'Maeve, is it?'

Maeve's face softened momentarily with relief.

'Ellen?' she enquired from over her half-moon glasses, eying her from top to toe enveloping and intimidating with her stare. 'You've certainly changed.'

Considering Ellen had been a young child when last they'd met, it was practically guaranteed that she would look different now, twenty-two years later.

Ellen said nothing, simply trusting her smile as an appropriate response. Maeve glanced expectantly behind her niece, looking for Anna. Her eyes narrowed, a furrow forming across her brow when her expectations were unfounded.

'Your mother,' she shot accusingly, 'where is she?' Rummaging around for the second time, with eagle-like eyes, Maeve's search discovered something she'd been consciously avoiding. Two airport security guards were walking their way.

'Never mind.' She shoved her old suitcase and the battered biscuit tin into Ellen's arms, turned on her heel and began a hasty trot towards the exit sign. She mused, *'I often forget some people are naturally rude.'*

Kate waited a full two minutes before stepping from behind the coffee machine inside the café. Sighing with relief that her sister and aunt had finally left; her frayed nerves craved a strong expresso. She'd already discovered the café served carrot cake. A treat awaited.

It was one thing to accidentally run into her Aunt Maeve in the gift shop, quite another to meet Ellen here too and in the airport of all places. She cringed; that was certainty a close call.

How could she possibly explain her presence to her younger sister when she hadn't even the answers straight in her own head?

Ellen, Gemma and Kate had planned a get-together later that evening (sister's night out thing). Kate consoled herself that avoiding her sister and Maeve now, would evade further questions later. She had no desire to bring unwanted attention her way.

Now, time to find that carrot cake.

CHAPTER EIGHT

'I think I have a hangover,' Ellen moaned, holding her head for fear it would roll off. 'I'm dizzy and my stomach hurts.'

Fergal nodded in agreement while cooking breakfast for the family the following morning.

'It doesn't surprise me,' the dark-haired, swarthy, five-foot-six man said as he stirred the eggs on the pan, hoping against hope they wouldn't stick and burn again. 'A wino wouldn't have gone through as many bottles in one night as you lot did.'

A short tempered, speak as you see it man, Fergal wasn't in the habit of sitting on fences, Aries style. If something displeased him, he'd say it without hesitation.

Ellen groaned, dreading what the answer would be before she even asked the question.

'How many empties?' She enquired with her face squeezed, preparing for the worst. 'Please be kind.'

'Eight,' Fergal puffed. 'And a bottle of gin.'

'Flying heavens… *eight* you say?'

'Yep. Every one of you were steamin by the end of the night.'

'Holy Saint Germain.'

'I know,' Fergal agreed. 'Praying does sounds appropriate. Take something to redeem the consumption.'

Joining her sons at the kitchen table, Ellen sat in confused disbelief. Both boys smirked at one another niftily. It was unusual to see their mother in this state. It took great determination not to tease.

Instead, Matt (eldest), offered his help. He poured Ellen a glass of fruit juice, sliding it her way. The sunlight from the window caught and then emphasised the red sheen across his brown hair.

Coupled with his large brown eyes, narrow cheekbones and sharp chin, the fifteen-year-old was, in his mother's opinion, turning into a pretty handsome young man. One that any girl would be lucky to have.

James, at the tender age of twelve years and seven months, was so like his bigger brother that if it weren't for the age difference they could easily be mistaken for twins.

Apart from James having blue-grey eyes and a rounder shaped face, they were practically indistinguishable. Every parent believed their children to be special. Ellen was no exception.

It was clear from infancy that both boys would be tall; the height gene ran in Ellen's father's family, and it looked like they'd inherited it generously.

By the time Matt had reached double figures in his years, he was already an inch above his dad's head. James was mirroring that trail as they spoke.

So, it was little surprise to either Ellen or Fergal when both Matt and James showed favour with basketball from the get go (and James with golf). It seemed fitting they should give their creativity to the sport.

It had become the basis of their lives, with school, social and family commitments fitting into it, rather than the other way around. Fergal and Ellen encouraged their interest, happy to support the administration of it, providing finances, kits, lifts and equipment when required.

'As long as they have a smile on their face that's all that counts.' Ellen reminded Fergal when he complained at the price of the new season basketball kit. 'We'll manage.'

'Ever the optimist,' he grumbled. 'Rarely the realist.'

Now as Ellen accepted the cool juice from Matt, she sighed with a feeling of tiredness that felt alien to her these days. She remembered it from her teenage years gone by though, when her desire was to drink every drop of alcohol in Ireland.

Holding the cooling glass to her forehead, in the hope of soothing the pain within, she slowly tried to piece together snippets from the previous night.

Bit by tiny bit it came back. Once she'd safely (and thankfully), dropped her Aunt Maeve at Anna's home, declining the offer of tea and scones inside (she'd had enough alone time with Maeve on the journey home thank you kindly), Ellen hooked it back to her own place in eager anticipation of the girl's' night ahead.

She'd rather have risked her mother's wrath at not coming in with Maeve than have to spend extra time with the woman; her part was well played for that day. Besides, she justified, there was only so much negativity the human soul could endure in one long hour, and she'd had her quota for the week.

Gemma and Kate called around eight o'clock. Ellen was sure of the time, simply because the arrangement had been made from the previous week. After much deliberation (should they eat out, should they buy in, or should some of them cook…) the decision not to venture out in the cold won.

They reached a quick compromise. The recently opened Indian restaurant in the town was given a call, and an order was placed. When some of the nicest food that any of them had sniffed in a while was delivered, the driver was rewarded with a generous tip.

'Gemma brought three bottles of wine,' (what was that about) Ellen told her company now, doing the math in her head and fingers. 'Kate brought one… so…'

Fergal rolled his eyes disapprovingly. He was pissed (pun intended). From their personal wine stash (that he'd painstakingly build up) four bottles were gonners. Not sure if he was more annoyed because he wasn't part of its demise, it stung either way.

'We're down four bottles and a full litre of gin.'

'The full litre?'

'Every last drop.'

'Good gracious.'

'Indeed.'

'I can't believe it,' Ellen felt genuinely flabbergasted. 'Seriously,' she defended against her son's sniggers. 'I couldn't have had more than four glasses of wine. I don't remember having any gin…'

'I can't believe it either,' Fergal snapped angrily, while at the same time considerably pleased with his breakfast success. He carried the overcooked eggs to the waiting audience with a pride made up of mixed emotions and a festering temper. 'All I know is that Gemma couldn't stand up by the end of the night.'

'I saw that okay.' Ellen sighed its truth. 'Nothing new there then.'

'Not a thing.'

'Ummm.'

Twenty minutes later (the breakfast was so far staying down), with both boys and Fergal off on their respective commitments, Ellen decided her hangover wouldn't get the better of her day.

Moby was thrilled to bits his walk wasn't compromised and leaped into the car's boot with gusto. A brisk walk around Delaney Park would do them all the power of good.

Rose couldn't help the smirk when she noticed Ellen's pale face, despite the effects of the hill's climb.

'You look great,' she teased cautiously. 'If you're going for the sickly-grey look, you've pulled it of nicely.'

Ellen smiled weakly, sticking her tongue out in response.

'Behave,' she warned, 'or you'll get to wear my breakfast.' The walk had resurrected things in that area.

'Good night then?'

'Not sure and please… don't shout.'

'Very good night then.'

Conversation between them was minimal. Moby and Andrew picked up their games from yesterday, this time with some frisbee action and a little bit of dance in celebration of him catching on first go (Andrew, not Moby).

Grey clouds threatened a problem (they'd no umbrellas), while nearby grazing cows huddled together as a sign of rain ahead. Ellen's temples pulsed while Rose rubbed her knee to ease discomfort.

Minutes later, the first signs of rain showed up. At first, they were tiny skiffs, which was no big deal. Seconds later they were huge button sized drops. Ellen felt a relief for the beads of water falling (soothing the head). Rose was far from amused.

'Goodness,' she declared, standing hastily and a little more quickly than her ageing body was comfortable with. 'I can't risk Andrew getting soaked.'

In the same way that it hadn't taken long for the rain to make its presence felt, it took an even shorter period for it to pour. The heavens opened, inviting the wind to come with it. The games began between the two making it virtually impossible to maintain a conversation and walk at the same time. After a while, it became harder to remain optimistic, so each of them, including Moby, stopped trying.

By the time they'd reached the car park, Rose had no hesitation in accepting Ellen's offer of a car lift home.

'Great stuff,' she told her, with as much enthusiasm as she could muster at the mercy of dripping clothes. 'I can't see how we could get any wetter. At least it will save our feet.'

'That's the spirit.'

The McGrath's small, whitewashed cottage, sat nestled between several large pine and beech trees, with green pastures as far as the eye could see. The bumpy lane that took them there, amply supplied as it was with potholes and small bumpy hills, simply added to Mother Nature's delights. Until now, Ellen had never known where Rose and Andrew lived.

'Wow,' Ellen said, admiring the scene that greeted her through the misty car's windscreen as she peered between the wipers. 'This is lovely, Rose.'

'It is,' Rose felt blessed and said so. 'We're blessed to live here.'

Insisting Ellen come in for a cup of tea and a dry down, Andrew was delighted the invitation extended to Moby.

'The floors will get mucky,' Ellen warned, giving Rose the chance to retract her offer. 'When Moby's wet, there's quite a pong.'

'That's not a problem,' Rose responded lightly. 'I'm not a bit house proud, Ellen,' she smiled away the notion, 'as you'll no doubt see, when you enter.'

The Cancer-born woman preferred her home to be lived in rather than have it as a show house.

'I love your décor,' Ellen complimented her over scones, tea and a towel dry later as she sat in the room that combined both the living space and kitchen in one. 'The colours and textures blend well.'

It appeared their bedrooms were at each end of the house as two oak stained doors completed the entire structure. Rose had been right though, Ellen noticed immediately upon entering the three-roomed cottage. The place lacked tidiness and needed a bit of a spring clean.

'Life's too short to spend time cleaning,' the older woman declared as an excuse for the dust on the window sills and the stains on the tiles. 'I prefer to prioritise and,' Rose gave reasonable warning, 'if you need the toilet, it's across the yard.'

'Thanks, I'm set.'

Ellen sat much longer than intended. She felt cosy, comfortable and very at home. It was nice to feel that neither an air nor a grace was needed.

Speaking to Rose, Ellen felt like she was confiding to her grandmother, a kindred spirit. It was reassuring to know that chatting openly with someone she trusted and could speak freely too, with neither judgement nor criticism, was both refreshing and healing.

'I love my mum dearly,' she told Rose truthfully. 'I know she means well but,' she hesitated to find the right words. 'If I bring up my issues with Fergal to her, she always takes his side.'

Rose nodded understanding.

'You update her,' Rose offered an explanation that Ellen might not have otherwise got. 'It's her job to tell you what she didn't get around to doing. Now you're the one in charge of following up with your own perspective.'

'How so?'

'By bringing a new, fresh generational change to fix old karmas and problems.'

'I'll have a think about all that.'

'It might help.'

'Yes, thanks.'

As often happens when things feel uplifting and pleasurable, time trotted on quicker than racing hooves across a padlock. Deep in conversation, neither woman noticed the late hour.

'I don't believe in coincidences,' Ellen added to the latest topic. 'I feel you and I were meant to meet when we did,' she pondered. 'My life is transforming considerably. New beliefs are attracting different friends and letting old ones go. It seems a little frightening, uncomfortable almost. It's like a force I

70

can't and don't want to prevent. I seem to be craving something on a deeper, more meaningful level.'

Rose agreed.

'I agree,' she confirmed. 'Transformations in ourselves can cause fears for those closest to us as well.'

'I know.'

From the law of attraction, harsh soul lessons and Karmic Debts, Rose and Ellen shared opinions, insights and life experiences.

'I'm learning about elementals.' Ellen had never confided this to another living soul until now. 'As well as the probability of alien life force.'

'Those are head scratching topics.'

'They can be but it's exciting at the same time.'

It was late afternoon before the weather decided to let up. Andrew and Moby were exhausted from their play. Andrew watched television while Moby slept beside him.

'I should go,' Ellen stood to leave. 'School collection beckons.'

'Fair enough.' Rose grabbed her walking aid. 'I'll see you out.'

Once inside the car, Rose touched Ellen's arm through the open window,

'Don't worry about Fergal, it will all work out fine,'

'It hasn't been easy.' They were pulling apart bit by bit. She felt powerless to stop it happening, while at the same time not sure she'd any control over it in the first place. 'How did you know, Rose?'

'I've a heightened sense for these things.'

'You mean you're psychic?'

'Aren't we all in one way or another?'

'Umm. I do a bit of that myself.'

'I know,' Rose smiled confirmation. 'It was apparent from the day we met.'

'Oh… you didn't say.'

'Not my place, dear.'

'I see.'

It felt a bit surreal. All this time Rose knew about Ellen's heightened perceptions and kept it quiet.

Her journey home was filled with mental tension and a saddened heart for what she felt sure lay ahead. Rose's parting words sang a sombre tune in her head that she couldn't shake.

'It's not the letting go that's the hardest; it's the holding on.'

The old should be released to allow the new to enter.

CHAPTER NINE

Anna was trying desperately to adjust to having Maeve in her home. She seriously was. However, it was proving harder to do than she was comfortable with. In fact, it was close to impossible.

Anna, along with her late husband Eddie, had always prided themselves on raising their family as independently and spiritually minded as possible. It was simply their way and one they had both agreed upon, long before any of their children were brought onto the earth.

Consequently, their four children were well used to mentions of Angels, Archangels, Ascended Masters, Goddesses and Spirits Guides since they were born. It was part and parcel of their upbringing and as natural to them as the water was to fish, as wool was to sheep or as Cairo was to Egypt.

Anna was born under the sun sign of Gemini, the twins, ruled over by the planet Mercury. Apart from the communication factor this planet governed, amongst its many other traits, spiritualism shone strongly.

Having her moon in Pisces afforded and greatly attributed to her psychic gifts as well. She was no stranger to the unexplained or even supernatural activity from early childhood.

Considered by most to be "odd" or "weird",' the young child wouldn't be deterred, even when it meant playing alone or sitting alongside adults at lunchtime lest she got picked on by those of her own age.

Often discouraged by her parents not to practise or even speak of such things as seeing, hearing or communicating with deceased relatives, the stubborn and self-assured child would not back down from what she knew to be her right and her truth.

Anna stood firm on a solid foundation of belief and trust, which at times required bravery far and beyond her years. Luckily for her, she was an old soul, with many previous physical lives under her belt. Her essence was strong.

'We're never truly on our own,' she'd tell those who cared to listen. 'We're always supported.'

When her older sister Maeve left home as a new bride to live in England, Anna's only thought was to wish her well. The sisters were like strangers anyway (the years of Maeve's bullying) so missing her company was secondary to having her very own private bedroom, at last.

The two girls were as different as chalk and cheese. It was no great loss to see Maeve go. If anything, it was a relief. Her older sister was an intense stickler for their parents beliefs and conditionings, all based on the era they were raised in. Maeve had the habit of doing all she was told to do, without questioning why.

'It's the order of things,' Anna's mother answered her wonder at Maeve marrying so young. 'Time for Maeve to settle down and be a woman, just as I did at her age.'

'Why does she have to settle down to be a woman?' Anna asked innocently. 'I thought you could be a woman no matter what.' (That little snippet earned her a week's grounding for being '*so darn cheeky*').

The fact that love was a secondary consideration to how things should be, didn't seem to annoy or disrupt either Anna's mother or Maeve. She simply followed society's structure and its discipline.

Swearing she would never allow herself to follow suit, Anna fought hard against "the order of things". Such strength was gained and shown through her independent nature. She knew there was more to life than living under the control of man-made rules. Earthly dictatorships held no restrictions for her (unless she chose it to). And so, it was.

Avoiding confrontation, content to deal with things her way, brought freedom where it mattered most. The world was awash with many possibilities. She would not be denied or restricted from them. She wouldn't adapt, even if her very life depended on it.

Hand on heart Anna's rebellion against what was expected was actually doing quite nicely thank you very much until at the tender age of twenty-two, she met and instantly fell in love with Eddie McDowell.

Handsome, caring and physically sturdy, Eddie had the full package. Anna was smitten as early as his first words of, 'I'll have a coffee please, two sugars and light on the milk,' right up to, 'will you marry me?' she was a sucker for his charms, his bouncy bum (yes that counted) and his bulging biceps.

'It was my last day working in the café,' she often told the romantic story to their children. 'If I'd left a day earlier to find work in Denmark, we might never have met.'

Anna and Eddie discovered that love at first sight was possible. Their courtship was staggering and passionate; their marriage date was set for six months after they'd first met.

Despite Anna's mother refusing to attend the registry office ceremony, appalled that a church service was not part of the nuptials, Anna and Eddie married on a quiet, fuss-free Monday morning, basking in nothing but their own happiness and joy.

Apart from some usual minor disagreements, differences of opinions or personality clashes, sharing their lives together was the success story that most couples dream of.

With the arrival of their first child Gemma, two years into their marriage, it seemed their relationship thrived on the added responsibility of parenthood. As their family grew and became six, it appeared life was as perfect as it was going to get in this third-dimension consciousness with their spiritual beliefs to help lift and comfort them in times of need or, as Eddie called it, 'spiritual backup.'

Even on his deathbed, after a shocking diagnosis of colon cancer, the last words Eddie had for his caring wife carried with them the loving theme throughout their relationship. 'Thank you for such a great life,' Eddie told her. 'You completed me.'

'Call with me as soon as you can,' Anna made him promise before he left. 'Just make sure it's not during '*Friends*' or I won't be able to give you my full attention.'

Before such a promise could be made, Eddie left his physical body with a puff and a chesty pant. To the very day, each time the American sitcom came on television, Anna was sure to sense Eddie at her side, watching the programme with her.

Eddie recommended Maeve come back into Anna's life. A suggestion made during a particularity emotional episode when Anna wished she was with Eddie in the spiritual dimension and that her time on earth be cut short. This was a few months after his passing and as the full moon shone brightly in the May night sky.

'I don't want to be here anymore,' she wept. 'Please lift this pain of loss away.'

In response, a clear picture of Maeve jumped into her mind's eye, shocking Anna.

'She's virtually a stranger to me. Why show me *her* of all people?'

The picture persisted for days ahead. Washing dishes, cooking meals, Maeve's face. Doing laundry, supermarket shopping, it happened. Toilet trips (the long kind) ditto.

'All right, all right!' She finally succumbed. 'Enough is enough.'

Anna's desire to have her sister close may have waned before Maeve's visit but she knew she had to at least try. Maybe, she prayed, the scoundrel had wised up in her old age and things would be different.'

But alas, leopards and their spots never changed. Now, with Maeve's arrival into her home less than twenty-four hours ago, Anna stood with every positive intent she could muster behind the locked bathroom door. Her back was placed firmly against it, in the event it could be prized open by sheer maliciousness alone.

She pleaded intervention, Angelic or otherwise (whomever could help should), while at the same time enquiring what she'd ever done, in this lifetime or any other, to deserve the hell she was going through now.

'I'd rather lick a mouse's tail than feel like this.'

Anna was well informed of Karmic Debts. She also knew a thing or two about the wheel of life, the hand of fate, the consequences of applied actions, physically or otherwise.

She was no dozer (although she did enjoy an occasional afternoon snooze, but who didn't?). What she didn't understand was why.

Holding onto the door handle, practically afraid to breathe, she felt like crying.

The woman currently sitting in her kitchen, with the radio turned up to its fullest volume, blasting out the half-hourly news reports and enjoying her third slice of homemade cake, was horrendous. She was the biggest nut-bag ever and a total bully. How could anyone be so mean and not get that they were? It defied Anna's understanding.

From criticising every fitting and fixture in Anna's home to moaning constantly about her difficult past, the woman had nothing positive to say about anyone or anything.

Personal insults of how badly coordinated the furniture was placed in the 'whole house' or 'how undignified the dressing gown hanging on the bedroom door' (it was a kimono from Harvey Nichols that Kate treated her to for her last birthday and she loved it) were only the tip of the iceberg.

The real killer came when Maeve criticised the (non-existent) dust over 'her dear brother-in-law Eddie's photograph,' and the 'poor man,' (whom Maeve barely knew), 'turning in his grave at how little he was thought of.'

That last little gem had been the deciding factor. Anna saw red. This swine of a woman was unbearable.

She should either leave the room, or risk sitting trial for murder down the line.

Completely oblivious to the fact that Maeve's 'bad luck', or 'doomed existence' was entirely of her own making, Anna had long since stopped trying to tell her so. Was it really only hours since she'd arrived? It felt more like twenty-two years and counting.

'Please enlighten me, Angels,' Anna pleaded, her whispers faint in the scale of noise coming from outside of the confined space. 'What lesson am I to learn from this horror of a woman, and,' she warned, 'it better be a good one. This is tough.'

Trying hard not to judge, yet failing miserably, Anna wanted to scream.

'Anna!' Maeve's shrill voice sounded down the hallway, causing Anna to jump and recheck the bathroom door was locked. 'Come along,' it instructed. 'I've buttered you another piece of my prize-winning bread. Shift it before I eat it myself. You'll be sorry if you miss out.'

Anna whimpered the cry of a wounded animal resigned to its dreaded fate. Slowly unlocking the bathroom door, she renewed her prayer.

'Please intervene quickly Ascended Master Paraviti,' the Hindu goddess would inspire a positive change. 'Or I'm sure to die of food poisoning.'

How could that bread have won first prize? Anna asked herself as she pushed saliva around her gums and shielded herself in white light in preparation for what lay ahead. Since the first dreadful piece had entered her mouth, she'd had indigestion and heartburn, the likes of which she'd never experienced before.

'Help me,' Anna's pleas persisted. 'Or I'll be a goner by the morning.'

CHAPTER TEN

Thump, thump, thump, clatter!

Gemma O'Neill startled awake from her alcohol-induced sleep with a heavy head and an ache at the side of her temples that the Devil himself would winch from.

She rubbed her mascara-stained eyes, causing the blackened bits from old make-up to spread on to the bags beneath, where they nestled between the premature wrinkles formed there.

'Feckin hell,' her voice was hoarse, her mouth as dry as Gandhi's flip-flop. 'What the hell is going on?' Like a raging bull, she saw red. In one quick movement, she grabbed the duvet end, flung it across the bed and sat up. The sudden movement induced dizziness, the likes of which she'd encountered many times before.

Thump, thump, thump!

Gemma heard her twin sons giggle from the kitchen below. As much as she loved them, she knew without any doubt, that if she owned a lasso and some duct tape, nothing would stop her from rounding them both up and silencing the four-year-olds for the rest of that day… or at least for an hour… or two… or three…

'Little buggers!'

Seconds later she stood up. With the aid of the bedpost, the clothes-laden chair and the dressing table's edge, Gemma managed to open the bedroom door. She reached the banister in the landing at a snail's pace, each step harder to achieve than the last.

Ignoring the squeaky sound of guilt, permanently lodged at the back of her head, that always remind her how she was skirting around her parental responsibilities, she threw caution to the wind and sucked her breath in, preparing for eruption.

'Donal!' she bellowed, her shout reaching down to the bottom of the stairs. What the hell is going on there?'

Where, Gemma seethed, *in this torment of a house, was her useless lump of a husband anyway?* She waited for her outburst to be acknowledged with an irritation she could match on many previous occasions.

The man must be deaf, she believed, to not hear such noise and at that immense volume too. Judging by the vibrations it was causing, Gemma was sure the neighbours in the next street heard it as well.

Thump, thump, thump, clatter… giggle… bang! Something crashed to the floor. Gemma heard a whimper. One of the boys was hurt.

'*Donal!*'

Donal O'Neill ignored his wife's calls for the second time, for reasons that were tenfold. He listed some in his head as he shovelled pupil exercise books into his briefcase and prayed the year-three students didn't report him to their parents for some of the comments he'd hurriedly written on their work.

Donal simply hadn't the time to thoroughly check last night's homework's properly. Between making dinner, loading laundry into the machine, ironing school uniforms for the kids (and a semi-clean shirt for himself) and then collecting both the twins and Tara from swimming club, his time was greatly compromised.

Scarce in the hours that were needed to properly devote his expertise to the work, Donal had taken a shortcut and given grades based on time restraints instead of academic achievements.

He may have got away with such behaviour years ago he thought now with a worried frown furring across his forehead, when life seemed simpler and teaching was a pleasure and not a chore.

Now, it seemed his skills extended more to the children's parents than to their kids, judging by the number of complaints the school received daily.

'My son doesn't have learning difficulties you fool!' The father of a twelve-year-old pupil fumed to the head mistress. 'I want the teacher responsible for reporting him to the board sacked immediately!'

Donal had never felt as under-appreciated in his career as he had done this past four years. It was a daily struggle to continue in his current work yet paying bills in the hope his own children would have a brighter working future kept him plodding to school each day, despite the rumours circling that he might be gay.

Now, as Gemma's foghorn voice called his name for the third time, Donal was resigned to the fact that he'd drained the guts out of pretending he hadn't heard her from the start.

He flung the living room door ajar. It bounced off the two-seater sofa in the corner, firing it back to him, narrowly missing his large, straight, protruding nose; the very same one that had earned him the nickname "Concord" both inside and outside of school.

'What the hell do you want?'

The man was stressed beyond belief, and it hadn't even passed eight-thirty. 'I'm busy here.'

The large bundle of books held under his arm began to slide from his tight grasp. One by one they hit the stairs below. He let them fall to their destination without restraint, like a coyote giving up its catch to a lioness.

'Have you gone deaf or what?' Gemma asked, sarcasm lacing from her chapped lips. 'Do something about that bloody racket coming from the kitchen or I swear I'll…'

'You'll what?' Donal challenged. 'Dare to do something about it yourself?'

Thump, thump, thump, wallop, crash, bang, wailing.

'See,' Gemma felt victorious, 'I knew something would happen… go,' she instructed Donal hurriedly, 'If there's a trip needed to accident and emergency it won't be me making it.'

'Shocker.'

Donal dropped everything he'd been clinging to and raced towards the kitchen, preparing to go into paramedic mode.

He'd recently updated his first aid skills, via compulsory attendance at school, and was rather looking forward to putting some of the knowledge into practice now.

'Bitch,' he couldn't help but whisper as he left the scene. 'Go back to bed. Bloody drunk.'

Satisfied, when three minutes later turned into four and the crying had silenced to a mere drone, Gemma began her return to the room she'd recently left. Her stomach heaved and she felt nauseated to her gut. Going back to bed seemed justifiable and the only sane thing to do in her current state.

Circling around, she caught sight of herself in the long, wall-mounted mirror on the landing. Hair roots darker than coal, a bouncing belly protruding through the short pyjama top and toenails longer than a small stick, Gemma knew she should be peeved at what the picture was telling her. Surprisingly, she wasn't really that perturbed.

From the same mirror's reflection, Gemma noticed her thirteen-year-old daughter Tara coming out from her bedroom on tiptoes. Assuming her mum had left the landing, Tara panicked as she started back at Gemma.

Mother turned towards daughter for an early-morning showdown.

'What's with all the make-up, madam?' Gemma enquired through slit-like snake eyes, (while at the same time admiring Tara's glossy gold eye shadow). 'Did your school turn into a brothel or something?'

Tara giggled, despite the seriousness of the situation. Her face soon changed from a smirk to a groan as she began to plead her case.

'Pleeease, Mum,' she begged. 'All my friends are allowed to wear make-up. I'll get bullied if I'm the only one without.'

'Not a chance.' Tara's case fell flat onto the carpeted ground as Gemma gestured towards the room the teenager had just left. 'Back inside and take that muck off your face,' she slurred. 'You look like a clown.'

'Cow.'

'What?'

'Didn't say a word.'

Once back in the comfort and security of her warm bed, Gemma sighed a groan from somewhere deep in her gut. Being a parent had never come naturally to her, she thought. It was hard work by any standards.

She was no Mary Poppins either. Gemma smiled at the thought. Her caring skills were purely selfish and always would be. Hands down she'd quite happily let Mother Teresa carry on with her healing and caring for others, without complaint or competition from her corner. She wasn't sure if Mother Teresa had passed away but regardless, the principle held grit.

Pulling the duvet tighter around her neck for warmth, Gemma prepared to go back into the slumber she'd so rudely been dragged from.

Her tummy rumbled and growled from lack of food, while her bladder begged to be emptied, lest its flood gates opened involuntarily. It was no stranger to that truth on many occasions before.

'For the love of Jude!' It was now or never for the toilet trip. 'Is there no peace and quiet to be had this morning at all?'

On the way to the bathroom, Gemma caught sight of Tara halfway down the stairs. She could have sworn if challenged to do so, that her daughter's face was still plastered with the offending concoctions she'd been reprimanded over before.

On the brink of chastising her again, Gemma's bladder began to leak, forcing her to pounce faster than a blue wildebeest into the bathroom. At the same time holding onto her groin for fear more pee would escape, she hopped inside the small cubical.

'Oh, to hell with it,' Tara was off the hook and didn't even know it. 'I'll get her good for something else down the line.'

As things turned out, Donal didn't get to practise much of his newfound medical knowledge. On his entrance into the kitchen, his sons were rolling around the ground wrestling one another for the biggest saucepan to bang.

Apart from the small clump of blond hair stuck to Ruairi's jumper and the ripped t-shirt Rossa would surely need to change out of before school (but wouldn't,) no blood or bruising was in sight.

Once separated, Donal instructed both boys to find their school bags, take the offered money for a canteen lunch later (on account of not having time to make their requested peanut butter and jam sandwiches) and get 'their fighting butts into the car' or they were all going to be 'very late indeed.'

Tara had escaped earlier, preferring to riffle some loose change from her dad's pocket in favour of asking for some, (that she'd later use to buy single cigarettes on the school's black market).

It was one thing attending the very school her father taught in; quite another ball game to arrive in the same car with him as well. She'd walk there with friend's thanks very much. She was no nurd, even if Concord was a massive one.

With the bang of the front door and the initial hesitance of the car's ability to start first go, the majority of the O'Neill family left the building by 8.53 a.m. to be educated in a way neither one of them preferred to be, if given the choice.

Back in bed, Gemma could have cried with relief that another morning's drama had eventually concluded. The tick of the bedside clock was the only sound to interrupt her rest now. She could comfortably deal with that no bother.

There were, however, two extra issues to be completed before dreamy slumber could be achieved. These would be pleasurable and rewarding rather than annoying and irritating.

Reaching for the bedside phone, Gemma placed a call to the nursery where she worked. Leaving a message not to expect her in today again on account of the 'dreadful flu' she was still suffering from, she felt little guilt at its untruth.

'Screw it,' she reached under the mattress, extracting a warmed half bottle of vodka, kept there for "emergencies." Unscrewing the cap, she drank half the contents.

Fifteen minutes later she was dreaming of pina coladas, palm trees and swarthy skinned men fanning and frolicking with her under the shade while she leisured in the hammock.

Just the way she always wanted her life to be.

CHAPTER ELEVEN

Donal O'Neill sat in his car parked in the school grounds, ignition switched off, with his head held in his hands, slouched over the steering wheel.

He breathed several huge gulps of air into his (already) congested lungs (chest infection, never cleared in weeks), hoping for emotional relief. He'd heard meditation was good for what ailed. Maybe he'd give that a go sometime. It couldn't hurt.

The heavy set, five -foot seven man, bald (almost totally), with a handsome face, felt drained in so many ways, counting would be lengthy. Honest to heaven above, he'd just about had enough.

The strain of his job was tremendous because so much changed since the start of his teaching career almost thirty years ago. There was zero control in the classroom and proper, meaningful discipline was a thing of the past.

The sun sign born Libran man's vigour and enthusiasm had slowly and steadily dwindled over the years. His motivation to continue, fading faster.

Donal's confidence had also taken a serious hit, especially after the big scandal (five years back).

Just because he'd shown advances towards young Michael Rafferty, a year twelve pupil in his history class, suddenly he's labelled gay with a reputation spread all over the school and district combined.

Of course, there was nothing to it. A simple childish infatuation (on Michael's part) the whole thing was nothing but a student teacher crush. It was simply one of those things that many others have gone through before. No big deal.

Suspending Donal indefinitely, until an enquiry was carried out, saw a chunk of his fellow teaching colleagues fight his corner. Many had given glowing character references. For that, he would never forget their kindness, this side of a decade or beyond.

Michael was exempt from any further connection with Donal (when all proof proved non-factual). His parents insisted he was moved to a separate class. New subject choices were established for him and after a month or so, everything resumed as before for them both. This time, a trail period of supervision was added, which proved successful to that very day.

Donal was no fool. He knew those kinds of things stuck and that he was regarded as being gay amongst the pupils and some of the teaching staff as well.

Proof was needed to provide his innocence. Gemma and his children were the biggest part of that. It was hard to argue homosexuality when he'd a wife and three children that dictated a pretty solid and creditable response.

He'd made a point of taking Gemma to all the staff events, including a school trip to France back in the nineties.

He'd actively encouraged everyone to take photographs of the two of them coupled up and cosy looking together; like a newly married couple, excited and enthralled with nobody but themselves.

Gemma hated it of course. She'd shrug his arm away from her shoulders, refuse to dance at the Christmas dinner dance with him and actively ship herself off to get hammered with head of English Brian Cleland, twat that he was.

He was one of the people who consistently referred to Donal as the 'bent rusted spoon.' After a while, Gemma joined in, especially when she wasn't getting her way or fancied a spot of blackmail.

'I'll write anonymously to the newspapers and talk about the paedophile in the local school,' she howled at him when left to take the twins to school (he was in bed with a bad flu). 'Bent rusted spoon would have nothing on what would follow for you after that, fella.'

Suddenly an unexpected knock came to the car window, startling Donal into a new reality. He smiled a false cheer, rolling the window down to acknowledge Wanda Millar, the (reasonably) new maths teacher.

A pretty slip of a thing, fresh out of university, this was her first permanent position since. There was a bet going on amongst some of the teachers that she'd be gone by the new term. So far, his suggestion otherwise, was holding strong.

'Having a tricky old morning?' Wanda's large lips glowed jungle red lipstick, applied so liberally and thickly that Donal felt the nick name of 'Rubber Lips' was aptly fitting. 'I know that feeling well enough myself!'

'Me and the missus were out drinking last night,' Donal lied, knowing Gemma would murder him if she knew the untruths he talked about their false activities. 'Might have had a few too many I'm afraid.' He faked a sore head with a touch. 'We live and learn, eh!'

'Ah,' Rubber Lips nodded an annoyingly long understanding of his plight, trying to show an empathy to her fellow colleague. It just came off looking superficial. 'I'm no stranger to those nights myself. Come on,' she urged. 'If we're lucky, Bart will have left some coffee for the rest of us.'

'Huh!' Donal scoffed. Bart was vice principle and the most self-entitled fellow in the place. Staff-room beverages took a serious pounding when he'd finished filling his gigantic travel cup from the machine each morning. 'That selfish bugger thinks of nobody but himself.'

Naturally, he was right. Barty Farty (nickname given for obvious reasons) had scoffed the lot and old missus McAnulty (Home Economics) was in the process of making a fresh batch when Donal and Wanda arrived. They were a little worse for wear on account of the heavens opening up and pouring down before they reached shelter.

Most of the staff were there for the routine Monday morning meeting. There were a few stragglers (the usual culprits) running late, who'd no doubt blame traffic or some domestic duties for their misdemeanours.

Donal poured himself a glass of orange juice that had been left out of the fridge overnight, so it was far from chilled. He found a seat beside Sam Puddy (biology) and away from Wanda because enough was enough.

Sam acknowledged Donal with a nod of his head, resuming just as quickly back to the science magazine he looked to be engulfed in.

The usual topics for the week were discussed; bus duties, lunch supervision and who's turn it was to carry them out.

A few suggestions were explored concerning a solution to the problem of smokers in the bathrooms and litter bins been set on fire, from other members of staff.

After a bit of analysis, it was decided to leave the topics for another day. That suited everybody as most were eager to get started with their first class of the day.

'Oh no!' Donal was given bus duty all week long. He'd felt sure it wasn't his turn until the following. 'Ah bugger, what will I do?'

'What's up?' Sam joined him at the notice board on his way to class. 'You sound peeved.'

'Peeved wouldn't be in it.' Donal's voice was louder than was actually called for. 'Look,' he indicated his name beside the duty. 'I'd assumed I was off the hook for another while. I've my sons to collect from school. Gemma's working later and can't.'

'Don't fret,' Sam consoled. 'We'll get this sorted in no time. Give me a second.'

Sam disappeared to the far corner of the room and was seen chatting to Wanda for a few minutes. She looked serious, smiled and then nodded in Donal's direction. It was looking positive.

Sam returned supporting a pearly white smile that covered most of his lower jaw.

'Sorted,' he announced triumphantly. 'Wanda's free and single with few obligations. She's new here and eager to please. She'll do bus duty this week for you.'

'You're a saint,' Donal complimented from nothing but sheer relief. Gemma would hang him if he left school pick-up to her again. 'I can't thank you enough.'

'Oh, I can think of a few things as payback.' Sam scurried a quick glance around the room to make sure nobody was within ear shot. 'See you later.'

With a hurried wink followed by a slinging of his tweed jacket over his left shoulder, he left the staff-room and the strong scent of Valentio body spray behind.

Instantly uplifted, Donal threw Wanda an over enthusiastic wave, mouthed a big bold 'thank you' her way and left.

Some rumours had real solid foundation, often hidden behind a façade of normal family life. It kept the gossip buzzards at bay and the fear of judgement away from his shoulders.

Marriage after all, was a two-way street.

CHAPTER TWELVE

Kate was meeting Adam in the park at lunchtime for a quickie and it had started to rain outside, which was just rotten, stinking bad luck. She was fuming. Why did these things always happen to her for pity's sake? It was so unfair.

She slammed her pen on to the desk so hard it bounced up and slapped her chest, only to then fall to the floor and crack open.

She sighed a temper frustration, inhaling so deeply it caused light-headedness. All weekend she'd prepared for today's event. Not once in these plans, had she ever considered the weather.

Today too, she'd got up earlier than usual, even though she'd been awake most of the night with Aine, her youngest, who seemed to have contracted a bug with added temperature.

While that lazy lump of a husband of hers turned over in the bed for a second sleep, Kate had showered, dressed and got the girls up for school (amid a fight that involved Aine arguing reasons why she shouldn't be going there).

She'd prepared breakfast all before John made an appearance into the busy kitchen, wondering why there was so much racket to waken him in the first place.

Kate was looking forward to seeing Adam for days. She was excited to be wearing a new garter (he loved those), even though it was nipping into her leg since she'd put it on.

The bikini wax from Saturday was starting to cause a skin rash. The beautician was trying out a new moisture that didn't seem to be agreeing with her skin. It was itching like a poison ivy allergy 'down there.' She was not a happy bunny.

Nothing seemed to be working out as it was meant to be. Secretly, Kate was worried sick that Adam would lose interest and find someone else. He wasn't a man of patience (with any stretch of the imagination) and she'd seen Nelly Travers from the accounting department give Adam the glad eye on more than one occasion.

Okay she reasoned, so Nelly was due retirement soon, practically kicking up dust as they spoke. But still, a threat was still a threat regardless of age and should be taken seriously.

Adam Malone was a looker. With is long, straight nose (that had been broken on two occasions), blue grey eyes, brown side locks and a handlebar moustache, what he lacked in height was amply made up for in features. Her idea of Mister Dreamboat.

Kate picked up the pen from under her desk, banging her head on the way up ('uch'). She sat down on the TriFlex office chair, recently purchased for all senior staff members and swivelled it from side to side, deep in thought.

Sub-consciously scratching her groin area (the rash was doing a number), a new alternative venue for her and Adam was in the making. It would have to be somewhere discrete, away from the usual places the rest of the staff frequented at lunchtime... or did it?

Like the wallop on her head earlier, it hit her, only this time mentally. If most of the others left the government building from twelve thirty to one thirty (and again the following hour), why on earth should she and Adam? What was wrong with staying put? It had less chance of being caught than if they'd gone out.

Store cupboards, cleaning storage units and even bathrooms were lying vacant during lunch hours. Couldn't they simply avail of their privacy? There wasn't one solid reason she could think of now why they shouldn't. It was genius. A real humdinger of a plan. Adam would love it. She'd text him with the suggestion that very second.

Not convinced it's a great idea. His instant replay left her feeling deflated. *Way riskier than the park. We'll pray it stops pelting down before one. Ax*

You're not giving the idea a proper chance. Kate would be dammed if she'd give up that easily. *Think about it for a while, weigh up the pros and cons. It makes pretty good sense to me. Kx*

Fifteen minutes later her phone let her know she'd had a response. Half way through interviewing for a new personal assistant, the desire to read and answer the message was nearly as profound as the rash, that was by now ripping her a new one.

'I need to take this,' she lied to the skinny brunette sitting opposite, who'd the attention of every red-blooded male (and one female) outside in the common area, glaring in at her as they (deliberately and unnecessarily) passed by the glass window of her office. 'Excuse me.'

Not keen on your attitude, telling me what to do. Kate stopped breathing. *May be best to leave things altogether. Good day to you. Adam Malone.*

Was he serious? *Leave things altogether?* What the hell did that mean? Was he breaking up with her because she took the initiative? Oh, sweet and holy Jacob. What on earth had she done?

On the verge of throwing up, Kate hurriedly excused herself for the second time, racing towards the toilets at a rate equivalent to a photon.

Once there, bile and a little undigested breakfast landed in the bowl. Some kind of yellow stuff followed. Likely the lining of her stomach, she though, state she was in.

Minutes later things began to settle. Dampening a few disposable hand towels, she patted her cheeks and forehead several times with a cool cloth.

It was essential to gather composure and soon. She couldn't risk delaying a response lest Adam think she was agreeing to his earlier suggestion that they should leave it.

I'm wearing a garter and thong. Kx She waited. Five... six... seven... ten... eleven... sixteen seconds past and then bingo! Almost instant response.

See you in the park. Normal scheduled time. Ax Thank the Universal energies for such huge relief. Saved by the garter. Buying a size smaller had finally pay off. Kate assumed it would do that okay, just in an entirely different way.

Next plan was to find time to nip out and buy a thong. But first things first. Collecting a few new hand towels, Kate dampened them under the tap. She walked into the cubical, locked the door and went to town, scratching and rubbing the itch. Blood spots had appeared. The water made things sting but it was worth it all to know her affair was still functioning.

Later that day at approximately twelve forty-four p.m. the school rang to ask that she collect Aine from their care. She'd been throwing up all morning and seemed to be running a pretty serious temperature.

Family emergency, Kate cried as she text. *Need to reschedule. So, so sorry. Please don't be mad. Kx*

Me too. The response was instant this time. *Invited to golf match with Paul.* Adam's boss. '*Def have my foot in the door there!* He'd been seeking a promotion for months.

'Let's get you home and into bed young lady,' Kate hugged her rosy cheeked daughter, guiltier than ever at having sent her to school in the first place, all because she prioritised the time with Adam. 'I think when you're feeling better the new Barbie doll's house might just be coming your way.'

There was nothing like retail therapy to dull the senses.

CHAPTER THIRTEEN

When Anna saw Ellen's car pull up outside her home the following day, her whole body sighed with relief. At the same time, it allowed for a little trapped wind to finally find escape.

'Thank you, Archangel Uriel,' she acknowledged the answer to a recent prayer, 'I knew you wouldn't let me down.' Relief came in many different ways.

Maeve's routine was to enjoy an afternoon snooze. Anna had grown to devour the joy of her sister's slumber in the short time she'd bombarded into Anna's otherwise peaceful life. Secretly, she'd been tempted to fast forward the clocks an hour ahead, just to make it happen quicker.

'Hi Mum,' Ellen's call was loud and cheery. 'Where are you?'

'Shush!' Anna appeared from behind the bathroom door, arm's flapping in time to her hissing noise. 'You'll waken it.'

Ellen did a quick surround check, noticing immediately that Maeve was nowhere in sight.

'Don't you mean *her*? Ellen asked, 'and not *it*?'

Anna looked deflated.

'I'm not so sure,' she gestured Ellen into the living room and farther away from the spare room where the wickedness currently resided. 'Maeve may not be as human as we'd originally thought.'

As they conversed in whispered dialogue, it was clear to Ellen that her mother was either on the brink of insanity or loss of integrity, which in some worlds was far worse.

Words like "foul" and "insulting" were used. Others such as "insensitive" and "vindictive" were flung around with heated discourse. Anna wove her tales and fables, all connected to Maeve and the influence she had held over her younger sister since arrival.

'And,' Anna sniffled, on the brink of tears, 'she complains about everything. She sprays the whole house with air freshener every two minutes,' she looked despairingly at Ellen. 'I'm close to exploding, Ellen,' she confessed. 'These past two days have been nothing short of a great big nightmare.'

'Stay calm, Mum.' Ellen advised. 'We'll sort something out. Don't worry.'

Anna twisted her hands anxiously. At a loss on ways to cope, things were becoming terminal. Maeve's visit was having quite an impact. Ellen feared the drama may have a great deal of truth attached to it. Her mum looked older and worn in the space of hours.

The tales didn't stop there either. Apparently, the neighbours were privy to the destruction as well.

'She told Jean Jackson off' Anna's long-standing neighbour and a friend 'for doing nothing more than walking closer than needed past the gate.'

'Fair enough,' Ellen consoled as the rant came to a quavering end. 'Tell me how I can help.'

'Oh dear, I'm not sure…'

'We'll think it through and…'

'I'll hold her down and you put a pillow over her face.' Anna suggested, half serious with a jokey edge. 'We could dump the body in Lillie McCartan's garden and let her take the fall.'

Lillie McCartan was renowned for being the town's biggest gossip and happened to be one of Anna's least favourite people. This was on account of the rumours Lillie had spread last year that Anna was dating Frankie McEvoy, a married man of three and a raging alcoholic.

'Mum!' Ellen scolded. 'That's not helping.'

'Well,' Anna showed little remorse. It had been hell. 'McCartan's good for it.'

It was time to get serious. It was as clear as Canadian water that Anna wasn't coping as well as assumed. Despite her reluctance to ask for help in the past, Anna was in no position to hang on to that pride so deeply now.

'I'll mention it to Kate and Gemma,' Ellen suggested, forming a plan of action in her mind. 'Hopefully, they can help.'

It was further decided Ellen take her aunt walking around Delaney Park.

'I'll start in the morning,' she suggested. 'We'll arrange a time later.'

Before any further plans could be made, the living room door edged open with a squeak of its un-oiled hinges. Maeve's presence darkened the entrance. She looked annoyed.

'What's with all the talking?' She glanced from one to the other. 'My nap was disturbed. It's very upsetting. I'll be out of sorts for the rest of the day now.'

'Sorry.' It felt a lot like Ellen and Anna were being chastised by a head teacher for offences neither one had committed. 'We were trying to be quite so as not to disturb you.'

'Well, you've failed miserably. Anyway, you two see each other a lot. I'm not sure what the insistent nattering was about in the first place.'

Anna instantly fumed. She could put up with a lot but drew a line at being scolded in her own home and in the company of her daughter as well. *She'd* invited Maeve, not the other way around. It wasn't unreasonable to expect some decorum from her guest.

'Catch yourself on!' Anna's voice pitched high on account of confrontational nerves. 'This is the way things are here, Maeve.' The tone wobbled and she cleared her throat. 'It won't be changing anytime soon. It's a case of like it or lump it I'm afraid.'

'Yes,' Ellen injected when she saw the look of distain Maeve threw Anna's way. 'Seems like you've forgotten how we like the craic here. Now come on,' she gestured towards the kitchen area. 'Time for a cup of tea to wet the buds.'

Maeve pondered and then sniffed an indigent breath at being put into her box. She hesitated, deciding the next move. Should she abide with the request, or argue her case?

Her eyes darted from Anna to Ellen. They both looked defiant and smug. It was clear this battle was not her win. The look of determination on both their faces dictated there'd be no backing down. Decision instantly made; she'd let it slide… this time.

Reaching behind her back she retrieved the can of air freshener hiding there. Spraying two sharp squirts into the room. Anna and Ellen's nostrils were treated to the worst smell of chemical induced roses man, woman or child had ever known.

'Holy Moley, that's horrible.' The words were out before Ellen realised. 'Never spray that again.'

Maeve laughed a tittering chuckle. It sounded both high-pitched and squeaky, rather like that of a banshee.

'It was George's favourite scent.' Maeve squirted a hearty amount behind her (and towards Ellen in particular) as she walked into the hallway and then to the kitchen. 'I keep it to remind me of him.'

Conversation over their beverages was strained. Well, let's face it, strained was being kind. Long, lingering gaps filled the majority of their time together, with Maeve's noisy tea slurps devouring the serenity.

'I'd love to visit Croke Park while I'm here.' The announcement came out of the blue. 'Are there regular buses to Dublin by any chance?'

'There are indeed.' There was no chance in heaven Anna was driving her there. Two consistent hours (four round trip) in the confined space of a car, she'd toss her into the Liffey River for sure. 'I believe the service runs from Newry or from Belfast hourly.'

'Oh, super stuff,' Maeve faked a genuine smile. 'George loved it, you know, may the dear Lord rest his soul in peace.' She blessed herself to be sure. 'He'd visit it any time he was in Ireland on business.'

'Lovely.'

At Maeve's insistence, Ellen was staying for 'another strong but hopefully not stewed,' cup of tea.

'I've a surprise for you dear.' Maeve took Ellen by the arm, gliding her towards the guest bedroom. 'I've won awards for the very thing you're about to be privy too. Follow me.'

'Don't touch it,' Anna whispered into Ellen's ear, following closely behind. 'The dog ran from the piece I slipped him. Poor thing hasn't come near the fence since.'

Things definitely needed to change, and soon.

CHAPTER FOURTEEN

Conor McDowell looked more like his sister Ellen than any of his other sisters.

With mousey-coloured hair, naturally bleached in parts from the sun, a long straight nose and thick red lips, it was a challenge for anyone not to consider him a sexy specimen of the male gender.

Physical appearance was not high on Conor's list of priorities which simply added to his allure. It seemed that being naturally humble had its own attractiveness.

He stood now, deep in thought, on Nice's Des Anglais promenade, watching the weighty waves of the Mediterranean Sea crash onto the sands of the French coastal seaside town.

The sun shone hot, defying October forecasts. Apart from his Virgo trait to analyse almost everything to death, the good-looking male had been weighed down by a mixture of emotions, thoughts, desires and personal perceptions that he'd carried with him from home.

A lopsided grin spread across his face; who was he kidding, he thought? He'd been carrying this same stuff all his livelong life.

'Conor!' Philippe called from the roadside, disrupting his thinking and awakening him from the semi-dream state he was in, *'Ça va?'*

Philippe's old bicycle strained under his average size weight. The whining creaks and flattened tyres attracted the attention of passers-by and added a sense of humour to some of the holidaymaker's day.

Much too small for Philippe's tall body, his legs cramped under the handlebars. It was clear the Frenchman needed to be somewhere fast, yet his mode of transport was ill-equipped to make that happen.

'Ça va bien,' Conor responded with an uncertain cheer. 'You're looking good,' he mocked.

Phillippe peddled towards the tall villas, nestled into the cliffs ahead, smiling. The usual weekly visit with his grandparents promised food and financial treats ahead; they liked to spoil their only grandson when they saw him. His mouth watered at what was surely awaiting him.

Phillippe smiled a wider smile than before as he peddled. He felt fortunate to have the added bonus to his day having come across Conor too. An unexpected treat for him on top of the day's events made him think Jupiter's luck was shining strongly in his sun-born Leo chart that day.

Phillippe thought back to when both men had first met. It was the first week Conor arrived on French shores, looking like a fish out of water. He was standing at the crowded bar, tapping his fingers self-consciously to the musical beat the rock band was throwing about in such an ear-insulting mode.

The attraction across the noisy nightclub was instant between them both as their eyes locked and lingered in a knowing stare. It felt to him that they had known one another from before, yet Philippe was sure it wasn't in this lifetime but in many previous ones gone by.

Phillip made his way over to Conor through the crowd, touching his arm from behind.

'Vouloir dancer?' he asked, a bit more cockily than he felt, *'je suis assez bon au trot de renard.'*

The startled Irishman spilt his beer over the bar's counter and onto his own fingers with the help of Phillip's pat on his arm, which was more of a thump than anything else.

'Hey,' Conor wasn't sure if he felt annoyed or complimented that this tanned, dark-haired stranger was inviting him to boogie or had just tipped out a quarter of his drink. 'Maybe later, thanks.'

'Ahh, you... English?' Philippe spoke a broken amount of the language himself. 'You are to holiday here,' (he hoped not), 'or to lay?'

'Working,' Conor confirmed Philippe's hopes. 'And I'm from Ireland.'

As their night progressed, the music seemed to become bearable, based solely on the amount of alcohol consumed. When that night turned into the next morning and a breakfast of outdoor sunshine, fresh fruit and croissants, both men knew something special had transpired between them.

'I am feeling dis was meant to by.' Philippe stole a grape from Conor's plate and displayed the munched fruit each time he chewed. 'How's about ye?'

'I agree,' Conor spoke from an unsure position. 'And thank you for making my first few days here so comfortable.'

Now as Phillip cycled, a tiny frown furrowed his brow at the memories they'd shared. In the days and months since that fateful meeting, he found it difficult at times to read the Irishman.

This was never more so when Conor took on that dreamy, faraway look from some yesteryear place. It would happen randomly at times and more so after he'd finished a phone call from Ireland. Philippe could admit that it did fluster him somewhat, if pushed.

'Perhaps it's dreamy Neptune's placing in my chart.' Conor explained when Philippe enquired. 'My mum always swore I was more Pisces born than Virgo.'

But Philippe wasn't convinced. He knew a few astrological references himself and to him, Conor lived up to the traits of the sun-born Virgo personality quite well.

Prone to anxiousness and perfection, there had been times Philippe's reassurances that all was not as bad as it was being made out, were both intense and a little testing if he were honest. More time needed to pass to better gage the whole thing.

Running out of puff at an alarming rate now as he cycled, Philippe narrowly avoided crashing into a young child on the pedestrian crossing.

He was rewarded with a stony look and a one-fingered salute from her father as he struggled to straighten the small bicycle after the swerve.

Smiling apologetically, he ventured forth, unperturbed. His taste buds tingled at the thought of his grandmother's beef bourguignon. His legs peddled harder because of it and his stomach rumbled loudly from the lack of it.

Back on the promenade, Conor hung his head, still smiling at Phillip's unexpected visit. It had been good to see him but God — he sighed deeply now — he was so confused and felt pressurised.

Struggling for the longest time with the same mental block, the familiar tension entered his thoughts. What was he to do and how was he to do it? *Perhaps*, he thought, unconsciously biting into his lower lip. *The biggest question of all was: is it really what I want?*

Ireland was a small place to grow up in, a tiny island in the scheme of things. Renowned for its warmth, friendly people and charm, as much as for its scenic beauty and emerald-green fields, it was surely in league with Nirvana on earth — rainy climate aside of course.

It was also a place where everybody was somehow related to the next one. Where third, fourth and even fifth cousins counted. If someone burped in Belfast, they'd know about it by nightfall in Donegal. Where families helped one another out and where animals were respected (for the most part) rather than abused.

Conor signed and subconsciously chewed on his thumbnail. He'd always prided himself on being a liberated New Age thinker, or as his sister, Ellen had recently called him, 'an Indigo born' progressive one.

He knew, ego aside, that his mind was both an asset and a hindrance to him, which more often than not, flung great waves of confusion his way. Like now for example. How could he ever expect to return home one day, have a decent, carefree life, if this decision he was struggling with now, swayed the way he truly wanted it to?

'Frig.'

A group of young Welsh tourists passed by. The giddy females glanced Conor's way, shy for his attention yet reluctant to let the chance to flirt pass by.

Conor lit a cigarette. The grey smoke exploded into the crisp seaside air, creating a frenzied, dancing cloud around the females.

'Those things cause cancer.' A slim, dark-haired female called his way. 'You'll make yourself ill, handsome.' Her friends erupted in squeals of laughter at such boldness; this was someone who wasn't afraid to take a chance.

Conor grinned as a response, hoping this was all that would be required of him. He was in no mood for banter but at the same time, didn't want to be rude.

Maybe they'd think he was French-speaking and unable to understand their words. That way he'd be off the hook.

He noticed this girl was attractive with her long dark locks and brazen blue eyes but way too young for his tastes, and besides, he scolded himself, wasn't he in enough turmoil without adding logs to the already flaming fire?

He'd no desire to explore further, so remained silent to her taunting. The group walked on while discussing in great detail their friend's bravado.

His throat tickled and he coughed. Sitting down on the metal seat beside him, he felt the usual ache and dull heaviness that he'd been feeling for months in his left knee; fluid built up from an old sports injury, or so he thought.

He rubbed and stretched his leg, hoping this time it would make a difference. Added to this, his digestive system was causing problems that ached in a way he didn't care for.

His mother always had a cure for everything. At that moment he really missed her natural remedies. He'd stop and pick up ginger and lemon to make a tea and maybe grab some mint for later. The chef in the restaurant where he worked, wouldn't mind a bit. They were mates.

It wasn't so long until his work shift began. Stubbing the cigarette dead and leaving the tranquil, artistic, scene behind, Conor crossed the busy road reaching *'Le Restaurant du Bord De la Mer'* two minutes later.

He'd lived and worked there since his arrival in Nice with Philippe's considerable help.

Through the swinging doors, the heaviness of garlic and Stilton cheese greeted his nostrils, filling them with a sense of familiarity and a slight rumble from his empty stomach.

Before descending the stairs to his apartment, he picked up all required ingredients to make his tea, along with bread and cheese to fill the empty pit his stomach seemed to have developed.

The remains of Philippe's grandmother's three-day-old onion soup was stored invitingly in the small fridge, awaiting its companions, for a tasty meal. He obligingly honoured the request.

The meal finished, Conor felt considerably uplifted both mentally and physically. Standing from the small table, he pushed the empty bread basket to the side and rubbed his sandpaper chin.

It was time to shave the three-day stubble away. His reflection from the ageing mirror above the sink agreed. Smiling at himself he felt a confidence he hadn't felt in a while.

'It has to be done,' he spoke his thoughts aloud, clearing away the cobwebs one by one. 'You owe it to yourself to be honest, me old matey.'

A text message beeped from his phone. It was from Philippe.

'*À plus tard,*' he read aloud, '*et j'espere une réponse.*'

Conor was no expert at the French language. He'd picked up bits and pieces from Philippe. By adding them to his secondary school educated learning, it was a lesson in progress. He did however know the bulk of what Philippe's message required. He wanted an answer to his question when they'd next meet.

'*See you later.*' he texted back, playfully adding a little Gaelic for fun. '*Ionas gur feidir leat pog mo thoin as Eirinn.*'

Later on, when they were together Conor would explain the meaning to him and they'd no doubt laugh at the invitation he'd just issued for the Frenchman to 'Kiss his Irish arse!'

To heck with what others thought. Conor's relief was abundant at finally reaching his decision. To blazes with man-made rules and conditions as well. He would carry this choice through to its end, as proudly as his wobbly knee allowed.

It was time to stand up and be counted and he would start the countdown from his own personal soapbox.

So pleased with himself at that time, Conor barely felt the rush of cold air swipe past his face as his father's energies surrounded him in comfort and unconditional love.

All was as it should be.

CHAPTER FIFTEEN

The pre-arranged time with Maeve for their walk around Delaney Park was proving difficult for Ellen to honour. Fergal and James had delayed her considerably.

In a heated discussion, that began last night and carried into breakfast today, getting out and earning a living for herself was Fergal's abrupt (verging aggressive) suggestion. He was insisting it was time for her to 'earn her keep.' Like a red flag to a bull, Ellen tore into him.

She began by pointing out the many ways he was undervaluing her role as the homemaker. This however, not only fell on deaf ears but was laughed at as well. This infuriated her even more, to the point if she didn't walk away, thing would have turned physical.

Okay, okay so there was a slipper or two thrown (one hitting his leg) but it was done in temper and not to cause pain. The bedroom door was slammed so violently on her way out of the room, the window vibrated with its effect. '

In the midst of heated intensity, James debated a day of school for a sprained foot (basketball injury from the night before). Compromise was finally reached, a note to excuse participation in P.E. that day and a gentle nudge out the front door, so as not to miss the last bus, hobble or not (which wasn't so bad anyway).

Moby knew she was flustered. His submission when having his lead hooked, told the tale. They set of already ten minutes behind time in a panicked frenzy.

Ellen decided she'd calm down on the drive. No time for meditation beforehand. A challenging time lay ahead (based on what she knew of Maeve's personality so far). No need to add insult to injuries by not being prepared.

Maeve stood impatiently outside Anna's gateway, tapping her foot against the pavement and glancing at her watch as every two seconds passed by. She rolled her eyes skywards and pulled her mouth into an 'o' shape as soon as she recognised Ellen's car pull up in front.

Wearing a light-blue waterproof coat with matching gloves, scarf, hat and earmuffs, Maeve was ready for their adventure ahead (and for a blizzard if it appeared).

The car came to a stop. Ellen smiled, looking out of the windscreen. And then she prayed.

'Help me, Angels,' she begged through clenched teeth. 'Bring me calmness and direction.'

A starling flew across the car by way of instant response. She smiled a thank you to acknowledge the response, never not surprised how quickly requests could be answered.

'You look great,' she told Maeve as soon as the car's door was opened, staggering its truth. 'I envy your eye for detail. Not one of my stronger gifts I'm afraid. I'm useless with co-ordination, I tell you.'

Ellen's rambling continued, intentionally. 'I once paired black trousers with a navy top and yellow shoes. Complete disaster.' The white lie was told with fingers crossed behind the car door. She didn't even own yellow shoes and never had.

Maeve looked startled, then surprised, then suspicious. Her eyes narrowed to slits, wondering if she was being played or not. Getting inside the car, she buckled her belt.

'Thank you.' She answered, secretly pleased at the complement. It had been a while since she'd been praised for anything. 'But it's my timekeeping you should be envying Ellen dear, not my dress style. Perhaps I could give you a few hints on how to improve that. I've a feeling,' she placed her handbag under her feet, 'you'd benefit greatly.'

The drive to the park was nothing short of torture, consumed entirely by Maeve's complaints.

'It's the fact they bring disease everywhere they go,' she said, glaring at an oblivious Moby who was enjoying the scenery from the rear of the car, awaiting his chance to escape. 'You really should get rid of that beast you know. He'll bring rabies into your home.'

'But we love Moby!' Ellen felt offended. 'He's part of our family.'

'I'm telling you,' Maeve insisted. 'He'll be the death of each and every last one of you.'

'He's had all his shots.'

'Makes no difference. Rabies or salmonella. You choose.'

'Oh Maeve,' Ellen said. 'We're all fine. Moby's been with us from he was six weeks old and nothing has shown up yet.'

'Well, don't come crying to me when the inevitable hits.'

'I promise I will not.'

Once at Delaney Park, Ellen got out of the car a much more informed person than when she had got in. The state of the economy, the dreadful weather, the youth of today and the bad policing were all topics she felt better educated in, regardless of her desire to be or not.

'And,' Maeve concluded her latest grievance leaving the car's comforts, 'even though I told your mother the alcohol she drank from last night was really the devil's urine,' — Ellen almost gagged — 'she told me to climb into my own arse and,' she looked downcast and regretful, 'I'm sorry to say…' she hesitated, 'bite her!'

Practically running to the car's boot, lest she roar with laughter and be gunned down on the spot, Ellen opened the door and let the impatient dog out.

Moby agreed with his owner's whispers of 'fresh air being nature's saving grace.' His delight was to pollute the same air with a pee and a poop. The park was his personal playground and Moby liked to engage in its recreation.

As Angelically guided, Ellen placed a white light bubble around herself for protection and one around Moby, by way of rabies prevention. Assured they'd carry little or none of Maeve's grey energy with them, dragging spirits down, she wished the same idea had kicked in before now.'

It worked a treat. The older woman moaned and groaned as they walked. Complaints around the ground's surface, the coldness in the air, the number of birds chittering in the trees and the 'unnecessary need for a park so close to the ocean' were all seen by Ellen as nothing more than fear transported from another time. Maeve's heart was closed; her views restricted and her tolerance pitiful.

Twenty minutes later, with a well-timed interruption, Moby arrived at their feet clutching something in his mouth just as they'd begun to climb the hill.

'Hey dude,' Ellen greeted the golden-haired dog excitedly. 'What have you there?' She stroked his soft fur. 'Let's have a look.'

Prying the material from Moby's tight-toothed grasp, and hoping lockjaw wasn't an early sign of rabies, revealed a well-worn brown cap. Further investigations and a lift of the cap's hem showed Ellen that her suspicions were founded.

'It's Andrew's,' she told its finder and her aunt. 'One of his favourites if I'm not mistaken.'

Moby barked acknowledgement, causing Maeve to scream and subsequently run for shelter behind Ellen's back.

'That dog should be hanged,' she shrieked, 'and sold for parts.'

'Catch yourself on.' Ellen was losing it. 'He's as gentle as a feather.'

'He'll be going for my throat next.'

'I'm surprised nobody hasn't done that already.'

'I beg your pardon?'

'I'm sorry but seriously Maeve,' Ellen knew she was walking on some pretty rocky waves. 'You really do need to get it together.'

'Well, I never...'

Reaching the pond's bench (in silence on account of Maeve's huff. Thank goodness for small mercies and all of that), both Ellen and Moby were disappointed by Rose and Andrew's absence. It seemed that today their luck was far from plentiful.

'Mustn't be warm enough for Andrew,' Ellen surmised, a glimmer of regret etching her tone. 'His health is delicate. Let's sit anyway,' she suggested with an eagerness she didn't feel. 'We can do a spot of meditating.'

Maeve found sitting at the pond to be too cold and thought meditating was a waste of time.

'And,' she threw a nasty glance Moby's way, 'if I get soaked once more with his shakes, I'm sure to catch pneumonia.'

'That's very unlikely,' Ellen said, dismissing Maeve's fears. 'You'd have a better chance of being shot or run over by a car.' She glanced towards Maeve, 'Your choice.' The whisper was faint, its intended audience unaware. 'Let's go.' They'd drive around a bit in the heat of the car. 'Moby won't be too pleased but at least you'll be warmer.'

Ellen knew in her very heart of hearts that her mother would pound her if she brought Maeve back so soon. The whole idea was to tire her to almost unconsciousness. She wasn't sure that was even possible to do; this woman appeared to have the energy of a teenager and the constitution of a boar.

Taking into account the journey here and the amount of time they'd been walking, she'd say they'd been out thirty-five minutes, tops.

Ellen thought hard about what to do. An early lunch was out of the running on account of them both not hungry. A shopping trip to Ballygo town would have disappointed on account of today being half day closing for the shops of highest interest.

A movie… no, Moby wouldn't get access … a trot up the mountains… umm too cold again. What about back to the O'Hare house for tea? No again. It was untidy and would be open to harsh criticism. And then suddenly, it hit her!

'Hey,' she suggested eagerly, 'how about we head back to the car and go deliver Andrew's cap?'

Maeve sniffed angrily.

'I don't think so,' she rebuked, 'I'm not even acquainted with this Andrew fellow.'

For all she knew, her niece could well be introducing her to a murderer, a rapist or worse still, a member of parliament.

Ellen patted Maeve's knee encouragingly, standing up to indicate she wasn't for backing down.

'I promise he's *thee* most harmless soul on the planet,' she reassured Maeve. 'You'll love both Andrew and Rose on the spot.'

'I highly doubt that,' Maeve argued indignantly. 'Mixing with strangers has never been my strong point.'

'I see,' Ellen sighed, wondering if there was anyone stranger than herself. 'We could stay for tea,' she taunted hopefully. 'You'd be in the heat and out of this damp air.' Maeve pondered the latest suggestion and allowed time for it to digest.

'Fair enough.' She was sold. The thought of warmth, hot tea and indoors felt like cream on the cake, the icing on the sponge, chocolate on the éclair. She was willing to accept just reward for her solid endurance. 'But be warned,' she advised, 'I'm not staying if there's any funny business.'

And off they went. The triple cluster gathered their belongings and began the twenty-minute journey back to the car park in virtual silence, eager for the temptations ahead.

As they walked, one shivered with cold, one peed every five minutes and the other grinned from ear to ear with sheer relief she'd saved herself from a motherly trouncing.

Ellen prayed Rose wouldn't mind the intrusion.

CHAPTER SIXTEEN

The McGrath family couldn't have been better pleased with the unexpected visitors. Andrew was ecstatic. He released Moby from the car's boot seconds after it came to a stop. It was time to get their noisy games started and there was no time like the present.

'He hasn't been feeling great this past couple of days. That's why we didn't venture out around the park today,' Rose explained to Ellen at the opened car window. 'Moby's arrival should improve that enormously though,' she smiled towards Andrew and Moby's excited exchange. 'I'm truly delighted you called.' She really was as much delighted as Ellen was relieved to hear her say it.

Once Ellen introduced Maeve to Rose, Rose insisted both women come in for a cup of tea (phew).

'The way I see it,' she smiled knowingly towards the opened cottage door and then pointed her walking stick in that direction for emphasis, 'you don't have much of a choice.' Andrew and Moby were already inside, games commenced.

With a smile and an agreement, Maeve and Ellen accepted the warm invitation. The truth was Ellen could have given Rose a bear hug and a million kisses, for the suggestion alone. She really had saved the day and didn't even know it. The hope now was that Maeve behaved in a fitting manner that didn't have them chucked out earlier than expected.

'It wouldn't be such a great shame,' Maeve mumbled, stepping from the car and pulling her coat tight against the cold, 'if that brute of a dog stayed here permanently.'

It was as clear as a white quartz crystal, the moment Rose and Maeve sat down to tea and homemade shortbread, they were going to be friends. So apparently mirrored in character, the Cancer- and Aquarian-born women acted like they'd known one another for aeons of time.

Something fitted between them, like an instant bond. As absurd as it was to think it, much less voice it, Ellen swore they both looked alike, a distinct facial similarity.

'It's the shape of your cheekbones,' she tried to explain to a perplexed looking Maeve and a smiling Rose. 'You look more like sisters than strangers, meeting for the first time in such a long time.'

Giving one another tips for cleaner laundry and advice for lighter scone mix, the two older women chatted non-stop. It was like old friends catching up, reunited after years apart.

It wasn't just their looks either. Their closeness in age and their generational upbringing and outlooks seemed to mirror one another perfectly

Ellen was fascinated by it all. Rendered speechless, she felt like an intruder into their conversations.

Coupled with Maeve and Rose's chatter and the warmth of the cottage, within thirty minutes Ellen felt sleepy. Her eyes became heavy, and her breathing slowed. Inside another five, six seconds she moved her mind into a meditative, dreamy state.

Colours invaded her head: indigo, green, yellow and blue. She breathed deeply, filling her core with their glow.

It took minutes for her to reach the point in her mind that held onto the physical, keeping her grounded, while at the same time opening a channel to better connect to the spiritual dimension. It took an even shorter time for her to begin receiving messages from her guides.

Opening her eyes, she found the atmosphere changed. Ellen felt it and Rose knew it. Andrew and Moby left, going outside to find another game now that the drizzle had stopped, leaving a draft in their absence and a lingering odour from Moby's digesting breakfast.

The room filled with a heavy, soundless stillness into a silent tranquillity. They were in another dimension.

Rose stopped talking, encouraging Maeve to do the same. They looked towards Ellen whose mind was already in a state of higher consciousness.

'I have a message for you both,' she told them, her gaze concentrated past them and focused on the back wall to better hear what was being channelled. 'It's from the Spirit World.'

'At last!' Rose was thrilled to bits. 'Thank goodness. I've been waiting on this.'

'What's happening?' Maeve frowned a perplexment she genuinely felt. 'I don't understand...'

'Go with the flow,' Rose promised reassurance and added a wink. 'You'll see shortly.'

Clasping her hands in anticipation at what was to come Rose was beyond delighted that things were finally moving in the direction they appeared to be.

Once again, her perception was spot on about Ellen. She'd known since first meeting her younger friend that Ellen was a medium, a channel for other energies to work through.

The bigger plan was to send messages of healing and hope through her, so one day (maybe soon) she could help the world and its occupants. Ellen was a Lightworker, and this job was one of her major contracts to fulfil in this life time.

'Go ahead,' Rose instructed. 'I'm all ears, if not a little deaf in one.'

Ellen inhaled deeply before continuing. She felt a nervous and excited all at once but knew going backwards was not an option.

'It seems,' she began, 'that you two,' she indicated Rose and Maeve, 'have known each other in a past life... in several lifetimes in fact.'

131

Rose gasped and Maeve scowled. She moved her eyeballs around the room, feeling an uncertainty and yes, a touch of fear and vulnerability as well. Should she go now before things really got out of hand? If so, where was the closest escape route?

'Fate or destiny,' Ellen continued, 'call it what you will…has brought you both back together now for a very specific reason.'

'I knew it!' Rose nudged Maeve, startling her into a response that resembled a whimpering pup. 'I felt it the second we met. Didn't you too Maeve?'

'I… I… I think so.' Maeve thought nothing of the sort. She hadn't a single clue what was going on but didn't want to offend Rose. She'd been a proper treasure so far, but this carryon was weird. 'What did you feel exactly, Rose?'

'That we had a connection of course.'

'Well yes, I felt that okay,' and Maeve had. 'But I'm a bit lost with all that Ellen's saying.'

Rose smiled at a bewildered-looking Maeve, patting her shoulder reassuringly, hoping to dispel any fears she may be having.

'I'll say more later when Ellen's finished,' she promised. 'Please just go with it all for now.'

'Okay.' She trusted Rose, in-so-far as meeting her for the first time an hour ago. There was a connection between them okay, but Ellen was Anna's daughter. This was beginning to sound a lot like the past.'

'It was in England.' Ellen confirmed still in the zone. 'You both worked in service. I believe it was London... in a basement kitchen... you were... sisters!'

A chill entered Maeve's spine and travelled up to her neck, forcing the surprised woman to shiver under its spell.

Far from knowing what was going on; she'd never encountered the likes of this before (even with Anna), but there did seem to be something lodged deep inside, that spoke of a truth in what Ellen was saying. A button was being pushed, rusty in its use, but still, it held grit.

Maeve continued to listen with a perplexity that was second to none. Rose promised an explanation when Ellen was done. Prayers were offered it would be a logical one.

'This is a karmic connection,' Ellen proceeded. 'There is something needs completed from another lifetime. It's been carried over to be settled in this one.'

'Can you tell us what, Ellen?' Rose enquired. 'It would help to know.'

'It's already in progress Rose. Completely out of your hands.'

'Contracted stuff usually is.'

'Umm hum. If it helps, it feels to me like you were torn apart, forced to separate.'

'I wonder why?'

'If I had to guess I'd say, some friend of a rich friend wanted the help.'

'Seriously?'

'Yep. One of you were given to another household miles away. Didn't matter if you wanted to go or not. The choice was taken away from you both.'

'Which one of us went?'

'Maeve... called Nelly at the time... the new life was difficult... abusive.'

'Good gracious.'

'Indeed.'

If they chose to complete the karma this time around, the fear connected to the previous separation would be lifted and they would have a breakthrough, debt paid.

'Wow, just wow!' Wide-eyed and animated, Ellen glared at Rose. 'I can't believe I just did that!'

'Well, I can,' Rose said. 'I'm so pleased this gift of yours has finally found a voice.'

'It's like I couldn't stop it,' Ellen half listened to Rose, captivated by the miracle of it all. 'I knew it was in me okay but to come out as daringly as it did well, I'm elated.'

'And so you should be, dear. It's quite a significant step forward.'

'I've only ever delivered messages inside my own family before, never to strangers or with what has happened here today. It's you Rose.' Rose looked startled. 'Since I met you, things have developed into this.'

'There are no coincidences, Ellen. Everything has a reason.'

'Yes, I know.'

Ellen felt chuffed beyond description. Secretly she was a little empowered. So much so that Maeve's reaction to it all was a distant consideration, until her aunt spoke up.

'I hate to break the moment,' Maeve shifted uncomfortably in her seat. 'But I'm lost with most of what you're both talking about.'

Over the next few hours, the conversation moved from domestic chores to discussions on Angels, Master Guides, different religious beliefs, spiritual ones and then previous lifetimes. Rose and Ellen took turns explaining.

'The soul carries all experiences from the past into present life, including fears.' Ellen said from an understanding she didn't know she processed. 'We often carry blocks that hold us back from reaching our full potential. The roots can be from traumas or disturbances in previous incarnations.'

'These things can close our hearts off and cause us to feel lonely, frightened or isolated. At its worst they can make us lose sense or sight of the Divine Plan in everything.'

'An example would be,' Rose took over. 'If someone suffered a horrific passing... say they died in battle or were tortured beforehand, the experience from that, with all the emotions included lives on and becomes part of the persona when in a new life time.'

'I see.' Maeve didn't really but heaven forbid Rose would think her an imbecile. 'So, say someone had a fear of water for example. Now where would that have come from?'

'Well,' Rose and Ellen spoke in unison. 'You go ahead,' Ellen encouraged. 'I'm sure we'd similar possibilities.'

'Okay. I was going to suggest drowning or having some other negative memory stored connected to water. Well,' she asked Ellen. 'Have you anything to add?'

'Nope. You've covered it all.'

Time trotted on. Lost in a world of many topics, the three women chatted. When Ellen did check her watch, she sprang upright with shock.

'I can't believe it's three-thirty already! 'Mum will think we're lost. Time to make a move I think.'

Maeve looked regretful. Sorry their time had passed so quickly, it seemed unjust now. Although some strange things had occurred, she would find no hardship in sitting with Rose all day and night long.

But she had come to visit her sister. Conditioning down the years had taught loyalty, principles and endurance, even when desiring otherwise.

'Rose,' Maeve stood, gathered her coat and handbag, preparing to leave. 'I cannot tell you how much I've appreciated your company today. Might I visit again before my stay in Ireland finishes?' She knew it was presumptuous of her to ask but seemed not to be able to help it.

'Stay!' Rose was feeling deflated the visit was ending. 'We can have stew for dinner, there's plenty in the pot.'

'Really?' Maeve couldn't believe her luck. She checked with Ellen, assuming a scolding of sorts about honouring commitments, but none came. Instead, Ellen was very much on board.

'It's your decision, Maeve,' Ellen had to leave regardless. Matt and James needed lifted from school. 'I'll call back later this evening for you.'

'That's settled then.' Maeve was elated and tried unsuccessfully not to show it. 'I'm delighted to accept your invitation,' she told Rose truthfully. 'Thank you.'

The rarest of smiles crossed her ageing face, making her momentarily look younger.

And so, it was.

Ellen was to inform Anna of the new plans (Ellen felt her mum would have little to no objection). Moby was invited to dinner as well, which he had no hesitation in accepting.

'Trader.'

'And one more thing before you go.' Rose handed Ellen a floral-patterned serving dish. 'Be a dear and leave that at Flanagan's house. It's the big grey farmhouse at the bottom of the lane. You can't miss it.'

Apparently, Cecilia Flanagan was entertaining a potential son-in-law later that week and wanted to impress.'

Despite the television blaring loudly and some kind of haphazard jazz music coming from upstairs, there was no answer to Ellen's knock on the farm house door.

She decided to leave the dish on the door step instead of waiting longer than the five minutes she already had. All being well, it would be discovered before the day was over.

The drive home was filled with elation and wonderment. How amazing was it to be able to access and then relay all she had done earlier?

'It feels like I'm finally starting to evolve.'

For the first time in so long, a new direction was showing promise. The gut feelings she'd held this long with a real sense of new beginnings developing, seemed to finally be making themselves felt. She'd no desire to ever let it stop.

Fergal was home when she arrived later with the two boys. He was in foul form. A work contract that he was sure of getting, went elsewhere.

'That bloody Brian McKinney,' (an-up-and coming builder in the area), 'under-priced me again.' He puffed a cigarette to an inch of its life outside the patio doors. 'It'll be a quiet word in his ear I'll be giving him when we next meet.

Sorry he was having a tricky day, Ellen sympathised okay but honestly to heavens above nothing, absolutely nothing, was going to deflate her after today's events. She was on a high that would take a long while to collapse. Let the games begin.

Life's roller coaster, was indeed invigorating.

CHAPTER SEVENTEEN

'I hope you don't think me rude,' Maeve glanced towards Rose once Ellen had left. 'I'm very nervous about this whole past life stuff.'

'Yes,' Rose knew rightly. 'I'd thought that myself.'

'It's just,' Maeve hesitated. How on earth would she ever explain the experience with Anna growing up? This woman here now was just a dream. She'd no desire to undermine her or the beliefs she held.

At the same time, this nonsense couldn't go on. 'I've had considerable experience with this kind of thing before with Anna. Nothing good can come from it. There's no need to delve into the unknown. Goodness knows what kind of things could be raked up.'

'I understand. Rose had heard it all before. 'But when working from the Light, only positive effects go along side it surly? Fear has a way of finding a voice, no matter what. Let's not give it one now, okay?'

Maeve's memoires were close to her mind. She'd kept them so, often thriving of the nicest ones (after one of George's beatings), while rejecting the not-so-great ones (Anna and her bad behaviour).

She knew Anna and Rose were mates. Her sister mentioned it last night. If she were to slander her to

Rose, it wouldn't look good. Rose would think all sorts, maybe even chuck her out or label her a tell-tale, talking behind people's backs and all of that.

'Things happened when Anna and I were younger,' she glided in. 'Unexpected mysteries my parents were upset over. You must understand,' heaven forbid she wouldn't. 'We were simple, good living Christian folk. Anna's misgivings were verging witchcraft. The work of the Devil.'

'Umm.' Rose pondered. 'I know it was a different time sixty years back,' she'd lived through them herself. 'But unless Anna was slaughtering, sacrificing or causing others destruction, I can see no harm.'

'*She talked to the dead.*' Was she not getting through? Maeve felt fraught. 'All sorts of strange things were said. Relatives long since departed… neighbours that died before she was even born… she brought the lot of them up… and some other things too.'

'So, really what you're saying is that Anna is a medium like Ellen?'

'It certainly appears to be that way, given what happened today. Ellen has inherited the trait.'

'Personally, I believe Ellen's abilities supersede Anna's.'

'Doesn't that trouble you?'

'Not even one wee bit. In fact, I feel privileged to have both mum and daughter in my life. The world is a better place when it's in touch with its spiritual side, Maeve. We all have abilities like Ellen, some lying dormant within us. Forgetting that is detrimental to the soul's progress.'

'I certainly don't.' Maeve wouldn't entertain the very notion of it. 'It's unnatural if you ask me. We are human beings. Not some wishy-washy form of that.'

'Having physical bodies is only a small part of us. When we forget our spiritual side, we've become too humanised.'

'Let's make a fresh pot of tea,' Rose said as she noticed Maeve's thoughtful frown deepen into a scowl. 'You can tell me what it's like to live in Kent.' She grabbed the side of her chair to help her aching body's stretch up to a stooped position. 'I'm sure it's just delightful.'

They talked together over general things for another hour or so. Andrew and Moby joined them back inside on account of a heavy shower forcing their hand.

Maeve shared a modest amount of her life with George. Impressions were given to suggest it hadn't been an easy life, but Rose didn't poke her nose in where she was quite sure it didn't belong.

By the time Ellen called back to collect Maeve and Moby, the night sky had developed nicely. Its stars were glittering brightly, and the orange of the full moon's aura was lighting the way.

'I got delayed... *waylaid*, so to speak,' Ellen offered an apology. 'Matt and his dad needed some refereeing I'm afraid. I didn't feel happy leaving them both to argue the rights and wrongs of marijuana.'

141

'That's an unusual subject to have strong opinions on.' Rose frowned. 'I never heard the likes of it.'

'Umm, not as much as you'd think these days.'

'Really?'

'Um.'

'The subject was changed in favour of enlightening Ellen of how successful Maeve's prolonged stay had been.

'She's now converted to becoming a white witch.'

'*What*!'

Rose giggled a hearty cheer. They had touched on a few things over their time alone. Talk of New Age Practices, Paganism and Buddhism were given a fair shout. Maeve seemed to have taken a lot of the information in.

'I'm joking,' she chuckled to a gunked Maeve. 'Just teasing.'

'I'm a little more opened minded than I was before… shall we say,' Maeve surprised them all with her admission. Rose stopped laughing and Ellen's eyes widened. 'But I'm joining nothing and won't be for the foreseeable future.'

'That's a healthy start.'

'Well, it's a big jump forward for me indeed. As long as it's nothing too witchy or weird mind you but yes, closer to exploring more on the subject of… whatever it is you do Ellen.'

What a breakthrough. Ellen was shocked at how much her aunt had lightened up in one afternoon. It

142

appeared that this strange woman had many facets to her personality. Rose seemed to have worked wonders at opening some of them up.

Thirty minutes later, as Ellen and Maeve prepared to leave, Moby came bounding towards them in three large leaps across the room. Ellen, fully aware of Maeve's fear of Moby, panicked.

'Moby!' she warned loudly. 'Down, boy, down!'

Before either Moby or Ellen had a chance to react, Maeve laughed loudly.

'Ach, Ellen, he's just being friendly sure.' She smirked towards the golden retriever, cautiously reaching out to pat his soft furry head. 'Good boy, good fella.'

'Where's Maeve and what have you done with her?' Ellen addressed Rose from a place of shock. 'I've a feeling she's been replaced with a newer version.'

'Give my head peace.' Maeve used one of Rose's well used sayings. 'I'm learning so much in such a short space of time.'

With an invite given and accepted to tea the following day, and a promise of home-made scones and shortbread, Anna was included in the request. Maeve was thrilled that another day like today was secured.

The drive home was so different in comparison to their earlier journey to get there. Maeve chatted tirelessly about Rose and how lovely she'd been.

'Opening her home to me like that was simply amazing. I've never, ever had someone in my life that was so easy to talk too.'

Ellen felt sad to hear that alone. She was learning so much about his woman that wasn't evident before. Maybe her mum had exaggerated with her tales of woe about Maeve. Maybe it was Rose who'd worked wonders at bringing out the best in her. Either way, something was shifting.

The drop of at Anna's revealed the house in complete darkness bar the outside lamps and hall light lit. Ellen knew her mum's excuse of headache was fake. She was in bed reading.

'Tell her I'll catch up in the morning.' She made Ellen promote the deception. 'I can't face another evening of torture.'

'Goodness,' Maeve pulled her breath in. 'Looks like your mother's gone on to bed and me her only guest. How rude!'

Stepping from the car, Ellen walked her up the short pathway to the front door.

'It's unlocked.' She opened the door. 'The keys are in the lock for when you get inside. Good night, Maeve. Sleep well.'

'Ellen?'

'Yes?'

'Can I ask you a question?'

'Of course.'

Maeve looked shy. She hesitated before deciding to go for it.

'Do you really think Rose and I were sisters before?'

'I do.' Ellen nodded confirmation. 'From what I was shown, there was no doubt about it.'

'Interesting. Good night, dear.'

It seemed her aunt was intrigued. The tiny grin on her face replaced the frown from her brow.

Hopefully tomorrow that smile would widen.

CHAPTER EIGHTEEN

Rose opened her eyes and slowly looked around the bedroom. Still thick with sleep, she pondered for a few long seconds. What had wakened her?

Frowning, she squinted towards the bedside clock on the nightstand. She was told it was four a.m. It didn't seem that long since she'd gone to bed in the first place.

The air in her bedroom felt chilled. She shivered its effect wishing she'd added the extra throw considered earlier. The atmosphere, she noticed, was deadly still. Closing her eyes, she lay motionless under the thick quilt, waiting for the expected.

It wasn't long until she felt the familiar male presence, close beside the bed. Just as she believed he would come, right away she knew it was her father, long since departed the physical world.

Outside the window and into the open fields beyond, the silence was deafening. Time seemed to stand still, all movement ground to a halt. It felt as though the atmosphere thickened. She made a mental note of the freeze crawling up her spine, making her shiver.

The sheer strength of his presence, coupled with the force of the cool breeze across Rose's face, forced her eyes open for the second time. When the tingling touch graced her hand, she felt sudden fear but quickly replaced it with familiarity. It was impossible not to. There was something amiss. This was not just a regular spiritual visit. It had intent.

'Father,' she whispered into the silence. 'What is it?'

The same cool breeze swept across her face. Her eyes darted around the room, searching, questioning. Nothing. Gently she lowered her head onto the pillow again. Her heartbeat quickened.

This time the cool, still air, touched the top of her head causing hairs to stand on her neck. She tried desperately not to be frightened, yet his presence seemed to demand she should be.

'Please don't,' she pleaded. 'Just tell me what you want.'

There suddenly developed a distinct smell of something familiar from bygone years. She sniffed intensely, trying to place its source. It took a while to search her memory.

The scent continued, solid this time, lingering long enough to be recognised. Carbolic soap! There was no doubt. Her father's favourite brand to use.

She waited. The breeze swept across her face once again, only this time it lingered on her forehead, sliding down to touch her dry, chapped lips and onto her cheeks. She felt dizzy with its effect.

Rose was starting to feel annoyed. Enough was enough. On the verge of losing her cool, suddenly and very abruptly, the message hit her. '

'Andrew!'

She didn't hesitate. Throwing the bedclothes off her body, she raced as fast as her mature body allowed, out of the room.

It took her seconds to cross the middle room that separated their two bedrooms, staving her big toe on the side of the wood-framed sofa as she passed.

'Ouch!'

Flinging open the door, she dreaded what waited inside. The room was in pitch darkness from the heavy curtains. Winter ones, recently put up.

'Andrew?' Her whisper was faint. She just knew. The feel of the room, the stillness of his figure, and the silence of the atmosphere confirmed her fears. Andrew's physical body, devoid of his essence, lay still and heavy in the bed. His face was smiling. It was warm to the touch. The first thing she noticed.

'Andrew,' she sighed, resigned. 'My sweet boy.'

Standing with her hand on his cheek, her shoulders were slumped in sadness. She took comfort in knowing she wasn't alone. The strong scent of carbolic soap lingered in the air. The cool draught carried it past her face, time and time again. Reassurance all was as it should be.

One of her major soul contracts was now complete.

CHAPTER NINETEEN

Cecilia Flanagan was about to put the second batch of soda bread onto the hot griddle when she noticed Rose walk up the concrete yard towards her home.

The oversized plump, seventy-one-year-old, balding and toothless woman, left the uncooked dough sitting on the table, wiped her floury hands on the coat apron and then rushed outside to greet her neighbour.

Knowing instinctively from sheer body language alone that something was amiss, the ample woman threw her arms out in greeting.

'Ah bugger,' she comforted, 'it's Andy Boy, isn't it?' Cecilia's voice reached a striking, almost hysterical chord. She enveloped Rose into a vice-like grip as she wept. 'Has he gone, Rose?'

Rose nodded confirmation, as best as her head allowed, under the confines of Cecilia's upper arms and generous breasts.

'He passed around four this morning,' Rose confirmed against the sweaty armpits and the overwhelming body odour (resembling sour eggs). 'I came as early as was decent.'

It was never usually a bother that Rose didn't have a telephone, hell she even preferred not to. Often

149

considering them highly unnecessary pieces of equipment, she'd grown up in a generation of letter writing and neighbourly communication. Any news to be told was restricted to and by such means. It worked well then and she saw no reason why that still shouldn't be the case, until now.

'I should call Doctor Holmes,' she mumbled. 'We need to legally confirm he's gone.'

Rather than dislodge her captive from the grip, Cecilia hugged Rose tighter, causing Rose's walking stick to fall on the ground.

'I know that, me dear.' Cecilia wailed tears of sympathy. 'And afterwards you can take a nice warm bath.'

'That's not necessary, Cecilia but thank you anyway.'

Ten minutes later and at Cecilia's rather persuasive insistence, Rose drank the sugary tea handed to her as she rang the doctor's surgery.

'It's good for shock.' Another three spoons of sugar were added. 'Put's hairs on your chest and curls the toenails.' This woman, in her kindness, seemed to have lost the plot.

The recently installed telephone, was hidden at the bottom of the long, dark hallway in the Flanagan's home.

Doctor Holmes was genuinely sorry to hear of Rose's loss and Andrew's passing. Her family had been medically treating the McGrath family for many years. She knew their history well.

'I'll be out as soon as possible,' the middle-aged doctor assured Rose. 'Sit tight with Cecilia until I arrive.'

Following the doctor's advice, Rose sat with Cecilia, who chewed greedily on soda bread and slurped noisily from a large mug of tea.

'Quit hogging the butter, Rosie,' Cecilia demanded. 'Come on, pass it here.' Chubby fingers dripped with jam while thin, wispy, white hair, fell over rounded cheeks, catching crumbs.

Rose sighed and glanced towards Cecilia with a sadness. She'd known Cecilia and Arthur forever. To see how far gone she was, brought a sense of forlorn to her already overloaded heart.

It was obvious, for quite some time now, that Cecilia had the early onset of dementia. She'd been showing signs, on and off, for the past couple of years. Many had commented on it. Even Arthur, who was known to be a man of few words or opinions voiced his anxieties.

'The old girls lost it,' he told Rose last summer as they chatted across the hedge. He was on his way back down the lane from retrieving Cecilia. 'She's just walked towards the main road in her underwear,' he sighed its truth. 'Forgot to get dressed first. It was pure luck I spied her from the lower field. Lord knows what would have happened.'

Cecilia struggled from under Arthur's tight grip of her upper arm, while he in turn admitted he would be lost without his wife.

'She's my heart and soul,' he confided with uncharacteristic affection. 'My life wouldn't be worth living if she wasn't around.'

At the time, Rose's sympathies went towards the ageing couple and the challenges that surely made up their future together. Right now, she struggled to find the same degree of empathy.

The emotional ache in Rose's heart burdened her physical one. Her realistic head tried to make sense of how life would continue without Andrew in it.

It was difficult to comprehend. Having spent a lifetime seeing to his needs, looking after his every demand and nurturing his ailments, her life had been suddenly forced into change. Fear gripped her being: what was to happen now? The unknown often seemed daunting. Shock was numbing her other senses.

'What are you frowning about Rosie me old girl?' Cecilia enquired through a muffled mouth of bread and a lake of marmalade jam running down the side of it. 'What's eating at you, Fickle Fingers?'

Rose smiled sadly. Lifting her eyes from the kitchen's cracked and stained floor tiles, she rested them on Cecilia's face.

'I was thinking of Andrew, Cecilia,' she told the hungry woman. 'I'll miss him so much.'

Cecilia nodded, eyeing up the last of the bread lying on the board.

'Ah yes,' she smiled, placing an indulgent knob of salty country butter onto the bread and grabbing it. 'Just how is Andy Boy keeping?' She was transfixed with food anticipation, 'It's been a while since he's been down to visit you know. I've his favourite bread and butter pudding growing a mould as we speak. You could take it to him when you're going. It'll sweeten his tooth and gas his belly a treat.' she winked skilfully. 'It's hiving with rhubarb.'

Rose couldn't find the desire or even the words to respond. She brought her attention back to the floor. Cecilia was so wrapped up in pouring herself more tea and lacing it with a generous shot of brandy that she didn't miss that Rose hadn't responded anyway.

Time somehow trotted forward. Twenty minutes later and just as Cecilia was beginning the second verse of 'Andrew Boy' (changing the name from 'Danny' to 'Andrew,' solely for Rose's benefit), the telephone rang, bringing all music to an abrupt halt. Thank the Lord above for small mercies.

Rose silently offered a grateful prayer to the Angels for the swift intervention she'd been requesting since the first words of the song were sung. She was deafened and fearful for her long-term hearing.

'I'm five minutes away from your home,' Doctor Holmes told Rose loudly against the roar of the open road. 'I'll meet you there.' This provided a great source of relief.

'Arthur will be wondering where I've gone,' Cecilia informed her companion cheerfully, letting Rose know she'd be joining her. 'I'll leave him a note to heat up the goat's cheese and marmalade tart in the fridge. He needs a good wholesome breakfast for the day ahead.'

Rose silently smiled at the taste test Arthur had in front of him. Little did she know Cecilia's latest culinary delight would be considered decent by the hungry farmer, compared to what he'd had presented for dinner yesterday evening.

It didn't matter how much garlic butter was spread over the pig's tongue; there was just no disguising its unique woody taste and jelly-like texture.

As the two women began their short journey down the pebbled, narrow lane towards Rose's cottage, Cecilia insisted on continuing her song exactly where she'd left off. With her head held high in the direction of the tall trees, even the early morning birds were thrown into silence at the howls.

Cecilia roared out her tune, puffing and panting in between. She even managing a skip and a trot as she walked. In her world, things were just dandy.

'You can take that bath we talked about later,' she told her deflated companion, nearing the cottage. 'I'll make sure Arthur gets the ducks out of it first though.'

Today was a difficult day.

CHAPTER TWENTY

'It's really lovely of Rose to invite us for lunch,' Maeve commented from the back seat of Ellen's car with a grin as wide as double patio doors. 'She's such a little treasure.'

Anna glared at Ellen from the front passenger seat, wide-eyed with surprise.

'That's a nice thing to say, Maeve,' she responded. 'I think so too.'

Since Maeve's visit with Rose, Anna could see a substantial change in her sister's behaviour, a real lightening of sorts.

The judgements and criticisms she'd become accustomed to hearing, had lessoned considerably. The air freshener blasts had decreased, which was of great relief to them all. The remainder of her prize-winning bread was binned in favour of fresh, shop-bought pastries.

'My life has entered a new, brighter phase,' she'd told Anna that very morning on her way out of the steam-filled bathroom. 'I've a skip in my step and a bounce in my tummy like I've never felt before. Things are looking up.'

'What's brought this on?' Anna asked cautiously, lest Maeve's inner beast come back from its hiding place. 'I must say I have noticed the change.'

'Meeting Rose,' Maeve's smiled happily. 'It's all down to her.'

'Well, I'm going to wrap Rose in tinfoil and keep her fresh forever. This is the gem we've needed all along.'

'Indeed.'

Now, as the car turned onto the stoned pathway and drove towards Rose's cottage, Ellen frowned at the sight ahead. The lane was bombarded with cars parked along its hedgerows. Some were even filling the fields on either side.

'What's all this?' she asked confused. 'Is Rose inviting half the country to lunch as well?'

'I thought it was just ourselves.' Maeve's obvious disappointment showed. 'I was looking forward to another long chat.'

'I thought that to, Maeve. Rose doesn't normally go in for big affairs.'

She managed to drive the car towards the small house ahead. Serious manoeuvring, and some questionable clutch-work was required, to avoid a collision.

As they neared their destination, amongst shouts from the passengers of 'watch that wing mirror,' and 'pothole to the right,' Ellen's nerves were frayed.

'Is that a hearse?' Anna squinted ahead against fuzzy eyesight. 'What's going on?'

Parked outside the cottage's gate sat a long black hearse; with one of the drivers outside of it, having a sneaky smoke.

All at once Ellen's breath left her lungs. Her hands froze on the steering wheel while her foot stamped forcefully on the brake, bringing the car to a stuttering, abrupt stop.

'Oh God,' she exclaimed. 'Rose!'

Abandoning both car and passengers, Ellen shot from the vehicle. Seconds later, she was inside the cottage. It took a minute for her eyes to adjust in the darkened room, squinting hawk-like, seeking out her target.

'Please no, no, no, not Rose.'

'Ellen.' Rose broke the silence noticing her friend's appearance. Sitting in the corner of the filled room, Rose faced the open doorway. 'Over here,' she instructed. 'I'd forgot you were coming today.'

Ellen closed in the space between them with four steps. They embraced; one from the liberation of fear and dread and the other enjoying the support of the touch.

'Andrew's gone,' Rose's voice sounded weak and desolate. 'He passed earlier this morning.'

'I'm so sorry,' Ellen felt sudden guilt at her relief it wasn't Rose. 'You're going to miss him dreadfully. We all will. How can I help?'

'Just being here means the world.'

'I always will be.'

For the first time that day, since finding Andrew's limp body, Rose felt tears spring into her eyes. Stunned at the unexpectedness of what had happened, the shock of it had rendered her impassive until now.

As Ellen held onto her, huge sobs began to travel up from her midriff, pouring out through her throat and wailing through a husky voice. Her body fell limply onto the chair she'd recently left, deflated and depleted. Ellen knelt to console her.

'Oh Rose,' she sympathised. 'I know Andrew was your world.'

'He was.'

'He'll be with your Spirit family now. Please don't worry about that.'

'I know but it's hard.'

'Yes.'

Doctor Holmes appeared at Ellen's side. She'd been watching the scene unfold while sipping the whiskey-infused tea Cecilia Flanagan was handing out like water. '

'It's delayed shock,' she diagnosed. 'I'd a feeling this might happen.'

Opening her leather case, Maureen extracted a small brown bottle, with no more than four pills inside. 'They're mild sedatives, Rose,' she advised. 'Taking one now will help get you through the night.'

Despite Rose's objections, Ellen and Maureen Holmes managed to persuade her to take the medication.

'It'll take the edge off until things settle a bit,' Ellen suggested. 'Some rest works wonders.'

Fifteen minutes later, Rose was showing signs of recovery. The sedative was beginning to work. Maureen Holmes addressed Ellen.

'I'll ring later,' she informed her, 'to see how things are.'

'Of course,' Ellen understood the doctor had other patients to attend. 'I'll keep you posted if needed.'

As the doctor turned to go, confident that she was leaving Rose in capable hands, she collided with Anna and Maeve in the small doorway.

'May I ask,' the doctor enquired of Maeve (she already knew Anna) in favour of keeping overcrowding to a minimum, 'are you family or friend?'

'Family,' Maeve assured her, oblivious to the fact their blood was different. 'We'll make sure she's well looked after.'

'That's a lie,' Anna whispered as the doctor departed. 'Neither you or I are family at all.'

Maeve clicked her tongue with frustration.

'Rose and I were family in another lifetime,' she informed a puzzled-looking Anna. 'I'll explain later.'

It seemed that with Andrew's passing, new life was beginning.

Seeds of change were ready to spread roots.

CHAPTER TWENTY-ONE

Andrew's funeral was small, dignified and prompt.

'I don't like fuss,' Rose insisted to those who asked. 'I can't justify the need.'

Apart from a handful of close friends, four or five sets of neighbours and a few genuine mourners, the attendance was small. Most folk paid their respects and then returned to their day's activities afterwards.

Moby O'Hare behaved impeccably, granted permission inside the church at Rose's insistence. He was, after all, Andrew's biggest mate. He'd as much right to be there as any of his human counterparts.

The little church, located four miles away from the cottage, was far from packed as everyone took their seat. As the congregation waited for the service to commence, they were treated to the music from the old organ, badly in need of re-tuning. The town's organist blasted out her version of 'How Great Thou Art.'

All sympathy cards and wreaths were declined in favour of saving the planet's trees. Donations were also made to charity. 'The Healthy Heart Association' was significantly better off too, as the last generous contribution was made in the name of Andrew

McGrath. Seeing as the very same illness had shortened his life, it seemed fitting.

'I know everyone means well,' Rose commented to Ellen just before the service, 'but I don't need cards or flowers to remind me of Andrew. I'd rather help save our planet or find a cure to help others.'

Apart from a few tear-filled eyes and the odd cough to unblock a choked-up throat, the service passed quickly and quietly. Andrew's body was laid to rest under a cherry blossom tree in the graveyard behind the church.

Rose paid a bit extra for the plot, but money was of little importance where Andrew was concerned. She looked forward to the spring when the blossoms would surely bloom in abundance on his grave.

Moby laid his paw on the soil when the last of it was filled in. It was his final send-off to a friendship that was fun and a playmate who wasn't afraid to have it.

Matt and James waited with him until he was ready to leave. Treats of water and wafer-thin ham encouraged him back to the car when asking nicely had failed.

'My heart is breaking.' Ellen confided to a stern looking Maeve (who was trying not to cry). 'I'll miss him so much. Moby will too.'

'I know.' She'd met Andrew only once but still, it was so sad to see Rose this dejected. 'It's difficult to let a loved one go.'

'Well, they don't really go,' Ellen said from the wisdom of a medium. 'But I know it can seem that way.'

'When you talk like that, it sounds strange, Ellen. the sense of loss at a parting can be overwhelming.'

'I know. You're right. Sorry, didn't mean to sound insensitive.'

Most surprisingly however, were the days preceding the funeral. Many hidden qualities were brought to the forefront, especially where Maeve was concerned.

Insisting that she would stay with Rose the whole time and beyond, Anna felt sure that nothing short of the threat of a gun to her head would deter her sister otherwise.

'She needs my help,' Maeve insisted, even after alternative outside help was offered by Doctor Holmes. 'I just know this is the reason I came back to Ireland in the first place. I won't leave her in this time of need.'

All Ellen's family, including Kate and a rather hung-over Gemma, attended the funeral. It was for Rose's sake they made time to do so, as well as a sign of respect for Andrew's life.

'I never actually met him before,' Gemma told the stranger in the church standing beside her shivering because of the cool morning air. 'I heard there was free booze after the service, so here I am.'

A disappointed, Gemma left as soon as it became apparent the strongest beverage on offer was coffee. The neighbour from down the lane wouldn't share her hip flask's whiskey. Gemma felt her sympathies were expressed to her fullest extent as she closed the cottage door noisily behind her.

'Would you like me to stay over with you tonight?' Ellen asked Rose as the last of the mourners took their leave. 'It's not a problem at all.'

Before Rose had a chance to respond, Maeve intervened. Busy clearing away the last of the dishes and covering the uneaten food with foil, she already had a plan in place. Patting Ellen's shoulder on her way past to the kitchen, she confirmed the arrangements.

'No need for you to stay, Ellen dear,' she informed her niece firmly. 'I'll be here tonight and,' she looked enquiringly at Rose, 'if it's okay with Rose, for the foreseeable future, until things settle a little anyway.'

'*I should be staying on my own,*' Rose's sensible voice informed her, '*but it's early days yet.*' Secretly, she was pleased Maeve offered.

'Hand me your mug, Rose,' Maeve ordered, reaching to retrieve it. 'I'll make you a fresh coffee,' she hesitated briefly in concentrated thought. 'If I can prise Mrs Flanagan's flask from her hands for a second or two, I'll make it an Irish one.'

Maeve was in her element, finally finding a confidence she'd buried many years ago. A conviction that was stolen from her during her married years when life had been tough. All that time spent feeling unhappy was gone now. There was little use in looking back with regret.

She'd paid her dues, many times over (and the rest). Today was the first day of the rest of her life. This time it would be different.

Divine Timing was in charge.

CHAPTER TWENTY-TWO

Life continued as normal. The days after Andrew's funeral were full of their many events, some happy and some not so much.

Maeve and Rose coped well, finding a routine in the daily life that Rose was now forced to adjust to without Andrew.

Ellen called every morning to bring fresh bread and milk and the occasional bunch of flowers, to help add colour to an otherwise bland day.

'They help lift the energies,' she informed a complaining Maeve who insisted there were other things more important to spend her money on. 'And if you see flowers as a waste of anything, you've missed their meaning entirely.'

Now, on the first Sunday following Andrew's passing, when Rose insisted Ellen stay home and share time with her own family, she was having breakfast with Fergal.

Their two sons played basketball outside on the driveway for the first time in a long time, now the dust had somewhat settled, and the rain had afforded them a dry day.

'Sundays tend to feel long don't you think?' she asked a tired-looking Fergal, not long out of bed. 'Maybe we could have cinema trip and lunch out later?'

'It'll have to be your treat,' Fergal shot back, helping himself to another succulent sausage to dip in the runny egg (unaware they were all vegetarian). 'I'm as skint as a flint.' Not feeling in great shape from his usual weekend socialising, both his wallet and energy had taken a serious hit.

'That's okay,' Ellen replied, 'it's just the change of environment I'm after. We could go for a walk instead.'

'Oh,' Fergal slapped the side of his head. He dropped his fork on to the kitchen floor at the same time. 'I promised to help Mum in the garden today,' he lied. 'She's weeding the flowerbeds out the back.'

He'd rather have had an afternoon of drinking and Gaelic football if the truth be told. The pub had bought the licence especially for the event. It promised to be a humdinger of a game with a good crowd in attendance.

'Laundry and floor washing it is then,' Ellen said, sounding a cheer she didn't feel. 'The boy's' school uniforms need laundering anyway.'

'Great. Thanks for the info. You go ahead and enjoy that.'

Fergal lifted the dropped fork from the floor. It now contained a chunk of Moby's doggie hairs. He went to look for a replacement, grumbling at how the dog shouldn't be allowed in the house in the first place.

166

He felt as guilty as he felt torn. *Should he have stayed at home today and taken his sons out for the afternoon? It had been a while since they'd had any family days out so maybe it wouldn't hurt to sacrifice the pub and match just this once.*

The shrill of the phone from the hallway echoed through his delicate head.

'Frig!' This morning was turning into something he hadn't bargained for. 'Answer that bloody thing will you!'

'Certainly,' Ellen oozed sarcasm. 'You sit down and rest yourself there.'

'It's Gemma,' she informed Fergal seconds later, as her sister hiccupped down the line. 'She's hammered.'

Fergal sighed with relief that he had indeed made the right decision to go to the pub after all. There wasn't a chance in hell he was hanging around for his sister-in-law's latest drama. Chances were strong that he'd be roped into helping in some way if past history was anything to go by.

Decision made and his heart feeling lighter because of it, he smiled as the butter melted on his new piece of warm toast.

In the hallway and oblivious to her husband's delight, Ellen listened as Gemma stuttered and muttered down the other end of the line.

'Whose dis?' Gemma enquired lazily, 'Dat you Ell?'

'It is,' Ellen confirmed. 'What's up?'

Gemma burst into tears. Heavily intoxicated from the litre bottle of vodka she'd recently consumed; both her words and wails were exaggerated by the drinks effects.

'Dat bastard left,' she wailed uncontrollably. 'He's taken da weans wit him.'

'Okay,' Ellen hesitated. 'Are you sure Donal and the kids haven't just gone visiting?' It wouldn't be the first time Donal O'Neill had left Gemma sleeping all day long as he and the kids made the most of the Sunday activities. Dublin Zoo, cinema, walks with picnics. The list was considerable.

'Noooo Smarty Pants,' Gemma drawled. 'He left a note.' She burped down the line. 'Da frigger's gone for good.'

It appeared, after further investigations, that Donal had been contemplating leaving their home for quite some time.

'He kept saying he was gonna go,' Gemma admitted. 'But I thought he was bluffing.'

'I'm on my way,' Ellen said. 'Give me half an hour.'

'Don't tell Mum or Kate,' Gemma instructed. 'I'm not in the mood for their ridicule and lectures.'

'Fair enough,' Ellen complied. 'But they'll find out sooner than later.'

'Bitch.'

'Sorry?'

'*Switch*,' Gemma lied. 'I can't find the lamp *switch*.'

Fergal smiled condescendingly when Ellen entered the kitchen. She tried to ignore his smugness, having seen it many times before, especially where Gemma was concerned.

'Don't start,' she cautioned at her husband's sneer. 'It's easier to judge than to find a solution.'

'She's a drunk,' Fergal said, ignoring the command. 'There's nothing a good kick up the arse wouldn't fix.'

'Are you serious?' Ellen looked disgusted. 'Do you honestly think you're being helpful?'

She felt so mad at his obvious lack of empathy. Drinking was often related to unresolved emotional issues. Addiction was a cry for help.

'It doesn't do to criticise,' she told her husband as he maintained his conceited expression. 'And besides,' she lifted the car keys from the windowsill and grabbed her coat from the hook, 'often the ones who have the most to say, are the very ones who have no call to talk in the first place.' He could put that in his pipe and smoke it.

With the self-satisfied smile still holding rank on his face, Fergal finished his breakfast as Ellen's slammed the door behind her. She was so fed up and mad at him.

Secretly she was more upset that once again Gemma was calling the shots on her planned day of relaxation ahead. Ellen had recently bought a new transgression meditation CD and was hoping to check it out. That was now put on the back burner.

Inside the house, Fergal made his plan. He'd take the work van and park it at his mother's house. His mum would cover for him in the event questions were asked. The fifteen-minute walk from her house to the pub would help build his appetite for the first afternoon pint of Guinness that day. The very same one that was causing his mouth to water now at the mere thought of it.

'Shit!' He'd forgotten about the boys, 'Frig sake.'

After careful consideration... *should he take Matt and James with him, should he get his mum around to sit or were they really old enough to look after themselves*, the choice was taken from him, as Matt insisted he was no longer a baby.

'Go,' he instructed his father, knowing how his Granny O'Hare didn't like to be kept waiting, especially where gardening was concerned. 'Mum will be back soon anyway.'

'Well, it's on your head if your mum gives out,' Fergal shirked all responsibility otherwise. 'So don't come crying to me if the shit hits the fan.'

'I never would.'

Fifteen minutes later Fergal left, Matt searched the fridge for snacks and James scored his tenth basket that morning. It seemed all was grand on the surface of things.

Yet it was the bigger picture that told the tallest tale.

CHAPTER TWENTY-THREE

Ellen's arrival at the O'Neill family home was accompanied by a host of Angels, Archangels and Ascended Masters, by request.

'I know you won't interfere with free will,' she told her companions. 'I could do with your help regardless.'

'Bugger,' Gemma panicked at the sight of Ellen's car outside the window as she rushed to clear away the evidence, she'd been drinking all morning. 'Frig, fart, crap!'

It took seconds to clear what she needed to into a nearby bottom drawer with a clink (empty vodka bottle), and a minute for Ellen to ring the doorbell.

Gemma refused Ellen's hug.

'Get off me ya big lezzy,' she mocked. 'I'm not that desperate!'

Entering the living room, Ellen found the least cluttered free chair and sat down. She watched Gemma pace back and forwards across the room.

'Please don't,' she pleaded with Gemma as she prepared to light yet another cigarette, from the one she'd just finished. 'I can't stand the smell.'

'Frig sake. No fun in ya at all.'

Flumping down on to the waiting sofa in a bit of a huff, Gemma looked annoyed. The house was an untidy mess. Empty crisp packets, overflowing ashtrays and shelves layered with dust, spoke of weeks of neglect. It was clear from this fact alone there had been ongoing problems for a while.

'May I read Donal's note?' Ellen edged towards Gemma lying sprawled across the cushions on the sofa like a rag doll. 'I didn't catch all you said on the phone.'

Gemma searched the back pocket of her tracksuit bottoms and extracted the note.

'Here,' she thrust it under Ellen's nose, narrowly missing its tip. 'Good luck making sense of his scrawl.'

It was blunt, short and to the point. Gemma was right; it did take a bit of deciphering (a three-year-old's efforts would have been easier to make out).

'I've... had... enough,' Ellen read aloud slowly. 'Your... tinkering sorry... *drinking* is out of control... meek, sorry... *seek*... help. Donal.'

Gemma leered forward and snatched the paper from Ellen's hand. This sudden movement only seemed to encourage a fit of hiccupping and she gasped for air.

'Told ya,' she confirmed hotly between bellows. 'Da bastard's done a runner.'

Ellen looked sadly towards her oldest sister showing a sympathy she truly felt. Gemma looked pathetic with her hair all shapes, its dark roots black as soil. Discoloured and bitten finger nails were down to the quick. Her clothes had seen many better days. She

172

looked twice her age even though she was only in her early forties.

Her inner beauty was as well-hidden as her outer one was repressed. The word "hag" lingered around Ellen's head for a brief second. She quickly checked herself. Nobody behaved this way if everything was wholesome.

'Gemma,' Ellen suggested, shrugging of the distress she felt as best as she could. 'Why don't we get you dressed and make something to eat?' Getting her sobered up seemed the first step to take. Ellen reached out to help her stand.

'Don't touch me,' Gemma snapped, 'or I'll pinch you till you cry.'

'I'm only trying to help.'

'I said don't. *Back off!*'

Silence followed the confrontation as Gemma's foul mood festered and Ellen's felt deflated. She found herself regretting taking the phone call earlier, or at the very least wishing that it had gone to voicemail.

'You were always a real cow you know,' Gemma hissed angrily, looking up at Ellen from her seat, spitting venom through her saliva-filled mouth. 'You with your bloody big house and your perfect little family.' She stood up, staggering from the effect of her early morning cocktails.

'Everybody thinks you're bloody perfect but,' she cautioned with a point of her finger and a sway towards the seat she'd just left. 'I'm on to you Missy.' She wiped her chin dry with the back of her hand. 'And don't you forget it.'

With the threat issued, Gemma drunkenly fell back, completely missing the sofa and landing on the floor. Her foot tucked under her bum taking the full weight of her body.

'Ahhh!' She shrieked, writhing with pain. 'I've broke my friggin' ankle!'

'Oh, for goodness' sake.' Ellen reached the end of her patience. 'You're your own worst enemy, Gemma. Honest to heaven's above, your own worst enemy.'

Amid cries of 'take it easy,' and 'call an ambulance,' Ellen managed to help Gemma onto the sofa, get a frozen bag of peas and reassure the crying woman that she didn't feel that an x-ray was needed.

'It's sprained,' Ellen placed the bag of vegetables onto the slightly inflamed ankle. 'Put this on it to stop the swelling.'

'You a doctor now?'

'No. I'm a realist.'

'Huh. Give me the bag. I'll do it myself.'

'My pleasure.'

It wasn't very difficult for Ellen to admit that her oldest sister was a mess. After the insults Gemma had thrown her way, it would have been forgivable for her to leave and force her sister to sort out her own problems.

174

Instead, she held on, naively hoping a solution might present itself at any moment while realistically resigned it would not.

'Archangel Michael,' she whispered the prayer to the Angel of karmic ties. 'Give me strength to see this through.'

Minutes passed, while Ellen thought, Gemma's moaning and whimpering reminded her of a child's. She felt a pang of compassion. Decision made. She had little option than to take her back home.

'I'm taking you to my friggin big house.' She shouted to be heard over the crying woman. 'At least there in the west wing,' she quipped, 'your cries will only be heard in the dungeons.'

Ellen had a fair idea of what lay ahead in making her decision now. Fergal would object for sure; Donal wouldn't be greatly pleased either and Gemma would be quite a challenge to put up with.

Yet she knew something needed to be done and this seemed to be the only alternative available at such short notice. Maybe as her mum got to hear of Gemma's plight, she might show mercy and intervene.

'I'll gather some of your things from upstairs,' she said before departing to do just that. 'You'll need a couple of changes and your pj's.'

'I'll get them myself.' Gemma tried unsuccessfully to stand; 'I don't want the likes of you sticking your nose through my bits and pieces... frig this bloody leg... ahhh!'

Ellen resisted the urge to snap back, though she could easily have let the words sitting on her tongue have a field day, she didn't.

Instead, she helped Gemma back onto the perch she'd unsuccessfully risen from and left the room.

'I deserve a friggin' medal for this.' Ellen whispered, making her way to the stairs. 'Either that or a water pistol to soak her breathless!'

Some of Gemma's greatest challenges lay ahead. It was just a matter of waiting to see what developed for her.

Meanwhile, Ellen had trials of her own to face, starting with what awaited her back at the house.

'James has hurt his head badly, Mum,' Matt informed Ellen via phone call to her mobile. 'There's blood everywhere and a gash down the side of his ear.'

'Where's your dad?' Ellen wondered why Fergal wasn't dealing with this. 'Put him on Matt, please.'

'Ummm.'

Something equivalent to World War Three, in domestic terms, lay ahead.

CHAPTER TWENTY-FOUR

Under such sad, trying circumstances, it was difficult for Maeve to confront the intensity of delight, pleasure, contentment and happiness that she was encountering with each second she spent at Rose's cottage and in Rose's company. Difficult, yet far from impossible.

Maeve smiled with the sweetest of grins before she fully opened her eyes to greet another beautiful day. Her glee had little to do with the sunny rays outside but definitely not all of it.

Another day, realising she really wasn't living in a dream state brought a sense of euphoria never know to her before. This was reality. She was in a permanent state of bliss.

'Pinch yourself, just to make sure it's real.'

Gone (yet far from forgotten), were the days of dark, depressive mood swings George flung onto her, when his own temperament could endure it no more.

It was finally adios amigo to the hundreds of sleepless and disturbed nights of torture when his drunken slumber induced snores equalled to the volume of an articulated lorry's horn. The liberation felt enormous in its multitude.

What was more, relief had come to her with Anna's complete understanding of Maeve's decision to stay at the cottage. The dread she held over telling her, was completely unfounded.

'Of course, you must stay with Rose.' Anna dismissed Maeve's guilt_with a wave of her cake-filled hand. 'It's important that you do what feels right. Come on,' she encouraged, with Maeve's packed suitcase in one hand and her car's engine started in the driveway. 'You must do what feels right for you.'

The truth was that Anna was secretly pleased to have her home all to herself again. It was obvious the two sisters were far from compatible, especially as live-in companions. The new arrangement suited all involved wonderfully. A true blessing in disguise.

And so it was.

Ignoring the cold air now, Maeve bounced out of bed, her ageing form finding vigour it hadn't experienced in a long time. Andrew's bedroom may not have been decorated to Maeve's taste, but it felt like she was in her own idea of heaven regardless.

Reaching for her suitcase, a relic of her late husband's many work trips around England, she prepared to dress. Today she would choose her favourite outfit to wear on account of feeling so happy.

She picked up the navy checked skirt and cream jumper, unfolded and shook them several times to their fullness, in the hope of erasing some of their creases.

Humming the tune of *When you Were Sweet Sixteen* by The Fureys, Maeve reached under the rest of the clothes in the case, hoping to successfully find clean underwear.

Retrieving what she believed to be her "Sunday best," her attention was drawn to the edge of the red envelope, tucked far into the case's lid and under her passport and flight documents.

'What's this?'

Extracting the envelope took effort on account of it lodged under a tiny rip in the lining, but she managed. Her humming came to a halt when she began reading aloud.

'To my darling George,' it said, 'my true love.'

Squinting from the absence of her glasses, she reached across to the nightstand and found the sought-after spectacles there.

The paper inside was the same colour as its envelope. It had the faintest smell of perfume, its staleness causing Maeve to reject its scent by holding the letter farther away from her offended nostrils. She continued to read out loud.

'My darling George. This is the most difficult note I've ever had to write. Please be assured that I love you now, as I will love you forever.'

Maeve's heart skipped a beat. Gasping for air, she breathed deeply, willing herself to go on, while at the same time afraid too. What should she do? The shock alone was causing confusion. Seconds passed. Then she continued the search.

'I cannot leave Barney,' she read on. 'The cancer has spread to his lungs. He desperately needs my help.'

The loud pounding of her heart caused Maeve to pause for a second time. She could feel the thumping of its beat, pounding in her ears. 'The plans we had for moving to America cannot go ahead, my darling. It is with a sad and heavy heart I must put our ten wonderful years behind us and move on.'

Apart from the signature 'Molly' wrapped inside a hand-drawn heart at the bottom of the page, Maeve could read no more.

As she sat statue-like, staring at the wall, her mind went blank. A queue of thoughts lined up to be explored, yet not one materialised.

Sheep bleated in the background; hungry birds cheeped from the trees. A gentle breeze whistled through the gaps in the floorboards. It chilled her toes and blew stray threads on the curtain's hem, back and forth.

Maeve was empty. For the first time ever, she felt bottomless and drained of all thoughts or feelings. The letter slid from her limp hand, landing on the floor with little sound, just a mere flutter.

The tears that left her eyes, fell unchecked and unnoticed.

An automatic response of desolation.

CHAPTER TWENTY-FIVE

Rose was up out of bed, washed, dressed and anxious to begin a new day.

Getting used to her new circumstances, she forced a smile, raking the range ash-free. Humming while she worked, the tune of 'Boolavogue' took quite a beating.

She was deep in thought. It never ceased to amaze her, she pondered, that no matter how many years a soul lived, there were always new challenges, bringing with them chances for advancement.

All given lifetimes, she believed, brought the soul's progression forward, its aim to reach a state of supreme enlightenment, eventually ascending into the collective pure light of Source. She tried to live by its truth.

Surely, if nothing else, it was a human destination, to live as a spiritual being. Facing and overcoming challenges and practising acceptance and trust instead of judgement and anger, greatly facilitated strengthening that aim.

Becoming masters of our own soul, as she understood it, was key.

'It's not about how hard life hits us,' she preached to those who cared to listen. 'It's about how hard we can get hit and still keep going.'

Rose had often heard it said the biggest, most difficult and taxing obstacle in one's life, was best considered a friend. Ultimately it would build and toughen the soul, providing the lesson needed for growth. She tried hard, from day to day, to live by the change she wanted to see in her outer and inner world.

Rose was no stranger to pain, emotional, physical or mental. With many difficulties and ample amounts of strife under her own pink, flowered belt, she knew how life could pack a punch.

'It's damned difficult to stay positive when you're grieving or struggling,' she whispered now, to no one but herself. Yet the wise woman, knew it was important to at least try.

Life without Andrew felt empty. It felt different, almost odd. In her darkest moments, it felt unworthy of her efforts to continue living it. She wasn't strong enough to end it, even in its cruellest instants.

Knowing she'd simply return at another time to learn the same lessons over, it seemed the best plan was to stay put and face what needed facing now, in this part of her soul's journey.

Rose knew Andrew would make contact when the time was right. She was prepared to wait until then. In the period of waiting, the patience of wonder, Rose found comfort in calling on the Angels for their unrelenting, loving and unconditional support.

'Archangel Azeral,' she asked the great overseer of helping the soul's deliverance into spirit again. 'Help me find comfort now, with Andrew's flitting departure.'

She knew, trusted, that this caring, quiet and composed Archangel would stand over her, supporting her and cleansing the ache in her heart. She believed in its certainty and so created that reality.

And so it was.

Rose continued to lose herself in her thoughts, deep inside their core, as she cleaned and prepared for the day ahead. There was food to cook and logs to stack.

Sometime later, with the fire providing a degree of heat and breakfast about to honour her empty stomach's demands, Rose pondered Maeve's absence. It was unlike her, Rose thought, not to have made an earlier appearance.

In the short time of Maeve's stay, the two women had already managed to develop some kind of routine in starting a new day together.

Rose had expected Maeve to be up, dressed and ready at this stage. It seemed a little unusual she hadn't made an appearance yet.

Shrugging her thoughts away in favour of breakfast, Rose spread a liberal mound of honey on her buttered toast. Her mouth watered at the prospect of eating the delight as she spread it across the bread and into its corners.

A huge mug of strong tea threw steam across the table, promising a suitable accompaniment for the wheaten bread treat.

At first, Rose thought the whimpering sound was coming from the stove; a whistling pot shouting for attention or a little field mouse living behind it. She listened, looking intently for seconds before dismissing both possibilities.

Temporarily rejecting all food, her eyes darted around the room looking for the sound's source. They led her to Andrew's old bedroom which had now become Maeve's new one.

Leaving the table, curiosity pushed Rose towards the closed bedroom door. Nosiness propped her ear against it.

'Maeve,' she enquired gently with a soft knock to accompany it. 'Is everything all right?'

Lack of response prompted her to turn the door's handle to open. Its rustic squeak subconsciously reminded Rose to oil the hinges and maybe invest in a new door handle while she was at it, but nothing too fancy.

It had been a while since Rose experienced this type of grief. Andrew's passing, although surprising in its finality, hadn't come completely out of the blue. His weak heart, diagnosed from the age of twelve, dictated an increase in the possibility.

Yet the sight that awaited her beyond the open door rendered her speechless and momentarily motionless.

She waited, wondering what to do. Should she leave Maeve to her private time alone; could she leave without being accused of insensitivity?

Had Maeve even registered she'd come into the room? Maybe there was time to escape and wait for her companions company in her own time.

At that moment, Rose wished she had learnt to be a more impulsive decision-maker for times like these. It would have made life easier to navigate, instead of this feeble indecisive back and forth motion.

Finally, and with a degree of relief a decision was reached, she walked towards the weeping woman to offer comfort if she could.

'Boys a dear, what is it?' Maeve was sitting, curled up in the foetal position, in the farthest corner of the bed. 'Tell me how I can help.'

She glanced towards the floor, noticing the letter lying there. Without invitation, she lifted it, along with Maeve's underwear and spectacles. Placing all items onto the bedside stand she was secretly glad the underwear was fresh and not yet worn. Not that she was squeamish mind, but still...

Then she waited. Sitting down on the bed, she rested her hand on Maeve's arm, occasionally stroking it, consolingly.

All thoughts of honey, tea and bread faded into insignificance despite the rumblings of her empty stomach which now seemed louder in the silence of the still room.

Waiting was key.

CHAPTER TWENTY-SIX

Gemma limped down the hallway of the O'Hare home the following day, silently praying she wouldn't fall after or preceding each step she took.

She wasn't sure if it was her blackened ankle or the alcoholic withdrawal symptoms that made her feel dizzy. She was sure, however, that there was no happiness to be gained regardless. Reaching the kitchen, she opened its door.

'Hi,' Ellen greeted her with a cheerfulness she didn't feel, 'Come in, we're having a bite to eat.'

'Uck. None for me.'

Ellen was fuming inside and hoped it didn't show outside, but it did. Both boys had noticed the tell-tell signs; the bangs of cupboard doors, the sharpness in her tone and the screech when she called the hot grill an 'ass-hole' for burning her thumb. They'd also received weekend grounding for the part they'd played in letting their dad leave the previous day.

Fergal had long since left the house that morning, after yet another shouting match where Ellen threatened Social Services.

'I don't care what age they are,' she shouted at a man who was pale from drinking all yesterday afternoon

187

and into the small hours of that morning. 'They are still underage and that's against the law.'

James' plastered and bandaged face brought further validation to her plight. Not only had his ear blead but he was likely due a black eye when the swelling settled.

Gemma edged into the kitchen and closed her eyes. She breathed deeply, hoping against hope she could make it as far as the nearest chair without tripping or throwing up. It seemed like such a long way of, the possibility of success was significantly limited.

'I need help,' she pleaded. 'I'm so bloody woozy… Hey,' she noticed James' wounds. 'Wat happened you, Boozo?'

'Sport-related injury,' James answered from the voice of a true sports-man. 'Four stitches and no P.E. for three weeks.'

'We'll smoke a joint later for the pain,' Gemma suggested. 'There's nothing to beat it.'

'You'll do no such thing.' Ellen confirmed firmly. 'He's way too young for that carry-on.'

'Sorry kid. The Pleasure Killer here says no.'

Matt and James were delighted with their visitor and the drama she'd brought to their home. It elevated school morning breakfast to a whole new level.

'Why are you feeling faint, Aunt Gemma?' Matt enquired to the sniggering delight of his younger brother. 'Had a bit too much to drink yesterday did ya?'

Ellen glared a warning look towards her sons, while Gemma offered each of them a middle-finger salute accompanied by a silent profanity that invited them to leave the room at double speed.

'Gemma!' Ellen cautioned. 'Mind your language!'

Even though Gemma had been with the O'Hare's less than twenty-four hours, her presence was well established.

Clothes flung limply across chairs, unwashed coffee mugs randomly abandoned, side plates and saucers filled to capacity with cigarette butts, were only some signs she was there.

Already Gemma had made their house her home. She'd fitted right in. She was enjoying comforts she hadn't received in such a long time, and it felt good.

'Chuck that immersion heater on,' she commanded Ellen. 'I feel like taking a hot bath this morning. It'll help this,' she stuck the offending foot out for all to see. 'It's killing me.'

As soon as Matt left to catch the school bus and a sniggering James had gone to his bedroom for a morning of PlayStation games, Ellen suggested it was time for her and Gemma to talk.

'Ahh, do we have to?'

'Yes, we do. Have some green tea with lemon,' she told Gemma, who was perched tightly against the electric heater. 'It might help clear your head.'

The detoxing tea was rejected immediately.

'I'm not drinking that crap.' Gemma was adamant. 'It's pure dung.'

Her sixth cup of coffee that morning was subsequently produced minutes later. Ellen knew there was little point in defending the green tea's many healthy properties, so she didn't even try.

'I've called on Archangel Michael for cutting family karmic ties and Raphael for healing the heart,' Ellen said. 'They will help where they can without interfering with free will.'

Gemma didn't share her sister's beliefs. Far from it. Scoffing she made a tutting sound and rolled her eyes heavenwards.

'Don't start all that stuff again.' She'd had enough growing up with it. 'If you're going to talk, and I really wish you wouldn't but if you are, keep it real, man.'

Time passed quickly between them both, yet it seemed to take forever before they managed to get to a place where they could constructively work from.

In childhood, teenage years, even into her twenties, Ellen had regularly been accused of gullibility, occasional stupidity and often bluntness by this woman in front of her now.

She had hoped with maturity and wisdom, all such behaviour had long since been given the heave-ho. Yet it seemed, as she sat listening attentively to Gemma, it definitely had not.

It appeared Gemma was either stuck in the past or that she had never moved beyond the age of sixteen. Ellen was getting the brunt of some very pent-up, unspent anger, in the form of spittle, blames, occasional screaming and for the biggest part, untruths.

'And if it wasn't for you and your big mouth telling Mum,' Gemma's loud accusation spat hurtfully through clenched, smoke-stained teeth. 'Jimmy O'Reilly would still be going out with me now.'

'But he was cheating on you, Gemma,' Ellen defended, unbelievingly tired of having to repeat herself over and over. '*With three other girls.*'

Gemma snorted, breathing heavily on account of her anger.

'So?' The livid woman stood strong on her wobbly soapbox. 'It was my business to deal with not yours. Jimmy and I had a good thing going until you stuck your big, gigantic nose in it.'

'Fine,' Ellen felt hurt, discouraged and mentally tired. 'I thought I was helping, and I don't have a big nose.'

'Wanna bet? A sword-nosed-bat would be proud of that thing.'

'Stop being childish. I'd forgotten how nasty you can be.'

'I can do better. Just try me. I'm not faffin about here ya know.'

Time out, Gemma paused to slurp from the oversized coffee mug, carelessly flicking wispy hairs away from her forehead where they came to rest in an untidy clump on top of it.

Burping loudly, the cigarette stump she'd been using as a pointing tool (that had long since burnt itself out), was squashed in favour of a new cigarette, extracted from the packet and lit up. Purposely she blew smoke into the middle of the kitchen and away from the patio door Ellen had opened earlier.

Gemma glanced shrewdly towards a patiently waiting Ellen. Then, aware her behaviour wasn't having the effect she thought it should, she quickly gathered amour.

Deep in thought, she hesitated, contemplated some more. Then she smiled a miniscule grin before bulldozing forward for round two.

'You made yourself Dad's favourite.' She spat the lie as convincing as she could muster. 'The youngest daughter doesn't cut it with me. You had to be his little princess' (air quotes) 'all the time, stealing attention from the rest of us.'

Ellen gasped. This latest accusation was unforgivable. This hallion of a woman wasn't getting away with that. 'That is so untrue Gemma,' she defended. 'Take that back.'

Achieving the success and the outcome she'd wanted, Gemma stood relentless, pleased she'd finally attained her aim. It felt good to be in charge.

'You'll say anything, even without foundation, won't you?' Ellen was angry. 'You're a danger to yourself and others with that mind of yours.'

'Ah shut your mouth. Think I care what you say?'

'You shut yours. It's only producing viciousness anyway. You're a colossal pain in the arse.'

'Right back at ya.'

Ellen hadn't meant to say what she did. This was getting out of hand but seriously, was Mars in her zone today? What was with all the anger and frustration? She needed time to re-set. A walk into the back garden (and a chat with Moby) would restore calm and balance.

Gemma slumped down into the waiting chair, looking every inch the victim. Dramatically, as she sat, her shoulders drooped and her head watched the ground, mournfully dejected.

Every now and again she checked if Ellen was looking her way. Of course, she might have known the dog was getting all the attention instead of her.

Maybe next time she was in the garden she'd open the gate and cause merry hell with him running around, in and out of every body's gardens.

The neighbours around here had sticks lodged in places sticks shouldn't be anyway. It caused them to think they were better than most. She'd give them something to complain about, rock their little starch filled world a bit. Do them no harm.

Silence filled the foul-smelling space (cigarette smoke) as the clock on the wall ticked and the fridge hummed, both echoing unimpressive tunes into the almost silent room.

A short time passed uneventfully. Finally, Ellen appeared in through the glass doors, looking a darn sight calmer than when she'd left. As far as she was concerned, she'd taken Gemma into her home to help. With a bit of maturity on both sides, maybe they could achieve their aim.

'I'll make fresh tea.' Ellen said. 'Then we'll try talking again, calmer and wisely.'

'Yippie! Mines a coffee and make it a strong one.'

If prizes were being handed out for patience (she wanted to choke this hateful woman), endurance (the insults were hard not to respond to, (especially the name calling) and setting new prescience's (less-offensive words used), Ellen would come first. This was tough.

If gold stars were offered for tears (false ones, fashioned to look real), name calling (fatso, ugly, twat and yes, a couple of hippos as well), and untruths told (about Ellen and others) Gemma would get the shiniest one.

Right on the brink of desperation (with hands held behind her back for fear of strangulation), Ellen pleaded help. She was out of resources. Someone, or something, needed to intervene quickly lest murder become a possibility. And then they did.

'Dad's here.'

'Christ…! Where?'

That stopped her. Gemma clutched her chest and Ellen's grey sweatshirt that she'd pulled on her that morning. She looked around and behind, seeking clarification.

'Beside you.'

'Frig off! Are you telling yarns again?'

'I wouldn't lie about that.'

'Oh, indeed you would. What about…

'Shush! Just listen.'

'Dead on wee girl. Who do ya think you're kiddin?'

Gemma looked sacred, despite the bravado. Her mouth continued to run off, but she'd been spooked. Thing was, when Ellen was outside earlier *with that blasted dog* (she liked Moby okay but was in foul form for niceties), Gemma felt a presence inside with her.

The smell of her dad's favourite aftershave glided across her face several times. She shrugged it off as nothing more than the incense burning from the hall wafting through, but deep-down even she wasn't convinced.

'Don't start that weird shit with me. You've been doing that since we were youngsters.'

'It's not weird. It's a gift.'

'Huh, so you say.'

'Would you like to know what Dad's saying?'

'Naw, you're all right thanks.'

Silence consumed the space. Both candidates reached an impasse. One wasn't willing to back down. The other wouldn't continue without spiritual intervention. Based on what Eddie was showing Ellen, Gemma was holding onto a lot of past pain.

Ellen stood to leave. Honestly, she'd wanted to do that an hour ago. Delaney Park beckoned considerably.

A walk around it's fresh air and natural tranquillity would be like a dream come true right now. Maybe James might like to go as well.

'Where you goin?'

'I'm thinking we're done here. Moby needs a walk.'

'What about Da?'

'I thought you didn't want to know.'

'I don't. Still, if he's a message for me I'm intitled to hear it.'

'Gemma you're incorrigible. Make up your twisted mind. Do you want me to go on or what?'

'I just said so, didn't I? Daa!'

Ellen settled back down. Moby sighed deflation, realising his hopes were on hold (but not altogether shattered) for another while.

She inhaled deeply, quickly grounding and tunning into the Spirit consciousness. Eddie smiled the comeback, eager to shed light where he could.

'When you and Donal got married.' Her dad asked that she start back then. 'Something happened days before you left for Mexico.' Their honey moon was delayed by two weeks. Everyone was given to understand it was flights and resort issues that were not colliding with their nuptials date. 'He said we've to bring that up now. You're still holding the pain connected to it.'

'How do you know about that?'

'I don't. Dad does.'

'He didn't know either.'

'Does now. Nothing is hidden in Spirit World.'

There'd been an unexpected, unwanted pregnancy. The date for termination expired after their month in Mexico. Things needed to be rushed through. The clinic was accommodating, yet insistent it should be right after their wedding. No time to waste. Nobody but the newlyweds and Anna were privy.

'Well, I can't think of a thing.' Gemma chanced her luck Ellen was bluffing. 'You must be making this stuff up.'

'I'm not and you know it. Shall I put words to what I'm been shown?'

'Ummm.' Gemma chewed on her fingernails (or what was left of them), eyeing Ellen suspiciously. 'Go ahead,' she challenged shakily. 'There's nowt to tell.'

'Your daughter in Spirit is with Dad.' Ellen knew the termination was not her business. 'He wants you to know she is safe. You named her Bella after his mother.'

Gemma burst into tears, this time for real. From a pit buried deep inside her very core, old pain resurrected. This unexpected turn of events had knocked her for seven. Weeping and wailing accompanied the tears, while snivelling and sniffing finally showed a conclusion was in sight.

The discussions began.

CHAPTER TWENTY-SEVEN

Maeve felt like a great big bulging, googly eyed Moran. Now, she wasn't feeling like one of the East African warrior groups that originated the name. More the guileless foolish kind, associated with the saying.

She'd been a fool. Used and abused in every literal sense of the word. Far from feeling angry (that would no doubt come later), she was at an all- time low.

Hurt beyond endurance, most of her pain felt physically lodged in the throat area. This in turn was blocking her usual creative thinking to find answers.

Why had this happened to her? Why?

Of course, she was no eejit. She knew others had been subjected to partner dishonesty and infidelity the whole world over and since the beginning of time. It seemed to be the human form.

Yet, she sighed its fact; she'd been a good person. She was no murderer, rapist, gossip, adulterer or anything else that brought ill repute to her soul, moral or otherwise.

She'd led a simple, some might say boring or mundane existence, especially where her marriage was concerned. All the while, her integrity held strong.

She and George had understood the responsibilities of married life, long before entering into the sanctity of it.

They'd been well versed in what was expected of them when the words '*till death do us part*' were uttered, much less the '*love and obey*' commitment.

A sealed agreement was established with a religious stamp and a mutual understanding by both the Lord above and the human below. Vows given to one another held grit.

Married life to George had seen little bliss from the very get go. Leaving her parents (and beloved Irish roots) behind, at the symbolic command radiating from the gold ring around her finger, was heart breaking. But duty called.

Crossing water, she'd never once experienced before, to reach her new husband's home place, brought fear of such magnitude.

Sea sickness was blamed for her vomiting when even then, Maeve knew the upset was caused by nothing but dread.

'Smarten yourself up,' George's words cut like glass. 'You're making a holy show of yourself and me included. Pull it together woman and go get me food.'

Wifely duties, inside and outside of the bedroom, were nothing short of brutal. For nearly forty years she'd endured treatment that even an animal never knew.

Rape was a word and deed associated to a great crime. In that respect her late husband should have been locked away from the get go. He was guilty of that corruption to her many times over.

Yet her upbringing dictated a wifely duty must be performed when required, regardless to her desire (or enjoyment) coming a very far second.

She hated no wait... despised... yes despised every second of the act, staying up into the early hours many nights until he was tired waiting on her and fell into a drunken slumber.

Finding out, especially in the way she had, that George was involved with Molly for ten years of their married life, didn't really cause her much surprise, if she were being totally honest. The man did what he wanted anyway most of the time. It was his way always and only. She was simply there for his convenience.

Maybe she should be thanking Molly whoever she was. Maeve pondered. After all, what George did with her saved Maeve having too. A whole decade of romance, sex and goodness knows what else, all going on, right under her nose.

His works trips away; had Molly gone too? The shirts she starched and ironed (to an inch of their lives just as he insisted, she should). The shoes she polished (using spittle instead of polish for revenge in her own way because he hated that). The new suits he seemed to buy a lot of. Was this all for Molly's benefit? It seemed so.

At the thought of it all, Maeve's anger rose. She felt as peeved as a cat without whiskers or a skunk without scent. The bare faced cheek of him to use anybody the way he had, much less her! How dare he!

I wish he was here now so as I could kick him in the big, floopy, flabby gut!

But alas he was not. The rat had done a runner like the coward he obviously was. She was to be spared the satisfaction of confronting him or the pleasure of issuing divorce. Boy, wouldn't that have been something? Life and its lessons could be cruel.

Rose had helped of course. Her new sister-friend (as she secretly called her), took time to explain the principles of karma along with the universal rule of 'cause' and 'effect'.

'You've either selected the harsh lessons for your soul's advancement or are paying back from another time.' Rose was so wise and prudent in her approach. 'Nothing happens without a tale to tell first, or a reason.'

That had helped. Well, it shone light and possibilities where, until that moment, only darkness and pain resided. Maeve got to see things another way, a glowing prospect that certainly would not have been an option if Rose hadn't been with her.

Without the hard-hitting times, she wouldn't be the woman she was now. It is only through adversity, strength endures.

Burning the photograph of George, scratched from the gold locket she carried around her neck (a gift from

Anna many years back), helped considerably. He'd put the picture there in the first place himself. Arrogance at its peak.

Inside the same necklace now, resided space for new beginnings, yet to be filled. The biggest slug of a husband anyone would ever have the misfortune to meet the likes of, never once give her a gift that didn't carry amusement for him (maids outfit, for obvious reasons. New saucepans when his potatoes stank of cheap tin).

Once on her birthday when she suggested they go out for dinner, he left the house, came back hours later, drunk and with a bag full of cleaning products.

'Scrub the kitchen clean,' he sneered drunken spit all over her face. 'Then maybe I'll let you cook me a bite to eat.'

Well, Maeve decided, she'd mourn all right. This time, instead of his passing, she'd grieve for the young girl all those years ago, who was forced by society's demands to marry and settle down.

Maeve would feel aggrieved that she didn't have the strength to leave him all down the years together.

She'd forever regret not throwing ice water over him (while he was in the bath) or burn his (twice weekly) steaks (none for her only him, on account of him being the only earner) to an inch of their life.

So many things she wanted to do, could have done, to stand up for herself but didn't. That was worth her memories. The sadness and sense of loss belonged there. Not with that brute of a human being. He was not a man but a beast.

What a twist of fate she should discover this affair while back in her Irish home. It was like things had gone full circle. Was she being offered freedom from doom in one hand, with a torch to light the way in the other? It seemed so.

Suddenly it began to make sense. A life lesson had been learned. A great awakening was occurring, moving restrictions from her life and giving her a second chance.

Maeve's tummy tickled, making her feel excited. She knew without hesitation; it was time to reclaim her power.

A certain person (mentioning no names any more), had taken of her what he needed to boost his own lack off. That option, from here on in, would never be available to another living (or not) soul. It was hers to claim back.

She intended to do just that.

CHAPTER TWENTY-EIGHT

When the call came to Fergal's mobile telephone, the busy builder wasn't completely surprised. He'd been half-expecting it so finally receiving it, simply brought clarification that his instinct was spot on.

A quickly arranged meeting in the local bar, allowed both brothers-in-law to rapidly resume their working day.

'I've nipped out during class,' Donal's whispered explanation was hurried. 'If I hang up abruptly, you'll know the principal caught me and I'll get a paddy-whacking.'

Later that afternoon, Fergal grabbed a shop-bought sandwich before making his way to Murphy's Bar and Tavern on the town's Main Street.

Stepping inside, he was surprised at how busy it was for a week day. He waited at the bar for Donal to arrive, ordering a half-pint of his favourite beer to sip on. This only created the desire to down a full pint of it and properly quench the thirst he felt.

It was a crying shame, Fergal complained, that he was being pushed to get the latest work contract finished by Friday, otherwise, he'd be tempted to stay here and make a complete day of it. His taste buds tingled, as the dryness increased.

He scowled a frown. Ellen had put him in the foulest of moods before he even had a chance to defend himself. She'd stuck into him earlier that morning, a man just out of bed and hungover. It was unforgivable.

Donal arrived minutes later, looking rather the worse for wear. After greeting Fergal with a nod and a grin, he ordered a double whiskey from the bar.

'With a vodka chaser behind it,' he issued abrupt instructions. 'Keep them coming until I tell you otherwise, sister!'

Leaving his briefcase and overcoat across a nearby stool, Donal addressed Fergal directly. His look was serious, his body language poker stiff.

'I'll cut to the point, chum,' he delivered a sharp slap to Fergal's back, spilling a reasonable quantity from his glass in the process. 'Are you good for a loan, fella?'

Drinks arrived with a steady glare from Millie the barmaid, still smarting from Donal's earlier rudeness. Her message was lost on its culprit.

Donal wrapped his chubby fingers around the offerings and smiled a welcoming smile at the drinks appearance. Fergal frowned.

'Aren't you working later? He asked. 'It's only school lunch hour.'

'That's not important right now,'

'It kinda is, mate. You've children to consider.'

'Look,' Donal felt flustered. 'Forget that for a second 'I'm looking two thousand big ones,' he addressed Fergal hurriedly before tipping the drink into the back of his throat with one greedy gulp. 'I'll accept a cheque.'

Fergal whistled utter disbelief through tight lips.

'That's a lot of money mucker,' he gasped. 'Why do you need so much?'

Donal guzzled the second of his drinks, this time with a hunger similar to a squirrel recently awakened from a long hibernation.

'Loan sharks.' He spat a shower of spittle over Fergal's jacket and the bar he leant against. 'Gemma likes her luxuries. The friggers are breathing down me neck.'

The silence of the establishment was interrupted from time to time by a group of women giggling and occasionally jeering to one another from their corner alcove. Their noise managed to dampen Donal's unnecessary loudness considerably. A saving grace on this occasion, Fergal mentally observed, yet surely annoying at others.

'Are the kids with you?' Fergal asked. 'Where the heck are you all staying?'

Donal burped, hiccupped several times and then licked his red, chapped lips.

'At my Ma's old house.' Donal confessed through whiskey-infused breath. 'Tara takes care of the twins after school. I take over in the evenings.'

Donal's mother had passed away earlier that year, leaving her home free for new inhabitants.

'Thank God the place hasn't sold yet,' he nudged Fergal's arm playfully. 'Otherwise, I'd be up the Swaney without a paddle, eh!'

Fergal's lips thinned with annoyance.

'If you spill my drink again,' he issued a severe warning. 'I'll take a paddle and pound you to a pulp.'

'Fair enough.'

Excusing himself minutes later, Fergal left for the bathroom, seeking some time to himself rather than a pee. Priding himself on being a patient man at the best of times, today, his endurance was taking a considerable bashing.

'I'll order another while you're away,' Donal informed him with a wink and another hiccup. 'It's your round this time,' he smirked good-humouredly. 'You tight-arsed old bugger.'

The various squeals and sniggers, courtesy of the female bathroom next door, added considerably to Fergal's irritation and anger at what had happened with Donal and the money thing.

He never did have a great deal of time for Donal, preferring to keep his distance for fear his bother-in-law by marriage would one day ask him the very favour he just had.

Listen to your gut more, he chastised himself heatedly. *For the love of God, stop being so generous.*

Finishing the task in hand, he sighed relief. As it turned out he'd needed a pee after all. Humming, he readjusted his clothes, thinking many thoughts at the one time. And then two things abruptly caught his attention, causing him to fall completely silent.

The wall between both male and female bathrooms was thin. It was impossible not to hear what was being said from the women there. When the name Kate McAllister was mentioned, Fergal's interest rose considerably.

Ballygo was a small town with a population of three thousand people, give or take. It was rare someone wouldn't be known of, talked about or related to many others in the place. Gossip fed a chunk of its inhabitants, fresh of the press or long standing, it didn't matter.

Today was Kate's turn. Fergal didn't know of anything going on with Kate to justify the chatter. It seemed he was about to be enlightened. Donal could wait. This was important.

'Her and Malone have been at it for ages,' the chat continued. 'I thought you knew.'

'No way, *that* sleaze-ball. Are you kidding?'

'Oh yes, Mister Inflated Ego himself.'

'Seriously… wow.'

'It's been going on for ages. They were seen together at the conference in Manchester last month. Apparently, they were caught twice before in the park, doing it and all.'

'Wow.'

The voices went quiet. Fergal zipped up his jeans but debated washing hands yet.

'I know she's no looker but honestly,' the talking resumed. 'Even *she* could do better than that perverted arse-wipe.'

'I agree. He's a friggin sight.'

Seconds later Fergal left the bathroom. Donal had consumed another two whiskeys in the time he was away. Rambling to some old geezer about unfair and unjust politics, Donal spat and slobbered all over the place.

'There you are big fella.' He slung his arm around Fergal's shoulders. 'I told this fine woman you were paying.' Millie glared annoyance. 'So come on, pay up before she has a fit.'

It was an hour later before Fergal left the bar, substantially less well off than before he entered it. The builder's bank account had taken a mighty thrashing.

He'd even been stung for Donal's taxi fare home. The man was in no fit state to be around children with the condition he was in. The phone call to the school's office faked a family emergency, letting him of the hook for the rest of the day.

'Frig,' Fergal pulled his collar up against the chilling breeze. 'I feel violated.'

Although Donal had promised to pay every cent back as soon as his mother's house was sold, past experiences had warned Fergal not to be holding his breath, lest he died of suffocation.

Fergal debated if divulging Kate's news to Ellen was a good idea. He weighted the pros and cons, hoping to reach a balance. He failed miserably. In the end, he decided to say nothing. His wife had severely pissed him off and this little gem was decent payback.

'It's not my business anyway,' he whispered to the sound of the van's wipers, switched on to clear the afternoon's drizzle. 'I'll stay stump.'

As far as Fergal was concerned, there was quite enough going on in his own home with Ellen's family already.

The last thing he wanted was to have two of her sisters disrupting his life. The one currently occupying his spare room was causing enough drama to justify a dozen people, as it was.

Gemma's presence was felt on many levels and in a very big way.

CHAPTER TWENTY-NINE

'You bitch!' Gemma glared at Ellen, all attempts to hide behind the lie gone with the reaction. 'How the hell do you know about that?'

'Steady on,' Ellen frowned at the offensive name-calling. 'There's no need for that.'

Ignoring her, Gemma continued, air billowing from her nostrils and fire heating up her solar plexus.

'Well,' she tapped her fingers on crossed arms, 'who told you about the abortion?'

'Dad!' Ellen felt like screaming. 'I told you,' she repeated. 'He's here with me now, from Spirit, giving me the information.'

'Bullshit,' Gemma sneered, 'I don't believe you.'

'Shocker.'

'It was Mum, wasn't it?' Gemma glared accusingly. 'That woman was always a big blabbermouth.'

'That's enough,' Ellen defended Anna in her absence. 'There's no call to bring Mum into this, much less insult her.'

Anna may well play the odd mind game. She was no stranger to emotional blackmail either but on this occasion, she was innocent. As a parent she'd done her job.

Gemma paced back and forth on the tiled floor, mumbling under her breath and occasionally stamping her foot in temper.

She scowled from between slit eyes at Ellen and threw out words like "weirdo," "insane" and "nuthouse."

'Well,' she exclaimed heatedly. 'You may as well continue,' curiosity was getting the better of her. 'What else are you being *told*?' She made inverted commas with her fingers in the air.

Ellen sighed from tiredness deep within her core. She knew this needed to happen to free Gemma up from the effect of her past but would have preferred to have continued with her counselling course than give any more time to it.

'You haven't forgiven yourself, Donal or anyone else for this, Gemma,' she offered from a sadness that was waning. 'What happened was meant to happen.' She listened to her father and the guidance of the Masters. 'The decision to terminate was made before you came into your current body. It was contracted.'

'Speak sense, woman!' Gemma snapped, glaring at her. 'I've no idea what any of that means.'

'Then sit down and calm down,' Ellen advised. 'I'll either happily explain or strangle you with the belt of your jeans. It's entirely your choice.'

'You'd try it.'

'Trust me Gemma, I'm on the verge of going. Don't push it.'

It took twenty minutes, with Gemma making three attempts to storm out of the room and then retract when she realised Ellen wasn't following her, before the younger sister finally seemed to be making some headway. Ellen was fraught beyond the tip of her endurance and stressed in a way she had never been before.

'Yes,' she confirmed for what seemed like the tenth time. 'What happens in a past life, must be accounted for in the next one.' She threw her hand up in celebration as Gemma nodded understanding. 'You've got it now, finally.'

'So, you're saying,' Gemma asked, mostly for her own benefit of saying it out loud. 'If I'd killed someone in a past life, I'd have to complete the karma of it in this one for...'

'Payback,' Ellen confirmed. 'Balance, justice, karma. What goes around must come around. It's the Wheel of Fortune; the Wheel of Life.'

'Right. I get it now... dead on.'

'Thank Buddha.'

Seconds of silence, blissful to Ellen's assailed ears followed, while Gemma established head space for the latest information to find a home.

She resumed her earlier abandoned seat. Placing her behind on it, eased the aching ankle considerably, brought on from all the prancing about she'd done. Its throbbing made her want to cry.

Instead, she gazed into a past she thought was long buried, yet never forgotten. A time in her life when being an adult, responsible for herself and her choices, was just finding momentum.

Memories tumbled out, flooding through her mind like a burst tap across a floor. She was raking up details long since locked in her mind.

Her wedding day, their first home; buying their first supermarket groceries together; filling out a new credit card applications as mister and missus; picking out bathroom carpet and tiles; pricing garden furniture that turned out to be way too expensive for their budget but a must-have for the barbeques they'd planned to host at least once a month. Time stood still for several minutes as Gemma indulged in the sudden nostalgia.

When it came to the stage of acknowledging the memories of that morning, she recounted how she'd woke up with the sudden realisation that her period was unusually late. Dread set in.

That feeling of fear when things were spiralling out of control. Their perfect world was yet to be completed in its reality. It seemed pretty horrific.

That one time, that single one night, months ago when they'd had unprotected sex, drunk from partying with friends. Birth control faded in comparison to a celebration shag.

'Just this once won't count,' Donal consoled when the condom box was found to be empty. 'Nobody ever gets pregnant the first time anyway.'

Their gullibility was guided and believed by the alcohol they'd consumed.

Gemma broke the silence with a whispered admission.

'We were way too young and immature to handle a family.' She spoke as though she were talking to a younger version of herself, the fearful, fretful twenty-something-year-old child she was back then. 'We were skint, living in a two-bedroom terrace and just about to start on our careers,' she reasoned. 'The timing was way off.'

The pregnancy test showed positive pink stripes that for many brought such joy. For her and Donal it provided nothing but fear and anxiousness of an unsteady, as yet unplanned-for future.

How life could suddenly change in polar opposites, from ecstasy to dread, from joy to despair! It seemed so unfair. Both she and Donal had to find a way to put things back the way they had been when everything seemed simpler, laced with soon to be newly wedded innocence. Nothing seemed right about what was suddenly thrust upon them. It had to change.

There were tears and confessions of secret drinking since, as well as old anger towards their mother for coming along to the termination.

'She shouldn't have let me do it. I've carried this with me, every minute of every day since,' she confessed. 'I can't let go of the guilt.' The tears that fell, were from old emotions, never expressed until now.

Ellen touched her sister's arm, comforting her.

'One of the hardest things we face,' she told Gemma, 'is the ability to forgive ourselves.'

'I agree,' Gemma sighed, drying her tears on an already soaked tissue. She lit another cigarette, inhaling deeply, deservingly.

'But I'm also finding it so hard to forgive Donal. He didn't fight harder to stop me going through with it.' Gemma shrugged. 'I know that sounds weird,' she smiled a sad smile. 'We made the decision to abort together but...' her voice quivered. 'I think some part of me wanted him to make it okay, to say it was all right to start our family that soon, you know?'

Ellen didn't really know but smiled an understanding smile regardless.

'It helps what you've told me,' Gemma reassured Ellen. 'I feel I can handle it better now, just from knowing I'd less control over making the decision than I thought.' She sighed a deep wounded sound from the darkest part of her psyche. 'Thanks, sis.' She drew conclusions never before realised. 'This has shed new light.'

'You've shared a deep-rooted scar today. I think that makes you pretty darn brave, Gemma.'

'Oh, my dear god, do you ever stop?' The old Gemma had made a comeback. 'You think you're Mother Theresa or somit?'

'I'll make fresh coffee.'

'Mines a gin and tonic ta.'

'Would you like arsenic with that or just some ice?'

'Huh. It wouldn't surprise me one bit if you added poison.'

'Me neither.'

Lunch time was signalled, via a rumbling of both their stomachs and they enjoyed a bowl of soup and sandwiches in silence.

Decisions had been made to attend counselling sessions and a promise to start looking through the phone book for the closest service.

'Right, Goodie Two Shoes,' Gemma's mocking continued. 'What about this therapeutic healing shit you're on about?'

'Well,' Ellen advised. 'You've a choice of mindfulness therapy or cognitive. They are both close by, in Ballygo town in fact.'

'I can't risk anybody seeing me going into those things.' Gemma was horrified at the very idea. 'What's the other options?'

'Travelling further afield.'

'Give me that here,' she snapped the tablet device of Ellen, determined to prove her wrong. When it turned out a decent thirty-mile round journey was involved otherwise, she reneged. 'Just get me booked in,' she instructed. 'Can't stand all this fuss.'

'You're the one making the fuss,' Ellen confirmed. 'And what, now I'm your secretary?'

'You started this crap.'

'You really are the limit, Gemma.'

'Glad you finally noticed. While you're on your feet,' Ellen wasn't really, 'bring me that blanket you've chucked over the back of the sofa in the other room. It's friggin freezing in this monster of a place.'

'Sir, yes sir!'

'Ellen sighed as she watched Gemma stub out her cigarette and slurp noisily on the last of her soup.

Maye she'd research bipolar disorder later. Just a thought.

CHAPTER THIRTY

It was Rose's idea they should go for the walk around the park. Noticing her new friend's tired, melancholic expression, she felt a long dander would do them both the world of good.

Besides, she debated, anything had to be an improvement to playing host to the atmosphere she decided to label "doom and gloom." It had hung heavily in the cottage all morning since Maeve's admission that her husband was a bit of a baddie.

'We can take a flask of hot chocolate with us,' she suggested with a smile, a wink and a lift of her eyebrows. 'We'll treat ourselves to some shortbread, for pure indulgence. The extra inches on the hips will help see us through the winter.'

Maeve agreed that it seemed like a grand idea, with a half-hearted nod and a drop of her eyes towards the ground. Having analysed and connected past events regarding George and his mistress all morning, she knew a walk would help clear mental cobwebs. It might even stop her from feeling like such a fool, even for an hour.

Brown, orange, yellow and red leaves carpeted the park's pebbled ground and pathways, as its many surrounding trees shed their leaves, preparing for the chilly days ahead.

'It's nature's equivalent to the red-carpet treatment,' Rose remarked, enjoying the natural beauty and savouring the scene in front of her.

Delighted at how uplifted she was feeling by simply walking in the open air, Maeve was defusing a mountain of tiny burdens as she trotted along.

'It's such a shame to step on the leaves,' Maeve confessed with a seriousness she genuinely felt. 'It feels destructive.'

'Don't worry,' Rose assured her companion. 'It doesn't hurt them and besides,' she grinned, 'I honestly don't think they mind.'

Rose inhaled deep breaths of air as she walked, greedy for its healing qualities. Maeve was doing the same thing, delighted she'd mastered the art of eternal cleansing just as Rose had taught.

'If you visualise white light flowing through your body with each breath,' Rose offered helpfully, 'it tends to give you an emotional lift.'

'If that's true,' Maeve set her tongue firmly in her cheek. 'I'll need a ton of it.'

'There's plenty for all. Indulge away.'

At the pond, Andrew and Rose's favourite spot, they rested. Since they were in a deep meditative state inside the natural wonders, it was nice to sit and indulge.

The sound of the water gently hitting the pond's edge, trickled through their consciousness, signalling tranquillity all around.

This continued for a while. Even the cold of the air sweeping up and down their legs, numbing their toes (despite the thermal, fur lined boots) and nipping fingers into a state of shock, didn't seem to detain the serenity of their paradise.

Rose shuttered a shiver from the cold (the chill had found her). She heard Andrew's voice floating on the current and saw him and Moby play, laughing delighted squeals (and barks) of adventure echoing around the park. She felt sad.

A tear escaped down her cheek. She wasn't sure if it was the cold that caused it or from the wounded emotion felt, but down it came anyway.

She wiped it away impatiently, annoyed at herself. She knew Andrew was fine. There was no need to fret. She'd see him again someday.

'You're allowed to cry,' Maeve noticed the wipe and assumed this visit was resurrecting old memories. 'He was your life for so long.'

'Boys a dear. He was that all right.' Another tear joined the last few. 'But I know he's never far away. Her voice trailed as more water escaped. She let it fall unchecked. It was good to release.

Time passed. The mood lifted. Rose opened her closed eyes and took in all the sights and sounds around her. She smirked. 'I love to sit quietly and hear the birds sing,' she admitted. 'It's like listening to God's very own choir. This whole scene is simply precious.'

Closing her eyes again, Rose inhaled deeply. She hummed a tune. It was one of Andrew's favourites. He loved the Dubliners cassette she'd gifted him on his last earthly Christmas.

'I love that song,' Maeve made out the 'Grace' melody from Rose's singing. 'It's both sad and engaging all at once.'

'Indeed. I don't carry a tune very well,' Rose said. 'But I do love music.'

'I'll say no more about it.'

Time passed and then more followed. The blanket they'd brought became their cosy friend, the snacks their internal thermal.

'This hot chocolate is the bee's knees.' Maeve drank greedily, delighted with its effect. 'The shortbread is to die for.' She munched greedily. 'I'll need the recipe.'

Rose smiled at the compliment.

'It's my Mum's recipe.' She tapped the side of her nose with a gloved hand. 'It's a family secret,' she warned. 'You've no hope of repeating the same bake yourself. My old, chapped lips, are sealed.'

'You've it written down in the cookbook behind the breadbin,' Maeve helped herself to another square of the delicious pastry. 'I can copy it down later.'

'Fair enough.'

Eating outdoors was something of an unusual treat for Maeve. She struggled to remember the last time she'd had a picnic in the open air.

The only memory she could come up with was in childhood with her parents and Anna. George and married life to him prevented such simple joys. She felt such a pity for the absence now. Maeve was learning so much in such a short space of time it was becoming infectious.

She glanced sheepishly Rose's way from the corner of her eye.

'May I ask a question?' she ventured and then watched Rose guzzle an ample intake of liquid chocolate down her throat as she nodded permission. 'It was something Ellen spoke of at Andrew's funeral.'

Rose wiped the side of her mouth chocolate free with her woollen gloved hand. Then wiped the glove clean on the grass below.

'Sure,' she agreed again, this time verbally. 'Fire away.'

Maeve swallowed a hot mouthful of liquid chocolate herself by way of Dutch courage, without the Dutch, before continuing.

'The word chakras came up several times.' She struggled with the pronunciation. 'What the heck are they?'

'Um,' Rose considered for a few seconds, unsure how correct her explanation would be. 'I'm a bit unsure myself,' she didn't like to admit its truth. 'As far as I know, they are energy points, vortexes throughout the body.

'Okay…'

'I do know the practice of balancing them originated from ancient India.' Rose felt cheered she remembered reading that somewhere. 'Eastern practices swear by them as a means of healing and balancing the mind, body and spirit.'

Perhaps she'd underestimated her own knowledge of the subject after all. That little snippet had come from nowhere and actually sounded very informed. *Huh*, she thought, *fancy that*.

'Ahh.' Maeve pondered. 'Okay.'

A few still, silent seconds fell between the recent words. Maeve nodded slowly but truthfully looked more confused than ever. Rose may as well have spoken in Arabic to her for as much as she understood the alien description.

'I'm afraid you've lost me.' She finally owned up. 'I haven't a single clue what you just said.'

Rose understood her confusion. The very mention of India, Eastern or vortexes of energy had been so absent from their conditioning in the Western world at the time they'd grown up.

Back then, priority was given to things such as not committing sins or going to church regularly. There was guilt (of unmeasurable amounts) if you didn't live up to the rules laid down. Control over what was acceptable to think and believe in was also paramount, regardless of individual opinions.

India seemed as far off as the North Pole. On a very rare occasion, it was a great treat just to go as far as Belfast City itself. Thirty-six miles those days seemed like two hundred now.

Geographical locations were not as easily bridged as they currently were. Trips out in bygone days required a lot of pre-planning. Routes were designed meticulously to allow for bathroom stops.

Sandwich fillings were thought through intensely, for durability and taste. New flasks were bought for hot tea along the way with a cake baked for the occasion the night before.

It was all innocently exciting. Rose still remembered the anticipation she'd felt days before her first young visit to "the big city." She hadn't slept a wink the night before.

She smiled now at the unexpected nostalgia from her past. It was just lovely that she had the chance to travel down a road that held so many fond memories. Hard though life was then (compared to now) it was a simpler time.

'I'm a little lost with it all too,' Rose patted Maeve's arm in shared comradeship of the past. 'Ellen will keep us posted though. She's starting into all that soon.'

'She is?'

'Presumably.'

'Righty-ho.'

As their feasting drew to a close (because of the absence of any remaining shortbread), it was obvious the dark clouds forming overhead were sending them both a message: either take your leave or take shelter! Any decision otherwise dictated a good old soaking.

'I suppose we should make tracks back,' Rose felt begrudging that their time was being dictated to them. Today of all days when Maeve needed the distraction as well. 'Unless of course you fancy doing a rain dance to deter the weather, Maeve?'

Maeve laughed giddily at the joke.

'Sorry,' she pretended a false disappointment, 'In the absence of music, I'm beat.'

They gathered up their picnic utensils into the hamper and after stuffing the blanket to within an inch of its life, it joined the cups and plates inside. The straps struggled to close under the demands made of it.

They each took a handle and walked ahead, balancing the wicker basket between them as they strained to quicken their step. The fear was it would start to rain any second. It was getting greyer by the minute.

'I'll sing as we walk,' Rose offered playfully, partly to say something and mostly to help keep the mood light. 'That should get our paws moving faster.'

Maeve said nothing as the seconds ticked by. Eventually, she glanced Rose's way.

'No offence,' she told her eager companion, as compassionately as she could muster. 'But if your singing is anything like your humming,' she looked skywards. 'You'll encourage a thunderstorm!'

They both laughed so hard and so heartily that Rose thought she'd burst her liver. Maeve's giggles were the cause of her peeing a little in her last pair of clean drawers.

'Stop,' she warned between bouts, holding her legs across one another for leakage protection. 'I'll have nothing clean to wear tomorrow.'

'Don't worry,' Rose told her. 'You can go commando.'

Maeve didn't have the slightest idea what Rose was talking about, but she laughed anyway. She'd be borrowing a pair of Rose's knickers tomorrow for sure. The leg crossing hadn't worked as intended and quite a bit of urine had soaked through.

By the time the cottage came into view, their clothes felt damp with drizzle and other stuff as well. The thought of a warm hearth fire and a game of draughts, lay ahead invitingly.

As they reached the front door, Rose gasped.

'Oh my,' her surprise brought them both to a standstill. 'I don't believe it… look.'

Lying on the front door mat were two tiny white feathers. If they didn't know better, they'd swear they'd been hand-delivered. Maeve bent down and picked them up.

'What do you think this means?' she held them gently in the palm of her hand. 'Is this something else I don't understand?'

Rose extracted one of the feathers from Maeve's hand and smiled a very contented smile.

'This one,' she explained to Maeve's puzzled face, 'means that Andrew has finally made contact.' She grinned from ear to ear.

'And yours,' she pointed to the one Maeve was now clasping tightly between her fingers for fear the breeze would carry it away, 'is a sign from your Guardian Angel that all is going to be just fine and dandy.'

The power of a simple sign, meant the world.

CHAPTER THIRTY-ONE

'Whey hey!' Dean, the office receptionist barged in through Kate's office door, pushing the tall bouquet of flowers in front of him and the door against the wall with a bang. 'Have you and your hubby had a tiff then?'

'Goodness.' Startled, Kate glanced up from the statistical sheet she'd been studying. 'Are those for me?'

Dean grinned cunningly.

'Sure are, Twinkle Toes,' he confirmed, assured he'd guessed their sender accurately. 'Looks like somebody's gonna be getting some tonight.'

Thrusting the flowers in her direction and then leaving the door slightly ajar, the young man made his way back to the reception counter.

He was marvelling in the fact that a tall, blonde, nineteen-year-old female had just entered the building. It was time to turn on the charm. Luckily for her, he had it by the bucketload.

Before she opened the tiny envelope attached to the bouquet, Kate walked over and closed the door.

There was no apparent reason her husband John would be sending flowers; he hadn't done such a thing for the longest time. Assuming they were from Adam, Kate wanted complete privacy.

'Enjoyed last weekend enormously,' Kate read silently. They'd had a hotel stay. *'We need to talk pronto. Give me a call ASAP.'* The card was signed 'Big Daddy.'

A worried frown spread across her brow. Her tummy jolted a sudden jerk, nervous. What did Adam want to discuss in such a hurry she wondered? He'd always been a man of few words, preferring actions to speak louder. It was one of the things he'd made clear to her from the start, with a pelvic thrust and a lick of his lips to emphasise its truth.

Curiosity and self-doubt automatically motivated her to lift the telephone and call. Maybe there was a problem with their pre-arranged dinner later that week, Kate reasoned. Although in truth if there was, she'd be considerably disappointed.

The red lacy, see-through underwear she'd recently purchased would surely go to waste. Yes, okay, okay so it was a cheap knockoff from the outlet and in the pre-season sale but still. It would be a shame not to wear it.

Adam's secretary answered on the third ring.

'I'll put you straight through,' she told Kate pleasantly. 'Please hold the line.'

Kate happily did, along with her racing fears. A few seconds and a blast of U2's 'Sunday, Bloody Sunday' later, Adam answered.

'Kate,' his voice sounded deep and sexy down the line, causing her heart to skip a double somersault and leap into overdrive. 'Did you get the flowers?'

She smiled a long, lingering heartfelt smile, the very same one that would warm the cockles of even the coldest heart.

'I did,' she replied through her grin, wrapping the telephone cord around her finger and swaying her hips to a noiseless beat 'They're perfect. Thank you, darling.'

The silence that followed was long drawn out and uncomfortable. Kate's concern at the stillness forced the smile from her face. Its replacement resembled a rather deep and anxious frown.

Something wasn't quite all right. She could sense it. Her astute female intuition rarely failed to let her down in the past. It was always so accurate.

'Adam,' she whispered apprehensively. 'Is everything okay?'

Hearing his long, deep sigh brought back the prickly tickle to her tummy.

'Everyone knows, Kate,' Adam told her sternly. 'We've become the office joke.'

Kate gasped.

'What!' Her jaw dropped and her eyes widened. 'Are you sure?'

'Of course, I'm sure. Do you think I made this stuff up? I'm no eejit you know.'

'I do and there's no need to be like that.'

'Sorry. I'm freaked out.'

'Me too.'

Panic welled within. Many thoughts flashed through her mind in one short, sharp episode. They'd been so careful; how could this be?

'Apparently, it's been public knowledge for quite a while,' Adam continued, having taken on an impersonal, curt, and business-like manner. 'We were seen together in Manchester and again up in Belfast coming out of the theatre... I told you not to wear that yellow polka dot coat,' he blamed her mercilessly. 'I just knew it would draw attention our way... you're such a fool.'

'Hey!' Kate protested, 'steady on there. It took the two of us to tango,' she puffed. 'Your red trouser suit wasn't exactly discrete either.'

'Whatever. Enough of this faffin' about. We've a real humdinger on our hands here.'

Suddenly, amidst the many other thoughts running through her head, Kate remembered the pact they'd made when their affair first began.

Her stomach soured along with the taste in her mouth. Her heart quickened its beat once again. The palms of her hands grew clammy and muggy. She knew what was coming and detested it to her very core. The dread was unbearable.

'We can't risk Clare finding out,' Adam's firmness spoke finality. He'd remembered the pact too. It was him who'd set it out, in written agreement, with a copy faxed to her office the next day to be signed and returned.

'You know I can't jeopardise losing my wife, Kate. She's already suspicious as it is. This would surely tip the scales against me, and I'd be cut out of her da's will for sure.'

'Well,' Kate's voice trembled. 'It's not all about you, Adam.' The money comment had stung deeply. When all was said and done, their affair came down to finances. She'd believed it meant so much more to him. It was the world to her. 'What about *my* situation... what about John?'

'Um,' Adam's mind was focused elsewhere as he flicked through the paperwork on his desk. 'We don't have time for any further discussion.' His words were cruel in their deliverance. Kate physically winced in pain. 'It's time to say adios amigo. Sorry Kitten Breath.' He was keen to end the conversation as soon as possible. 'But we're done. Slan and all of that.'

'But...'

He hung up.

Kate stood with the phone's receiver clinging to her chest. Stunned into statue like if she didn't move it wasn't real.

Her breathing slowed as the room revolved, tipping up and down and around again. Spots came and went from her focus. She was drifting into another place that was grey and then black...

'Kate! Kate!' Dean's voice echoed through the pounding pain in her head. She slowly opened her eyes, coming back into focus. She wondered why so many were in her office at one time. 'Give her space,' Dean ordered. 'She's coming around.'

Windows were opened, her blouse unbuttoned (exposing her underwear. *Had she worn a decent bra today?)* She was being fanned with a file across her face.

'You fainted,' Dean informed her to the sound of 'daa' behind him. The office junior that he'd reprimand later. 'What's the craic now, how are you feeling?'

'Like I've been dragged through a hedge backwards.'

'Drink this.' Waster was produced. 'It'll help.'

Wedged between the office chair and desk, her skirt was all shapes, pulled up to reveal the ample thighs she'd struggled so hard to keep hidden. She tried to move her head, but things started spinning again.

'Blood pressure tablets in my bag.' She'd fake that. 'Over there. Get my coat too please. Throw it over my legs.'

'You heard the woman.' Dean fed her more water as he yelled at Smart Mouth behind. 'Shift it.'

Things settled before lunch hour began. At her insistence, she remained in work. Dean kept a tight eye on her from his desk for a while. When things seemed to be normalised again, he went off for lunch.

When they'd all gone, she wept. The tears fell uncontrolled down her chubby cheeks, with a landing onto her arms and desk even a bungee jumper would be proud of.

He'd left her life. Gone for good. How could she bear to see him at meetings again without breaking down? The thought of it felt excruciating.

No more sneaking out after dinner for a quickie in his car. Gone were the weekend's away (the sheer pleasure of those would be missed most).

Hiding credit card statements from John (she'd paid for all the hotel stays). There'd be no more feeling special, feeling loved and wanted. It was all dropped from her life like a stone falling from a cliff. All vanished with a few simple words.

At that moment Kate felt tired. She was utterly exhausted from being the girl always having struggle to prove her worth.

She was the one who achieved moderate grades, never brilliant at anything but just all right at most things. Middle ground, never quite reaching the top and not delving to the bottom. Ordinary, like a packet of ready salted crisps, all the while envious of the cheese and onion picked before her.

And the guilt! God, the guilt. It was the worst. The lies she'd told to her kids, her husband, her work colleagues and worst of all, herself. The heavy-weighted emotions. They seemed to rule her life. Their intensity ran as deep as a well.

The telephone's ear-splitting shrill wakened her from her despairing depths. Startled into realising she was still at work, it took Kate a few seconds to ground her thoughts and become work minded again, or as close to it as the current events allowed. The caller was her boss, Declan McNally.

'You've a meeting after lunch, Kate,' he reminded her curtly. 'Don't forget.'

'I'll be there.'

'Dead on. I'll get those stats of you before we go in.'

'Yes. right. Okay sounds good.' *Oh, hell, the stats that were never finished!* 'Grand.'

Estimating she had at least forty minutes before needing to re-groom, Kate thanked Declan, replaced the handset and walked shakily towards the filing cabinet in the corner of the room.

Once there, she pulled the bottom drawer opened and peered inside the suitably named "junk drawer."

Odds and ends littered the depth of the large drawer. There were scarves used to dress up outfits in a hurry. Perfume bottles with small amounts of scent at the bottom. A pair of comfy, warm socks to have for a cold day, worn on her feet as they nestled, tucked firmly under her desk. Essentials for backup.

John's photograph lay below an ageing novel. It took Kate a few seconds to fish it out from under the tangled pairs of stockings, a supply she had stocked up for emergencies. Her husband's smiling face rewarded her efforts, making her smile back.

Placing the long since discarded frame back onto her desk she turned it to face her chair.

'I've been such a fool,' she chastised herself sadly. 'Now I'm paying the price.'

Wiping her tears away, she breathed deeply, grabbed her handbag and walked in the direction of the ladies' bathroom. Fixing the face behind the mask she'd been using for years would help.

Maybe, just maybe she hoped, she could breathe new life into the embers of her dying marriage.

It was worth a try and better than being left on her own.

CHAPTER THIRTY-TWO

During their game of draughts, Maeve switched on the table lamp and looked at the feather resting on her lap. It had lain in the same position since their return home from the park, (where later on she'd put into her empty locket). She glanced Rose's way.

'I've been doing a lot of thinking,' she rushed her focus back to the board and its game, lest her opponent read into her psyche and knew the depth she recently managed to let emerge. 'I've made a few decisions.'

Rose's only answer was to jump counters and steal one of her rival's points. Adding it to the mound of others resting by her arm, she silently congratulated herself on another deserved win.

Rose knew she rocked at board games; it was her thing. Allowing Andrew to win the odd time was difficult for her but she managed. No such privilege would be afforded to Maeve (or anyone else).

Being competitive was not usually a sun sign Cancer's trait but having a Mars in Aries placing in her astrological chart when she was born, allowed the aggressive and competitive side too shine. There was nothing like a little smugness to satisfy the human ego.

'May I share with you now?' Maeve enquired. 'I'm dying to say.'

Rose nodded clearance.

'Fire away,' she instructed. 'I'm all ears, if not a little deaf in the right one.'

Taking a gulp from her glass of orange juice and then clearing her throat, Maeve continued.

'I've decided,' she began, 'that I'm going to stay in Ireland for the foreseeable future,' her voice faltered. 'I have no desire,' she continued bravely, 'to return to my previous life in England now that...'

'Check!' Rose won another point. 'Sucker,' she teased. 'You lose.'

Maeve let the interruption pass with a click of her tongue and waited seconds for Rose to compose her original position.

'As I was saying,' Maeve continued, unrelenting in her quest. 'I'll be returning to Kent for a few days, to sort out practicalities.' She glanced timidly at Rose. 'I've already spoken to Ellen. She's taking care of flights and rental accommodation for my return.'

Maeve sensed staying with Anna was not an option. Truth be told she'd rather not anyway. There was a lot to be said for keeping independence. It helped close relationships to function better.

As Rose moved her counter into a dangerous position, she felt it was clear Maeve was not committed to their game. She was in the throes of a life transformation and many other things occupied her mind. Rose, on the other hand, was very much involved.

'I win,' she made the last jump, completing further moves forward and taking advantage of Maeve's lack of focus. 'Now, hand me my prize.'

The slice of lemon drizzle cake tasted that bit sweeter with the word "winner" scrawled across it. Rose savoured its taste, licking her fingers clean when it had all but disappeared. She slurped down the remainder of her tea, rinsing her mouth from the cake's crumbs in the process.

'Righty-ho,' she smoothed her skirt and wiped a stray hair to the ground. 'Now I have a few things to say to you.'

Startled, Maeve threw a surprised look her way. She'd thought the conversation was finished. She'd all but cleared the board game back into the box. About to walk over and set it into its resting place, she instead resumed her seat.

'Okay,' Maeve grounded her feet onto the floor. 'I'm all yours.'

'Your home is here,' Rose's brusque manner left little room for argument otherwise. 'I see no reason why you need to rent, buy or move elsewhere, and,' she continued, lest Maeve's attempt to respond would have air time. 'I need you here.'

'But Rose,' Maeve argued. 'This is *your* home, not mine.'

Rose felt insulted and actually said so.

'I'm insulted you see it that way, Maeve,' she admitted truthfully. 'You may only have lived here for five or six days, but already your presence belongs here and you,' her finger pointed accusingly, 'darn well know it.'

Maeve could easily have wept. When tears began welling in her eyes, she felt she should. Never before had anyone made her feel as useful and wanted as Rose just did. In the twilight years of her life, she felt complete for the first time.

'I don't know what to say,' she admitted through a choked throat. 'Thank you.'

'No thanks needed. We'll say no more about it.'

And so, it was decided. The cottage would henceforth be known as Rose and Maeve's home.

'I've a buttload of money from George's insurance pay out.' Maeve felt such excitement as they planned their future together, Rose's terminology already wearing on her. 'I'd love to add a bathroom with a shower to the house,' she suggested eagerly. 'We could bring it in line with the twenty-first century.'

Rose agreed that it was indeed a fine idea to do just that, with a giggle and a look of sheer anticipation for what lay ahead.

'I've never taken a shower in my life!' she confessed. 'What a treat.'

All further discussions were cut short as the cottage door flung open, bringing with it a cold blast of rainy air.

Cecilia puffed her way in through the doorway, shaking the rain from her coat and the last of the air out through her lungs.

'Rosie,' she wheezed, 'I've met my future son-in-law.' Splashes of saliva ran down her ample chins and dripped onto her heavily protruding chest. 'And,' she confessed, 'he's the finest looking man I've laid eyes on since John Wayne himself!'

As Rose made to hug Cecilia, Maeve clasped her feather tight to her chest. She silently thanked the powers above for their intervention. She knew for sure that without the help they'd provided, this state of sheer joy may not have been made possible.

One door had closed on her past and now a new, brighter door to her future was opening. It felt so good.

The last few days had been a nightmare, coming to terms with how much of a fool she'd been over George and the affair. Now this sense of liberation (and excitement) replaced that. How amazing.

For the first in her life, Maeve felt true love of the non-human kind.

It was divine.

CHAPTER THIRTY-THREE

It was ten past seven that evening before Kate heard John's key turning in the lock. Their two daughters squealed with delight and ran to greet him, both clambering for his attention at once.

'Hey, slow down,' John protested, secretly enjoying the attention. 'Let me take my coat off first, you hooligans!'

The steaks Kate cooked for them both were seconds away from ruination. She knew that if they weren't eaten in the next five minutes both she and John could kiss them a sweet, yet sorrowful goodbye; they had cost her a pretty penny.

'Righty-ho girls,' Kate instructed her daughters. 'You've said your hellos to Dad now off you both go and finish homework.'

The girls were not impressed.

'Do we have to?' Meagan protested in complaint, stamping one foot on the floor. 'I want to play with Daddy for a while longer.'

'Yes,' their mother's voice made it clear that there would be no negotiation otherwise. 'You know well and good young lady,' she scolded, 'that this was the arrangement we made earlier. I've lived up to my end of the bargain,' she told Meagan's upturned, pleading face. 'Now you need to do the same with yours. Shift it Bouncy Bum.'

With both daughters trudging towards their destination, without any sign of a bouncy bum in sight, she and John walked towards the kitchen and to the back of their home.

Once inside it was hard not to notice the carefully laid table, displaying wine glasses and candles. John hesitated in the doorway looking concerned and a little confused. He scratched his thinning hair, not from itchiness but as a subconscious sign of said confusion.

'What's all this?' he asked, a frown forming on his already wrinkled brow. 'Is it a special occasion or summit?'

Kate smiled, she hoped seductively.

'Sort of,' she offered, at the same time lifting the meat from the grill and opening the oven door to retrieve the food keeping warm inside. 'I'd like us both to have a talk.'

John's frown deepened. He could feel a burp rumbling internally, his usual reaction to uncomfortable situations and a throwback from childhood. It's how he'd earned the name "The Rumbler" at school.

'I'm not sure that we have anything to talk about,' John answered briskly, heaving a little bile in his throat at the potential confrontation ahead. 'It's been that way for a while now, sure.'

Kate didn't like the way this was working out at all. She could sense her husband's gut issues arising; his tummy was roaring from its depths like a wild, confined animal in a cage. She could sense his fear.

'Please,' she pleaded, at the same time burning her wrist on the hot grill, salvaging the steaks. 'It's important... shit!' The burn stung.

Hesitating, John edged his way slowly into the room. He shilly-shallied a little longer at the table than was necessary, many thoughts racing through his mind, giving him a ton of reasons to either leave or to stay. His instinct said, "do a runner," while his ego suggested he stay and hear things out. He felt torn.

Just as Kate was putting the hot dinner plates on the table, he sat down, decision made. He'd see how things went before legging it.

'You know what,' he declared, more to salvage some manly power than anything else, (his guts were dancing noisily for the world and their granny to hear). 'This is actually not a bad idea after all.' He'd business himself.

Kate rubbed her painful arm and smiled. The darn thing was starting to blister but she soldiered on, reluctant to mess up the opportunity now that John was agreeable.

This was probably the most they'd acted as a married couple in years. Even though it was hugely awkward, verging on cringeworthy, she ignored that for a favourable outcome.

'I've wanted to talk to you for a while myself.' John gulped down a generous mouthful of Dutch courage from the wine glass sitting on the table. It was quite an expensive Australian wine Kate had specially picked up on her way home from work earlier.

She almost groaned at how little regard John showed for its cost. It might as well have been a bottle of cheap supermarket cider for the respect he was giving it. She said nothing.

It wasn't until they were halfway through their verbally silent meal — with both parties not realising how hungry they were until they started to eat — that Kate bit the bullet.

She took another drink from her wine glass, cleared her throat and then eased into her well-rehearsed speech (a written copy of which was residing in her desk drawer at work should it ever be needed).

'It seems like an age since we've had this much time alone,' she spoke softly, and she hoped a little sexily. Realistically it just came off as falsely optimistic. 'Remember how we used to surprise each other with romantic dinners when we first got married?'

He didn't answer, continuing to shovel creamed potatoes into his mouth like they were going out of fashion. This was mostly from hunger but some from nerves. The morsels of food that hadn't quite made his mouth nestled on his chin and his chest hair. (The buttons of his checked shirt lay opened).

Kate wasn't giving up and wouldn't be put off that easily. She knew this man from bygone days. He was like every other male she'd ever met; easily manipulated by the charms of a woman, if it meant sex was at the end of the quest. Mind you she thought, she was making no such promise to him tonight. Laying some groundwork couldn't hurt.

Putting her knife on the plate, she reached across the table. Touching John's hand tenderly with the tips of her fingers, she then seductively ran the same fingers around the rim of her wine glass.

Cupping her chin with her hand, Kate threw her husband a suggestive "come to bed" look like she had used many times in the past on both him and Adam. It never failed.

John recognised it right away, even after its long absence. He gagged on the overdone meat in his mouth and had to gulp more wine down to stop the coughing. Snot and saliva shot from his nose and mouth, covering the table and the majority of its contents. The dinners were ruined along with any ambience that might have been building.

'Frig,' Kate's patience was simmering beneath frustration. 'Just the reaction every girl dreams of!'

The place was soaked, the food rendered uneatable. This was not going to plan at all. At the back of her mind, she was remembering why John and she had become distant over many full, waning, waxing and new moons ago.

247

They'd nothing in common any more, both developing at different rates and very different levels. Their paths no longer crossed, and, she felt sure, never would again. There was just too much of a gap between them.

He preferred a game of darts at the pub, where she enjoyed a night at the theatre and dinner in an upmarket restaurant.

John fought for a family holiday at a camping site while Kate argued a group cruise may just work out as cost-effective with the amount they were saving on food and drinks alone.

She preferred good manners and etiquette where he didn't seem to give a toss. Their differences had already spilt into their daughter's upbringing, as their parenting skills contradicted so often.

She could tell the girls were already showing signs of confusion. So many mixed rules and signals were constantly coming their way. Kate knew adolescence with them both was going to be a blast, and not in a healthy way.

John wiped his mouth, nose and brow with their "special occasion napkins," a wedding present from Kate's dearest friend to be used only at Christmas or dinner parties (on account of them being bought at Brown Thomas in Dublin and extravagantly expensive).

The coughing had subsided but the tickle in his throat continued. He got up from the table in the hope that a drink of water might help.

Slurping and gurgling, John drank greedily from the water tap across the dish-filled sink. Once he was confident things were settling, he felt reluctant to resume his place at the table. Deciding to stand his ground, high above Kate's sitting position, gave him a false sense of power.

'I don't understand what you're playing at here,' he gestured towards the dried-up and lukewarm dinner remains, 'but I'm not falling for any of it... Okay! Okay!' he admitted throwing his arms above his head making his point. 'The food was nice enough but that's where it all stops.'

Kate felt like screaming. Why had she ever imagined life could resume as before with this man? She was a fool, a complete chump to even think of having him as a partner again.

She was so far past his crude, rude and disrespectful ways; getting up close and snuggly with him for a second time felt like going twenty steps backwards instead of developing leaps ahead. In fact, she felt genuinely repulsed at the very idea. She now understood the expression "skin-crawling." This man would never touch her again.

Rejection was never a pleasant thing to go through, especially twice in one day. Yet honestly speaking, Kate knew at that precise minute she'd rather spend the rest of her life living a spinster existence than rekindle her relationship with this creature before her.

She was a sensitive Scorpio and born in the year of the rabbit., She knew the road ahead wouldn't be a walk in the park emotionally, but she'd cope. She'd take up hobbies like jet-skiing, or even bungee jumping, (well maybe not that but still) she'd fill her life with other things. Men would be off the agenda from that moment forward (for a while anyway).

And then there were the girls, her lovely daughters to focus her attention on. They'd get through this together and end up finding contentment as they did in the movies, living happily ever after… or something to that effect.

John walked towards the table and lifted his wine glass, draining the remaining contents in one gulp. He glanced at her out of the side of his eyes, by now glazed from the alcohol he'd consumed. He sighed.

'We're done, Kate.' He spoke silently. 'I know all about you and Malone.' Kate gasped. 'That's right,' John sneered, as he wiped the side of his mouth wine free with the cuff of his jumper. 'I've known for quite a while now.'

'Why didn't you say,' Kate asked, 'before now?'

'I didn't want it to be true at first,' John admitted honestly. 'But when the news reaches your mates it's kinda hard to ignore.'

The many nights he'd lay in their bed lonely, missing her so much and wondering where she was. Then later when he'd found out about her affair, via of work colleagues on a drunken night out, he lay in the same bed wondering and then picturing what she was doing. That little gem had topped the deceit, betrayal and dishonesty tenfold; it practically drove him crazy.

At times, he remembered now, he'd even blamed himself for driving her into this geezer's arms in the first place. Had he been a bad husband, lover or provider? Where had he gone wrong?

Was he not deserving of love? He sure as hell still loved her to bits, just as much as when they'd first met. Yet over time and the longer the deceit had continued, that love weakened, bit by bit, day by day and turned into resentment, verging on hate.

And now, after all the questioning, the agonising pain of betrayal and injustice he'd endured, to think a simple meal and a few seductive gestures could wipe it all away, was unbelievable and downright condescending.

John felt his irritation bubble beneath the surface. There was no time like the present to do what he'd wanted to do for months now. So, if he was going to do it, he was going to do it right. He had his own nugget to share.

'I've found someone else myself,' his voice wobbled on account of his guts playing havoc. 'We're in love.'

'Wow,' Kate gasped, legitimately taken back. 'Wow,' she repeated, allowing some time for the news to sink in. 'I didn't see that coming at all.' She was momentarily stunned.

Delighted that he'd somehow managed to shock her, John considered he'd delivered some payback to his cheating wife. Tiny in comparison for what she'd done to him he thought, but he knew to take his kicks where he could find them.

'Do I know her?' Kate asked as innocently as she could muster in such a short space of time. 'Is she local?'

'She lives out of town,' was all John offered. She could go fish. 'I doubt you've ever even clapped eyes on her before.'

All Kate could think about at that moment was the months spent feeling guilty. Such a waste of time and energy. The whole time John was having his affair she was having hers. Such irony.

The ticking of the kitchen clock sounded out louder than usual, as a dull, deadly silence filled the room. Neither party knew how to proceed. Kate was damned if she'd ask anything else about this new woman. Truth be told, she didn't really care to know much more anyway.

John would eat his three-day-old boxers before he'd give out any other information to this harlot of a woman before him.

He stood stubbornly with his arms folded across his chest, guarding his heart centre, lest Kate attack it for a second time. He wasn't convinced he could recover twice in one lifetime.

Apart from John's irritating sinus breathing, the room remained hushed. In a stand-off, both of them took time to process what had taken place so far. The oven sang a bell from its faulty timing clock. The television played from the other room, dramatic music blasting out every now and again.

Eventually, Kate spoke.

'How did this happen to us?' she asked herself more than John. 'All those years gone by, the kids, the holidays, the downs, the ups. Never once, in that whole time, did I ever think we'd end up here.'

John looked genuinely surprised at her naivety.

'I know how!' he offered heatedly as his stomach pains finally gave way and he let rip for several seconds. Ignoring the bodily function as if it wasn't happening, (yet secretly enjoying the relief it brought him), he continued, 'It started when you decided our lives together were over.'

Turning from the table he reached for his jacket preparing to leave. 'You just forgot to tell me about it first... bitch!'

The dramatic exit didn't end there. John stopped at the kitchen doorway and turned back towards Kate, who was holding one of the expensive napkins across her mouth and nose against the foul smell he'd left behind. He needed to hurt her the way she'd so cruelly administered such pain to him.

'I wish I could say you were a good shag,' he sneered its untruth because their lovemaking was always glorious for him. 'I certainly won't miss those flabby thighs wrapped around me anymore.'

With a march down the hallway and a trip over the girl's shoes on the way out, John was gone with a bang of the door behind him. The house held a deadly silence from the vibration for a few long seconds after.

The remark he'd made over their sex together hadn't stung her as he'd intended. Kate had never enjoyed that part of their relationship, right from the start.

It was only after meeting Adam and enjoying their many sexual encounters that she realised just how inadequate John had been all those years. He was the only man she'd ever had sex with so until then, she had nothing to compare it with.

Lovemaking was meant to be a wonderful thing, not a structured, timed and very short event. It was meant to feel passionate, exciting, riveting... even enchanting like it was with Adam.

It certainly was not meant to be boring and all about the man's pleasure. Spontaneous passion was the best. Not regularly scheduled for Monday and Wednesday evenings and 'maybe a Saturday' if John was in the mood.

'Good luck and good riddance,' Kate got up from the chair she'd been glued to for the past half hour and spoke down the hallway as if John were still able to hear.

'Wish your new woman all the best from me!' She felt scarily relieved conclusions had been finalised at last. God alone knew she was going to need all the help she could get in the days ahead.

Reaching to open the window to allow fresh air to enter, Kate stopped and looked at her reflection in the glass.

'You can do this,' she motivated her slightly deflated reflection with a belief she was really starting to feel. 'It'll all be okay.'

In response, the light of the full moon glowed back, screaming results.

CHAPTER THIRTY-FOUR

The call came as Anna was about to place a new batch of cranberry, white chocolate and cinnamon scones into the hot oven.

'Hello,' she reached the phone just before it hit voice mail. 'Anna here.'

There was some vague chattering in the background before any sense was made of the caller.

'Anna, it's Maeve,' Ellen had insisted Rose and Maeve keep her spare mobile phone in the cottage, since Andrew's passing. It just made good sense. 'Can you hear me?'

Assuring her older sister that she was most likely being heard in Norway, Anna confirmed that she could.

'No need to shout,' she told the nervous talker. 'I'm far from deaf.'

Although she was tempted to find an excuse, Anna could find little reason not to honour Maeve's invitation to visit the cottage later that evening. Apart from feeling a little tired and hoping for an early night's reading in bed, other plans were non-existent.

'Can't you tell me your news now?' She enquired hopefully. 'I'm not great at driving in the dark.'

Maeve insisted she'd rather see her face to face.

'I owe it to you,' she persuaded. 'Seeing as it was your idea I come to Ireland in the first place.'

'I'll be there by eight,' Anna promised. 'Let me finish up here.'

Two hours later the small Nissan struggled and bounced down the stony lane towards the cottage. Bumping and jerking inside, Anna was nonetheless rewarded with the delightful odour expelling from the freshly baked scones, wrapped in a tea towel and nestled in the car's back seat. Treats for their digestive systems later.

Up ahead, the glare of another vehicle's side lamps edged towards her. It seemed likely, in more ways than mathematically, that both cars hadn't a hope of successfully passing on the narrow lane together, side by side. One of them would have to yield.

'Not a chance, Buster,' Anna voiced her reluctance to pull her car into the side of the verge. 'You're gonna have to let me pass.' She pushed ahead, adamant in her refusal to back down.

Her opponent finally got the message. Seconds before they were likely to meet, the car stopped and reversed towards the entrance of a field, allowing just enough room for both vehicles to pass.

'Aha!' Anna's delight at having won the non-existent battle, felt rewarding as she continued on her journey. 'Thank you,' she mouthed to the other car's driver slowly passing by. Stunned, she recognised the driver right away.

'Oh hi!'

Staring back from the driver's seat was John McAllister. That in itself was not unusual at all. In fact, it was pretty normal, or at least, Anna thought it would have been if it wasn't for the red-haired woman sitting next to him.

Anna quickly calculated the scene in front of her. It was obvious, she concluded by how they were dressed, that they weren't off to milk cows. By the look of things, this was a date in the making.

Was Kate aware of this? Was there something Anna was missing? Many possibilities swirled around her head within seconds of each other. She actually began to feel dizzy.

Maybe this woman was the babysitter and John was collecting her so he and Kate could go out tonight. Maybe he was giving her a lift, a work colleague for a night out with the gang they'd be meeting in the pub down the road. The list of possibilities was considerate.

Don't jump to conclusions, she checked herself as she wound down the car window inviting John to do the same. *Everything's likely above board.*

But Anna knew it wasn't, the very second she saw her son-in-law's face. Apart from looking like he'd just swallowed pickled goat's cheese, John's face glowed crimson. It was too soon to tell if the colour was from embarrassment or from shame.

'Hello Anna,' the beetroot-coloured face brought out the whites of John's eyes. 'I didn't expect to meet you down this laneway tonight.'

'I'm visiting Rose and Maeve.'

'Oh right, of course, of course.'

John could feel his stomach beginning to contract for the second time in two days. He wasn't sure he was ready for Sarah to know about that part of him yet.

'I won't keep you.' He tapped his watch, indicating the need to get going. 'In a bit of a rush…'

'Off somewhere nice?'

'Umm. Need to get going…'

Anna had always liked John, not in a pally way but more from a personality compatibility point of view. She often found herself taking his side in his absence. Even when Kate complained about John to her or when Eddie voiced his concerns before their middle daughter had married him.

'He reminds me a little of you.' Anna teased Eddie on the morning of Kate and John's wedding. They were munching on some early morning toast and poached eggs before all the wedding fuss began.

'They'll be fine, Eddie,' she assured him with a squeeze of his arm. 'Don't be worried about his lack of manners,' she joked. 'If Kate's anything like me she'll have her man trained to her way of thinking in no time at all!'

Eddie rewarded his wife with a smudge of butter all down her forehead and onto her eyelids by way of retaliation for her words of wisdom. She was not amused one little bit.

Now, as Anna stared with bewilderment at the two faces glaring back, she knew something wasn't right. This was no babysitter or work colleague, she concluded. This woman was resting her hand on John's leg in a very non-babysitting manner and looked to be wearing a top so low her boobs were having difficulty staying indoors.

Was she even wearing a bra? Anna didn't want to stare but seriously, that chest could feed a family of four, breakfast, lunch and dinner for a week, hands down.

'Who's this,' she nodded towards the "Mountains of Mourne." 'Aren't you going to introduce us, John?'

John wasn't enjoying this encounter at all. Dam that slow tractor on the way here, slowing him up and making him later than the seven-thirty p.m. pick-up arrangement he and Sarah had made.

If it weren't for that, they'd be well on their way and not having to deal with this unexpected situation now. Divine Timing or synchronicity could be both a blessing and a bugger.

'Anna,' John began, 'this is Sarah.' He looked at Sarah. 'Sarah, this is Anna, Kate's mum.'

'Oh,' Sarah was surprised. Now she better understood the strain. 'It's very nice to meet you.'

'Likewise,' Anna lied, because she wasn't yet convinced she should be enjoying their introductions.

'Are you both off somewhere nice?' She repeated the question and watched John squirm some more.

John interrupted before Sarah could answer. His guts practically punched through his stomach. He could take it no longer.

'We should go,' he declared abruptly. 'We'll miss the start of the movie.'

Anna could hardly believe her ears. So, this *was* a date after all! What the hell was going on? She stared at John in horror.

'Anna,' John began, hesitated and then decided to take the best escape route he could think of on such short notice. 'You need to speak to Kate.'

He pushed the button, and the electric car window began closing, indicating further discussion would be coming to a close. 'A lot has happened in the past twenty-four hours,' he explained. 'She'll no doubt fill you in.'

As soon as he could put the car in gear, they were off.

In a state of dazed confusion, Anna reached Rose's cottage minutes later. Once inside Rose handed her a small measure of whiskey on account of her looking as white as the cotton sheets on a freshly laundered bed.

'Sarah is Cecilia and Arthur Flanagan's only daughter,' Rose informed Anna once she and Maeve were able to make sense of Anna's babbling. 'Apparently, according to Cecilia,' Rose eased the words out as sensitively as she could muster. 'Sarah has met her future husband-to-be.'

Because of Anna's recent shock, Maeve did the honourable thing and delayed telling her younger sister her own plans to relocate to Ireland in the weeks ahead. She figured it could wait until a more appropriate time when Anna was a bit more grounded and back onto the earth. The woman looked like death warmed up.

Gazing into the abyss while subconsciously sipping whiskey and pulling on a loose thread attached to her skirt, Anna was in no fit state to be dealing with much more than she'd been delivered with that night.

Maybe her world would make better sense tomorrow.

CHAPTER THIRTY-FIVE

The place smelt musty when she unlocked and opened the front door.

Maeve let herself into the hallway, side-stepping the mound of mail lying there. The whole house looked oddly strange to her, like it knew it was not to be considered home any longer. An alien abode now, its usefulness not required.

How had she never noticed before the way it was so dark and drab? It had taken her to leave it, just to see how last century and outdated it really was.

The décor was never changed in thirty years. Its wallpaper was practically colourless with age. The carpets were worn and threadbare to within an inch of life, all singing songs of doom and gloom.

Maeve didn't even feel like taking her coat, hat and gloves off. She didn't dare on one hand because of the icy cold in the place. On the other, because a hotel stay for her duration here, awaited check in. Hell would freeze over before she'd endure another night in this hole.

She walked past the antique coat-stand, slash dresser in the wide hallway. In the middle of it, the oval mirror was tinted with age spots (and a little crack at the bottom where George had banged her head of it for admiring a new hat bought at the car-boot sale. Apparently, this had made her "*vein*" and she'd "*committed a sin*").

Onwards to the living room, the door sang a creak upon opening. Fusty and stuffy, the gap in the curtains shone daylight into the living room, highlighting a sea of dust particles living there.

The brown sofa and chairs (outdated with their moulded plastic and wooden arms), were faded and torn with nothing more than wear and age. Anyone forced to sit in that room, Maeve sniffed its truth, would surely be depressed within one hour. It looked pretty bleak, even on a sunny day.

She knocked the side of her knee on the coffee table on her way past into the kitchen. It wasn't the first time she'd done such a thing and was annoyed now that the pattern was repeated.

'Bloody thing.'

A swift but sturdy little kick was payback for services rendered. She owed the table nothing and by the look of it, it owed nothing to anyone.

Rubbing her shin pain free, the narrow gap between kitchen cupboards and workbenches allowed for only one person to pass at a time.

The step down towards the table and chairs at the end of the room, still gleamed from her years of polishing it. It made her sad that such a personal touch still remained, indicating to her, a life less lived.

'This place is a sight.' She spoke to nobody but herself. 'How the heck could I ever have thought it was home?'

The kitchen had always been her least favourite room in the house. It was in this spot that most of George's abuse would take place. With numerous complaints over her cooking and dishwashing, name calling, and insults abound.

He mocked the cupboard layouts when he couldn't find a tin of soup or saucepan to heat water (to shave with). Worst of all, it was here she'd had her very first black eye. Her head bounced off the side of the units when she fell to the floor.

George punched her stomach so hard (*not pregnant this month again*) Maeve fell down with the impact. She'd stayed there for over an hour, only resurrecting when he'd left for his nightly pub visit at the local.

She shuttered bad memories down her whole body. Refusing to let tears surface now (he wasn't worth the effort), Maeve walked towards the dining area. Hanging on the wall there, was a black and white photograph of him and his mother. She'd hated it then and now was no different. Time to let it have a more deserving place to rest.

Leaving the kitchen to go upstairs, the broken glass frame found a new home in the bin, right beside the torn and tattered photo, thrown in just before it. She felt neither love or loss at its demise. It was completely inconsequential; a trivial item, lost on a ghostly reminiscence.

Inside the two spare bedrooms of the semi-detached house resided more outdated furniture. Old bed-blankets, worn mattresses (from George's drinking buddies' sleepovers) and faded head-boards, give her a feeling of disgust at the unpleasant memories they resurrected.

A weekend here, a fortnight there. *Come stay at George's house everybody*. With maid services day and night, who wouldn't!

Their own bedroom almost made her puke. A queen size bed (double was too expensive and George was no Rockefeller), where many nights she was pushed out of it in his bad temper, or from his drunken slumbers, onto the floor.

In hindsight maybe it was her saving grace. Away from his many nightly advances, that way her body was her own.

Now, on the other hand, Maeve had ways and means of getting her own back down the years. The woman had an Aquarian mind. Rebellion was practically her second name for pity's sake. Innovation, a natural given.

On the worst days (bruises, thumps, insults), his steak dinner might just have had the tinniest bit of window cleaner sprayed into the gravy. His creamy mash, flavoured with a hint of flea power or his tea, drank with her underarm sweat lacing the cup's rim.

Any tummy upsets, gastral problems or sore heads as a result, were blamed on a virus or flu.

Once, when he'd shaved her hair bald (because she'd let it grow longer than allowed), she took one of the sharpest kitchen knives they had, walked out the back door and slashed three of his new Ford Pinto's tyres.

He'd had fun with that okay. Three blow outs in one day, not able to get to a big three-day sales conference (which Maeve know realised was code for seeing Molly), he was livid.

And his suits, oh good gracious the suits! His pride and joy. A new one purchased practically every month, all under the umbrella of *'needing to be presentable'* in his job.

When finally, he'd saved enough for a (seconds) Gucci suit, it was a day for celebration. A bottle of cheap sparkling wine was purchased on his way home in one hand, the suit flung over the other in a fancy bag.

While the wine chilled in the fridge and George and his mate Alan cheered the football game on television to success, Maeve slipped to the chemist down the road.

Bisacodyl laxative was purchased under the pretence she'd been having trouble going herself (the assistant was a fan of George) and needed added help.

When the glasses were filled with sparkly liquid (none for her of course), Maeve held nothing back in giving George a generous quantity. Alan had a drop as well, considering how he'd barely acknowledged Maeve in the years calling at the house.

Three weeks later and their bowels were still trying to regulate. Food poison was blamed on the curry they'd had coming home from the pub one night. What they didn't know wouldn't hurt.

'A fitting sore backside for the arse that he was.'

And then the Gucci suit. Ironically, it had the worst stitching in the world. Pockets kept flapping off at the side (she was a dab hand at needlework). Inside trouser ones had constant holes developing where coins, pens and mints kept sliding down his inside leg.

To top it off, there seemed to be an ever-ending stench of something really bad in the material, even after dry cleaning.

Maeve had collected dog poop, tucked it into the trouser turnups and then sealed it inside tiny pouches. The idiot was so angry, the suit was thrust into the bin after the tenth wear with his promise never to buy another Gucci item again. Apparently, he was beginning to develop the nickname 'Poovader' and could take it no more.

Walking towards the big, brown wardrobe now (an old heirloom from his mother's house), Maeve pulled the dressing table stool over towards it, stood on it, wobbled a bit, steadied her footing and then rummaged around the top of the bulky, old-fashioned eye-sore, seeking her find.

Inside the large brown envelope finally recovered, was everything she ever worked for in this house and her marriage. The paperwork belonging to the assurance policy she'd taken out on George, the year after they'd wed.

George knew nothing about it. The weekly money given for housekeeping (she wasn't allowed to work on account of his manly pride), got stretched to an inch of its life to pay for the weekly contributions.

His steaks were more often rump than sirloin disguised in strong pepper sauce to throw off his doubts.

The copious amounts of coffee he drank, was mixed with a cheap branded supermarket one that saved on the labelled variety considerably.

Out of date bread that had lumps of blue mould developing, were toasted to disguise the staleness. While the cost of living "appeared" to go up weekly, with him grumbling about it and Maeve pocketing the surplus, she managed to save a tidy amount.

Now the policy was about to be cashed in, with many thousands of pounds paid out. Coupled with the sale of the house, which she'd already instructed the estate agents to put on the market, all profits for it would be filling her bank account soon.

She'd been guaranteed by the agent how much this area was sought after and that her property wouldn't sit idle for long. George hadn't made a will (must have thought he'd live forever), so next of kin fell for the lot.

With a final depressive look around the place, Maeve stood in the hallway, about to depart. She'd everything she ever wanted from this stinker of a place in her handbag. Anything required in the future would be newly bought and to her own taste.

In a final salute, the seventy something woman did one of the most uncharacteristic things she'd ever performed in her life.

On the verge of leaving, she turned around, lifted her middle finger and flipped it off in all directions.

The memories, the torments, the despair and the slumps she'd experienced in this place would not be forgotten but would be forgiven. She'd be dammed if other's bad behaviour would affect her for another day.

With a bang of the front door and a trot down the pathway, she never once intended a return. After tonight it was back to Ireland. That's where she truly belonged. She'd come back home in more ways than one.

Wasn't karma just wonderful!

CHAPTER THIRTY-SIX

'I'm staying,' Ellen told Rose's firmly. 'It's only until Maeve's flight returns and besides,' she told her dearest friend, 'I could do with the break away from my own place for a while.'

Truth be told, Gemma staying with Ellen was driving her insane. She was all for helping a body out in their time of need but seriously, clumps of bleached hair blocking up the drains, hand towels — (the good Egyptian cotton ones too) — streaked with self-tanning lotion was hard to endure.

Then this morning there wasn't a drop of milk, bread or peanut butter in sight for breakfast, in favour of snack time last night while watching *'The Bridges of Madison County'* for the fifth bloody time that week!

The woman was a pain in the butt, family or not. Ellen had a newfound respect for Donal for putting up with the likes of that. In fact, she thought, it was a small wonder he hadn't done a runner years ago. The man had the patience of Saint Job himself.

Rose saw the unspoken stress on Ellen's face. Her usual flawless skin showed wrinkles forming around her mouth. Her eyes looked a little puffier from lack of rest and the usual bouncing curls she tonged into place each morning were lacking some serious merriment. She touched her arm sympathetically.

'It won't last forever,' Ellen knew she was speaking about Gemma's stay. 'Use Archangel Michael's cloak for protection,' she told Ellen helpfully. 'That will keep your energy balanced and help finalise the family karma between you both.'

'I've the poor being tortured all week.' Ellen admitted shamefully. 'Please God we're coming to the end of the cycle soon, as you say.'

After a cup of tea and a rather questionable mug of cocoa, Ellen settled down into the peaceful slumber of Rose's open fire and comfortable surroundings.

She felt sleepy from the lack of rest at home. Gemma liked to shower, play music and wake up Ellen with silly questions at all hours of the morning.

'Do koala bears live in Japan? Does it rain as much in Seattle as it does in Ireland? Do Buddhists wear underwear?

Who the frig cared? Seriously. It had become so annoying that last night Ellen actually threw a slipper at her before she even had the bedroom door properly opened.

'Get out,' she'd roared, quite sure she'd wakened the whole house with her temper. 'Before I bloody kill you!'

Gemma snapped the door shut so quickly that she caught her coat cardigan in the act. Actually, it was Ellen's cardigan, borrowed without asking. Because of the darkness of the night, luckily, she hadn't recognised it to be hers.

As far as Ellen was aware, her new garment was still in the cellophane hung up in the wardrobe. She'd enjoyed a treat from the cashmere sale rack in Dunne's Stores in the city. A little surprise in store for her, still waiting to happen.

Now as Ellen enjoyed complete liberation from annoying sisters (and grumpy husbands… yes, another row had erupted between her and Fergal concerning Gemma's pending departure date), she allowed her mind to relax, chasing away as many everyday thoughts from her consciousness, gliding into a comfortable, meditative state.

Once her mind had left behind these mundane events, Ellen became aware of the gentle touch of Spirit beside her left arm. Her spiritual senses increased as she gave focus to the energy of the young man both she and Moby had considered a brother.

'Rose,' Ellen interrupted her older companion's stitch counting as she knitted a surprise return gift for Maeve in a great hurry. 'Do you have a few moments?'

'What's up?' Rose had little time to spare. 'Is it important?'

'Andrew is with me at the moment,' Ellen said. 'Are you up for a bit of a chat with him?'

'Always!' Rose was thrilled beyond words. She sat Maeve's gift to the side, deciding it could wait. She knew where her priorities lay. 'It's just so lovely to hear from him.'

Tears filled the older woman's eyes, representative of the emotional turmoil she'd endured in the days since his passing. This connection now was invaluable to her and nothing else, at that moment, compared in contrast.

'He's telling me that he's very happy and quite settled.'

Rose smiled at the reassurance, relieved beyond words he was safe.

Ellen continued, 'And he is with his grandparents, Josie and Joel.'

'Thank God.' He was in safe hands with her parents. Just as she'd hoped he would be.

Having spent a chunk of her life and most of his together, caring for his needs and providing a safe and stable environment for him to grow in, that in itself brought much-needed confirmation. He was being well looked after, even in the afterlife. If Ellen never delivered another word from Andrew, Rose was certainly going to sleep that much better tonight. Her heart too, would beat a steadier rhythm.

But Andrew was only getting started.

'He's telling me,' Ellen continued, 'that I'm to tease you about your teeth...'

'Haha!' Rose was elated, 'not *my* teeth, Maeve's false ones... well, I never! Boys a boys, I don't believe it.'

Yesterday, as Rose went on to explain, she'd knocked Maeve's teeth, steeping in a glass on the sink ledge, into the waste bin amongst the rubbish.

'I'm not kidding, Ellen,' Rose laughed heartily. 'They landed right on top of last night's dinner scraps. I fished them out, covered in tomato sauce and old spaghetti and washed them off, okay,' she consoled her guilt away. 'Maeve announced later that we'd maybe try a new tomato sauce next time we'd meatballs,' she sniggered at the well-kept secret, until now. 'She said she just couldn't get the taste of it out of her mouth!'

Once their sniggering had lapsed, Ellen continued at Andrew's insistence.

'Who's Bronagh... Smith... Sss...?'

'Shaw?' Rose offered and Ellen nodded acknowledgement.

'It's the 's' sounding name, so I'd say that's a good guess.' It wasn't unusual to hear the sound of a name from Spirit rather than the whole word.

'Well, I never.' Rose was once again euphoric. 'She's an old and very dear friend from bygone days,' she explained. 'She passed away so suddenly, maybe twenty years ago now. Her heart gave up. Seconds later she was gone.'

'Andrew showed me ice cream and chocolate sprinkles,' Ellen said. 'Then beside that, said to mention a bed... a new one... or something to do with another house... maybe a holiday?'

'Woohoo, yes,' Rose smiled at the fond memory. 'Bronagh would take Andrew to her house almost every weekend. She kept her spare room as his "holiday bedroom." Rose drew inverted comments with her fingers in the air, 'He was fed treats galore. Ice cream with chocolate sprinkles were his favourite and a real treat, mind,' Rose cautioned. 'I'd him on a strict diet here, so this was a real extravagance for him indeed.

'He'd come back with his mouth white with cream and his clothes flaked with chocolate.' Such simple things meant the world.

Further confirmation that Andrew was happy in Spirit form, came with the messages of finding a long-ago pet.

'The collie dog my dad had,' Rose confirmed. He also mentioned his clothes, showing Ellen a chunk of jumpers and trousers to represent the message.

'I just started clearing some away yesterday,' Rose said. 'It broke a tiny bit of my heart with each item that went into the box.'

'He said to tell you he sat with you on the bed when you were tearful.'

'I knew it, Ellen. I could sense him there.'

'He likes the photograph you chose for your locket,' Ellen concluded, 'and says he'll be in touch again.'

Rose had recently cut his photograph to fit that very morning. She clasped the golden jewellery around her neck. The tears flowed. This time they felt that bit more joyful than sad. She'd heard from him at last.

After a while, when things had resumed as before, they'd watched Rose's favourite soap programme on television. Rose then switched the TV off, set her teacup on the side table and turned towards Ellen.

She'd finally finished Maeve's gift, which sat wrapped in tissue paper on top of the table, awaiting her return.

'May I tell you something,' Rose asked. 'Something I've never voiced to a living soul before?'

'Of course,' Ellen agreed. 'You know it will go no further.'

'I do.' Rose cleared a tickle from her throat. 'Andrew was my nephew, not my son.'

'Oh' Ellen didn't even try to hide her surprise. 'I just assumed…'

'Everyone did,' Rose said. 'He was my sister Nuala's son, born in England, out of wedlock to a single mum back in the sixties.'

'Okay. That can't have been easy.'

'It was not.'

It turned out Nuala was disowned, put into service, shamed when news of the unborn baby was revealed. Disgraced beyond belief, England was hardly far enough for her parents to send her. It was all they could afford at the time.

'Little attention was paid to the fact she'd conceived through rape,' Rose acknowledged Ellen's intake of breath with a quick nod. 'Nor that the father was a first cousin of my mother.'

Despite the unjustness of it all, when Andrew was born, Nuala couldn't stand the idea of adoption.

'Mother and baby lived in squalor, a small bedsit, outside London.' Rose glanced dejectedly at the floor. 'Nuala then took pleurisy and died when her son was two years old.'

Her only sister passed without the chance for them both to make things right again. Regret was a useless emotion to hold onto, yet so difficult to remove with its effect.

It had taken years for Rose to forgive her parents for not allowing her to visit Nuala, even if it was to check she was all right.

Rose had to sneak handwritten letters and cards to the post, for fear they'd find out and confiscate them.

When the news came to their door, via telegram, of Nuala's death, there was no stopping Rose then.

Against her parents' wishes, Rose had to beg, steal and borrow the money to sail over to London. Having sent a returning telegram, Social Services expected the next of kin at "their earliest convenience." They were holding Andrew in care and in wait for Rose's arrival.

Three weeks post Nuala's passing, Rose brought Andrew to Ireland and to his grandparent's home.

'At first, they did all they could to reject him,' Rose remembered the tale like it had happened yesterday. 'In the end, they couldn't help but love him. He was such a sweet child, always smiling and so easily pleased; a proper little treasure indeed.'

After her parents passing, Rose raised Andrew as her own. It was of no consequence to Rose what others thought about, or of, them both.

'He may have been born from Nuala's body,' she told Ellen. 'But he was very much my son.'

Ellen felt privileged to have been entrusted with Rose's family secrets. Proud that their friendship had reached a new level because of it, Ellen couldn't have been given a nicer gift.

Around nine thirty that night, the cottage door flung open bouncing off the wall and causing the coffee table nearby to tremble with its impact.

'I'm back,' Maeve entered the cottage with a lively smile that would shame even the biggest laughing Buddha. 'I've finally found my true home and my forever family!'

Rose and Ellen hugged the excited woman, each wishing they'd remembered to buy some sparkling wine to celebrate the occasion.

'I've made you a gift!' Rose announced by way of compensation. She retrieved the wrapped package from the table.

Maeve smiled from ear to ear. She was secretly glad there was no celebratory Champagne; she was no drinker at the best of times. Sparkly alcohol tasted foul to her. Instead, she unwrapped the gift and held it up in full view for all to see.

'A new pair of drawers!' Rose was ecstatic. 'I've knitted them for you in the colours of the rainbow.'

'Good God Almighty!' Maeve was both flabbergasted and humiliated at once. 'Rose McGrath,' she scolded sternly. 'You'll be the death of me yet.'

The new beginning had truly begun.

CHAPTER THIRTY-SEVEN

'The hand that rocks the cradle, rules the world.'

'What?'

'The hand that rocks the…'

'Yeah,' James confirmed, 'I got that, world and cradle blah, blah. Not sure what it means though.'

'I'm talking about those unsung heroes in our world, James,' Ellen told her youngest son who was seriously wondering if his mother had finally lost the plot. 'Females… tho—'

'I see,' James interrupted, pondering a fast exit. 'Well,' he stood gathering his study books with him, 'I'll leave you and your cradle rocking in peace,' he smirked. 'Just make sure you don't shake it off its joints. Oh and,' he concluded his defence. 'Males can rock cradles too you know.'

'I do.'

On his way out the door, James collided with an anxious-looking Gemma, about to enter the very room he was leaving.

'Please God,' he whispered the prayer, *'don't let her start crying.'* There were only so many times he could pacify her, and the numbers were already counted,

by him and by Matt too. This time his luck was in, and they passed by one another with little more than a nod.

'So,' Gemma entered the room, bringing seething anger as company, most of which was stored in her rosy cheeks. 'Donal and the kids have moved back home.' She looked accusingly across the room toward a television-watching Fergal before turning her attention to Ellen. 'Why didn't you tell me?'

Ellen choked on the water she was drinking as she glared at her accuser's long finger pointed in her direction, held inches away from her face and giving Ellen a full view of the nicotine-stained wand.

'Because I didn't know,' she confirmed defensively, rubbing spilt water from her chin. 'Honest to God.'

'He knew,' she stuck her tongue out at Fergal, who replicated the action back. 'You're nothing but a big, long, gangly snake. You rotten son of a bit…'

'Gemma!' Ellen roared. 'That's enough.'

'Right back at ya,' Fergal was fit to be tied. 'If I'm a snake, you're the biggest loser in town.'

'That's not helpful,' Ellen tired soothing ruffled waters. 'Calm down both of you.'

The two of them heeded her suggestion. Seething vermin, Fergal turned pale with temper. Sick to his very belly of this whole situation, this pest of a woman was ruining his house and his time spent in it. There was no pleasure to be found in home time when she was here.

Gemma farted, a great deliberate thunder of wind entirely for Fergal's benefit. He'd complained all week about her lack of hygiene. He could put that in his pipe and smoke it for all she cared.

'For heaven's sake would somebody grow up for five minutes please.' Ellen pleaded. 'We need to get this sorted out.'

'He started it.'

'I right, dead on.'

'You friggin did O'Hare. Sure, aren't you known all over Ballygo for your gossiping.'

'*What*!'

'Please, please let it go,' Ellen pleaded to her husband. 'She's only saying it to rile you up.'

'I'm bloody not...'

'Gemma stop. *Please.*'

Seconds passed in silence (phew). Gemma threw out stinking looks while Fergal turned whiter than cotton with rage.

Ellen moved things ahead. She asked Fergal if he did indeed know anything of Donal and the children's activities. Fergal debated a while, realised he had an upper hand and decided to deal it.

'Donal was in touch,' he revealed deceitfully, wiping the condescending grin of his enemy's face. 'He and the kids moved back a few days ago. I've been to see them. Even helped stock up the fridge.' More loaned money he was unlikely to ever see again. Still, he couldn't see the kids hungry. It wouldn't hurt Donal's gut to have a few days food free, but not the youngsters.

He grinned triumphally directly at Gemma. Whatever she took from that she deserved. The people of Ballygo loved him. He was no gossip.

Gemma was fit to be tied and actually said so.

'I'm fit to be tied,' she told Ellen but meant it for Fergal. 'I overheard their conversation earlier,' she seethed through clenched teeth. 'Donal was the one who told Fergal to call at the house later... *our* house for frig's sake... while I'm stuck here, wondering where the hell they all are, if the kids are okay, if... if... they've missed me, if... can you believe it!'

'You reap what you sow.'

'Hey!'

'If the cap fits...'

Fergal switched the volume up on the television in the hope that hints would be taken, and certain people would leave the room and a man in peace to watch the car show he was so enjoying. No such thing happened. The madness continued.

Ellen noticed the telephone receiver handset in Gemma's hand.

'Are you thinking of calling Donal?' she asked. 'Is that why you're so wound up?'

Gemma hesitated, bit her lower lip and felt like squealing. Instead, she looked helplessly at Ellen, all shrieks and yells gone in the flash of a possible phone call.

The thought of speaking to him, after all the things she'd called him last time they'd spoken — or roared — at one another, terrified her to the very bones.

What if he never wanted to see her again? What if he was, at that very minute, in touch with Social Services seeking sole custody of their children? She'd die a death if all was lost.

So many possibilities had gone, lingered and stayed in her head over the past week that now she truly didn't know what to expect.

'I don't think I can,' she admitted what she'd been debating for the longest twenty minutes in her entire life. 'I'm not ready to eat dirt.'

It was over two weeks — fifteen days really — since Gemma had come to stay in the O'Hare home. A short time in some circumstances, yet considering what she'd had achieved in that time, compared to a month's events.

Under Ellen's watchful eye and insistence, Gemma had committed to a counselling programme, designed specifically for those with addictive habits.

Joining the local yoga class and resuming her working life in the nursery added to the substantial success she'd reached in that time. There was amazing progress being made.

Ellen told Gemma how proud she was of her every step along the way. At the same time, she prayed their shared time together would be over quicker than the crows flying overhead.

Ellen stood up and held the nervous woman's hands in hers.

'Maybe you won't have to eat dirt, Gemma,' she told the woman whose knuckles turned white under the telephone receiver's grip. 'Something tells me Donal will be delighted to get your call.'

'Fair enough,' Gemma needed little persuasion to do what she really wanted to do. She'd gradually started to show trust in herself and her efforts to reignite her life. Phoning Donal would encourage her confidence for the days ahead.

'Ask your Angel cards first,' she gestured towards the deck sitting close to Ellen. 'See what advice they offer.' This was another avenue Gemma was gradually finding faith in.

The first card out signalled an "Answered Prayer." The second card pulled revealed "Harmony."

'Go for it Gem.' Ellen advised eagerly. 'The Angelic energies are giving you a big thumbs-up! You can't lose with cards like these.'

'Really?'

'Seriously.'

'You're not jerking me about?'

'Would I ever?'

'Yea, that time…'

'Gemma, just do it. It'll be grand.'

'You're for a whip lashing if things go belly up.'

'I'll take my chances.'

She left the room. Fergal celebrated with a cheer and a roll of his eyes skywards.

'I swear she's lost the plot that one.' Fed up to his teeth he could take no more. 'If there's a God above, she'll leave tonight. A real nut job if ever there was one.'

It wasn't bad enough that Gemma was staying in his home, eating his food, using all the hot water and messing up the place with her untidiness. Now her husband had deflated his bank account and him with it.

Fergal knew if he didn't do something quickly, at that very moment, there would be an almighty row as his anger spilt out and over everything.

'I'm going for a few pints,' the grumpy man stood tall in a moderately small body, stretching his aching muscles back into a workable order. 'Don't wait up.'

Fergal left several minutes later with a bang of the door and a throw of his van keys into the waiting bowl beside it. He'd no intention of driving anywhere anytime soon.

It was time to drown some of his sorrows while he had enough change in his pocket to do it. A man was entitled to some luxuries, he mused. He was going to claim his.

The night ahead suddenly felt promising.

CHAPTER THIRTY-EIGHT

Fergal was crazy mad, even though his outward appearance told a different story. He managed to appear cool and calm, but appearances were often deceiving.

He sighed heavily walking along the pavement, on his way to the local bar. Greatly burdened with his thoughts, he was finding it difficult to keep up the act.

'Oh frig,' he stepped in dog poop. 'What the hell?' He was irritated all over again.

The glow on his cheeks spoke of anger, Aries style. Plodding forward wishing he could scream out loud, he managed to contain his frustration because of the mother and daughter walking past on the opposite side of the busy road.

Brought up to prioritise other viewpoints over his own, as well as to find power in social, financial and professional status, he was almost completely unaware of how such views managed to quench the true essence of who he really was. He simply followed his conditioning, without question.

Stepping into Murphy's Bar and Tavern some ten minutes later, brought fleeting distaste concerning the last time he'd visited the very same establishment.

The hope was that tonight, nobody (mentioning no names) would be expecting him to empty his bank account again.

He felt nothing but bitterness about this whole sorry affair. '*So much for the holiday fund.*' He could also kiss a solid goodbye to his undisclosed plan to go to Las Vegas next year. It would be quite a while before he'd manage to suck any of that money back.

However, his yearning desire to tickle some very dry taste buds pushed him towards the counter and away from the nasty thoughts surging through his mind.

The longing to escape for a time forced him to order a large pint of stout and double vodka to follow.

'I'm not working until late tomorrow morning,' he told Millie. 'I can afford to indulge tonight.' Being a self-employed builder had its benefits.

The bar was full of football fans, creating noise to deafen even the most ardent listener. Waiting patiently for their team to play, the rowdy men shared jokes, tales and opinions openly with one another and the general public, regardless of whether or not the recipients wanted to hear them.

There was the odd crude innuendo thrown in for good measure too. It was well seeing the gang was predominately male. Feminists would have chewed them up and spat them out in a mere second.

'They seem to be in good form,' Fergal shouted across to Millie. At the same time loose spittle landed on her cheek. 'I hope for your sake, the right team wins!'

Millie agreed with a wipe of her cheek and a frown across the bar.

'I agree,' she replied. 'We could be doing with the extra sales. My accountant's sending out warning signals as we speak.' The recession was hitting hard.

As the alcohol took effect, Fergal's mood lifted. Gone were his grunts and groans, vanished bit by bit with each slug consumed.

He'd even managed to become sociable with one of the rowdy fans. Frank Smith, a balding, tattooed, tall and heavyset man, father of three and in the process of a rather nasty divorce, slouched across the bar and shared his woes.

'The whore legged it off with another bloke six months ago,' he drunkenly confided, with an arm draped across Fergal's shoulders and a sweaty hand occasionally ruffling his hair. 'Now she wants me money.'

As they drank, emotions were revealed, the likes of which would never be discussed without the dizzy effect the alcohol provided. Frank felt bitter (even though his beer was a lager).

'She ate at my very soul,' he told Fergal, knowing that he had a sympathetic audience. 'I don't know what I did to deserve it,' his eyes welled with tears. 'I gave her everything I tell ya.'

'Maybe that was the problem,' Fergal offered. 'You did far too much for the woman, yet it was never enough.'

'You're right, big fella,' Frank agreed. 'I'm just a soft touch for love.'

As the night progressed, it became evident to Fergal that most of the football gang were either single, divorced or in the process of.

By the end of the evening, he wasn't entirely sure if it was the atmosphere of the night or the amount of drink he'd consumed, but on the walk home, he thought of how lucky his new friends were.

To be single meant to be free and devoid of responsibility to anything or anyone. Just imagine, he pondered, no mortgage payments, no car upkeep, or no woman to spend your hard-earned cash as if it were dust. Wouldn't that be something?

And then, there was the nagging. Holy Moley above, the nagging. If he had to listen one more time about his beer count (seven last night, five the previous) he'd howl like a wolf.

'*You need help, Fergal,*' He imitated Ellen with an exaggerated squeak. '*Here's the number for AA Fergal. What about counselling Fergal...*' His head was seriously done in with it all.

He was no alcoholic for pity's sake. He was tired telling her that. A working man deserved a slurp or two at the end of a day. If that slurp turned into a few more, then so be it. Nothing wrong with relaxing.

His thoughts turned financial. He tutted out loud. No matter how much he made, it never seemed to be enough. Extra was always needed for food. Enough, he estimated, to feed the entire island of Corfu.

Then more for new curtains, replacement bedcovers, carpets and even a dog blanket to keep Moby cosy. The list was endless.

And now, on top of everything, Ellen's family were sponging off him too. Was there no end to it all? It seemed not.

As he marched ahead, his mind raced into the recent past and the way his wife's attention was taken from him (and his sons) and given to Gemma and her family.

'Friggin ridiculous is what it is!' A man was entitled to the attention of his wife, especially in his own home. He'd definitely earned the respect as the man of the house; of that, he was more than confident.

Truth be told, Fergal puffed, he'd been quietly seething for a while, especially over having to shoulder the financial burden on his own.

Ellen wasn't earning. It was all down to him, burdened with the responsibility of finding the money needed to pay their bills.

Gemma and Kate seemed to be more important to Ellen than anybody else these days. He was peeved, no, no, strike that... he was seething. He certainly hadn't agreed to marry her whole family for the love of Jude, even if it felt like it.

And then there was their physical connection. Well, really, what physical connection? Okay, so Ellen wasn't so much the touchy-feely type but these past few years, anything of the sort had virtually disappeared. Only yesterday she'd dismissed his hand on her back with a shove and excuse she'd other things to do.

Stumbling and toppling along, the walk home was taking twice the time to complete. As more reasons to get annoyed piled into his fuzzy thinking, he kept stopping to properly allow the complaint to form.

His attempts to light a cigarette failed many times. The gusts of wind were too strong. They kept blowing the match out before it had reached its destination, like a birthday cake that had never got started.

A car passed by, spreading puddled water onto the footpath, narrowly missing his jeans and shoes. He shook a fist in their direction, mumbling profanities that suggested the driver might prefer to do something other than drive.

Marching on, Ellen bounced back into his focus. Becoming melancholy for a few seconds he realised that did love her… always had really, from the first time he'd led eyes her way. But seriously (back to frowning), yes seriously, what was with all this Angel stuff anyway?

Surly to heavens above it was bizarre (verging evil) to be communicating with the dead? Honestly, he could live with the odd bit of weirdness okay, but that was the thing.

Talk of Master Guides, Spirit World and those in it, was now replacing the peculiar titbits of the past and becoming everyday lingo. It was all rather uncomfortable.

Only last week, Ellen gave him messages from his much-loved grandfather, from the so called "Spirit World." She'd mentioned things only he would have known about. The litter of kittens found and rescued by them both when he was a lad of six years old.

The "secret" treasure (toy soldiers and three old pennies) they'd hidden in the upper field while playing a game of Pirates, was no longer that with Ellen's divulgence.

Suddenly Fergal was mad. Who did she think she was anyway? Slabbering all over his personal terrain, poking her nose into things he held dear.

The more he paid attention to his anger, the larger it grew and the stronger it festered. Manifesting a mighty rage inside, he was ready to spit spikes at any moment.

By the time he'd reached the turn towards his home, his mind was raking up perceived injustices from bygone years. Their roots began and ended inside his and Ellen's relationship and their marriage. He felt completely victimised.

'I'm not a b-bad person,' he stuttered for the first time in a decade, close to tears. 'Why should I put up with this crap?' he sniffed loudly. 'I deserve so much more appreciation.'

Reaching home, the mood see-sawed from anger to self-entitlement. He felt bluer than the morning sky, without a spongy cloud in sight. Struggling to unlock the door, under self-imposed awkwardness, the key took the blame. '

Moments later and after a lot of scuffling and scarping the door was yanked open. Ellen rubbed her tired eyes.

'Hi,' she greeted him, ill amused at the wakening. 'Having a bit of bother there are you?'

Given his current negativity, Ellen was the last person he wanted to encounter. Fergal pushed past, leaving her to hold onto the banister, steadying her foot under his force.

'Hey,' she objected, 'what's your problem?'

He stopped in his tracks, smirked a sly and rather distorted face, looking at her up and down, sneering.

'*You're* my problem!' He accused bitterly. 'But not for a whole lot longer. You'll see.'

Changes would be made. He was perfectly justified in expecting more. There was no time like the present to start putting his foot firmly on that very floor of change. Even if it was full of tiny, hard to see splinters, he'd take his chances.

It was time to bring out the big guns.

CHAPTER THIRTY-NINE

'Ah, hello dear,' Rose greeted Ellen with a wave and a smile, as she entered the cottage the following day. 'How's tricks with you today?'

'Grand,' Ellen lied because they really weren't. 'What's up here?'

When Rose's phoned to see if she was free earlier that morning, both Ellen and Fergal had been in the midst of a very heated argument, the likes of which they'd never had before.

Criticism towards Ellen's spiritual interests, money and finances, family commitments and even lack of respect towards him, were all on Fergal's agenda. Where it had gathered momentum, remained a mystery.

'And you've let yourself go too,' he accused. 'That weight gain there,' he pointed to her midriff, 'ain't shifting despite your efforts.' That hurt so much she wasn't sure recovery was a given.

Ellen's head was lost in the past, trying to justify root causes for the complaints. Honest to Moses himself she was struggling to know what, when or where these complaints were coming from.

Was Fergal right with his accusations, she wondered now? Had she been neglecting her marriage and her son's? Was she taking money for granted or *'so involved in herself and her sisters'* that she'd forgotten him? Her mind was plagued with so many thoughts that she just couldn't get grounded at all.

Gemma left the O'Hare home earlier that morning. She had stumbled on Ellen and Fergal's argument (it wasn't difficult to find, all over the kitchen and down the hallway for Joe Blogs and his gang to avail off).

Fergal made a strong reference about her stay ('that cow there, milking me for all she's worth'). It was both painful and awkward to hear, verging on shocking.

'I know where I'm not wanted.' Gemma stormed out (with a carrier bag full to capacity, stuffed with her things and a few of Ellen's). 'Screw you, O'Hare,' she told the angry man. 'I hope the hot water scalds the arse off you in the shower! You're nowt but a tight-fisted prat!'

It had not been a pleasant scene but in honest truth, Ellen was relieved to see Gemma go. Just a shame it had to be on such incensed terms. That she never wanted, even once.

'I've a favour to ask.' Rose brought Ellen out of her head and back to the present. 'Are you're up for it? You're looking a bit dazed there.'

'I am.' Back to earth with a bang. 'Ask away.'

Without another word, Rose left the room, disappearing behind her bedroom door. She'd left her walking stick behind, unneeded. The planet Mars was currently placed in her first house, adding vigour seldom enjoyed in its absence.

'I won't be a second,' she promised from afar. 'Hold tight.'

Huffing and puffing, she reappeared seconds later. Squeezing through the door, she pulled an old suitcase with her. It was filled to capacity. The seams were breaking free at the edges from its inside weight. There was no doubt this case had seen better days. Today was not one of them.

'This was Nuala's stuff,' Rose declared through puffs of hurried breaths. 'I want you to have it, Ellen.'

'Okay. Wow.'

Ellen wasn't sure what she was being presented with. Internally she offered a hurried prayer that it wasn't old, outdated clothes or something crazy like a bunch of wigs.

Rose trailed the rest of the case into the middle of the room with as much gusto as she could muster.

'Thank you for not helping me Ellen,' she joked sarcastically. 'This wasn't heavy at all.'

'Say no more about it,' Ellen shrugged. 'Not my problem you find it hard to ask.'

She was rewarded with a playful clip over her head and a gentle pinch from the Cancer's crabby nippers. Independence could be both a blessing and a drawback.

A decent hour later, Rose declared it was time for cocoa.

'I'll not bother,' Ellen declined. Fergal's reference to her weight gain had left its mark. 'If you've fruit tea, I'd love one of those.'

'I'll check,' Rose got up slowly and eased her aching bones gently into place (Mars placing has seemingly done a runner). 'You sit where you are.'

'I'm not sure I've much of a choice,' Ellen confirmed. 'I'm hemmed in by all of this wonderful stuff!'

The suitcase's contents had turned out to be hidden treasure, literally. Everything Ellen had ever wanted to explore in greater detail was inside.

Tarot cards, Angel, Unicorn, Dragon, Druid and goddess cards abound. Some packs were never opened, while others were so used, they were taped at the sides to avoid falling apart.

Books of all shapes, sizes and publications littered the space. She'd piled each one on top of another for better legroom.

Edgar Cayce's '*On Atlantis*,' Joseph Lumpkin's *The 'Book of Enoch*,' astrology, crystal and fairy bibles and even books on real past life regressions were amongst the many findings.

It would take Ellen a solid, consistent year to read through them all. She was delighted. These things were collectively worth a pretty penny or two. Nuala apparently had collected most from the second-hand stores or was gifted others.

'Are you sure you want me to have it, Rose?' Ellen asked for the fourth time that day. 'This is all so great. So amazingly unbelievable. Please say it's all mine again.'

'I'm not saying it again, Ellen, get a grip dear, but yes, take the lot. You're the proper owner of it all now.'

'Wow... just wow!'

Rose had been holding onto her late sister's things since Nuala's passing. Now finally being able to pass those riches on brought relief to the older woman that she couldn't explain.

She could trust Ellen to make the best of everything. Her young companion had the feel for the spiritual, psychic and magical in her blood. The tools would be put to good use and that was the main thing.

'I love that you've given me all these wonderful things,' Ellen hugged Rose tightly. 'But I love it even more that you felt I should have them.'

'Oh, that wasn't down to me, dear,' Rose wouldn't take credit where it wasn't due. 'Spirit decided you should have them. You needed the information they give.'

'Well, thank Spirit then. They never fail to surprise.'

'Indeed, they do not.'

Once they'd had the tea and some of Maeve's much-improved date bread, Maeve joined them. She'd been pruning bushes at the back of the cottage.

'Do you mind if I plant an apple tree in the garden?' she asked Rose gingerly. 'Maybe a cherry one as well?'

Rose shrugged indifference. 'Go to it Green Fingers,' she encouraged lightly. 'Lord knows there's enough space to have a full orchard out there.' The back garden was nearly as large as a small field.

Time passed. Ellen sorted through the tarot cards one by one. Maeve fussed over clearing the tea tray away and wiping down the worktops. Rose yawned and then switched the television set off, just as the morning programmes finished.

Rose glanced around her, first at Ellen and then at Maeve. She knew instinctively something was amiss. She's sensed it the second Ellen stepped into the cottage. She hadn't missed either, the way Ellen periodically stopped what she was doing and gazed into space, deep in thought. Something was up.

'Maeve,' Rose began. 'Any change you could take my turn at getting the clothes of the line? I can feel rain approaching in my very bones.'

'Oh goodness.' Maeve's new blouses and skirts were hanging there, and Rose was never wrong about the weather. She'd need to act quickly. 'This will be the third time this month I've taken your place,' she complained on her way out. 'The favour's getting stale.'

'You knew I was a chancer before you moved in,' Rose answered truthfully. 'I'm making no apology for the longer than average time you're taking to adjust to that.'

'Skiver!'

'It's why you love me dearly.'

'Keep saying things like that and folk will think we're a couple.'

'It matters little to me what others think. You know that. And anyway, we are a couple. A couple of divas.'

Maeve rolled her eyes skywards and then left the room hastily (in case the rain appeared).

'Righty-ho,' Rose turned her attention to a dreamy looking Ellen. Engrossed deeply, she was reading the latest book recovered from the case. Amazing insights into Atlantis were consuming her very mind. 'Ellen,' Rose prompted, unaware how deeply engrossed Ellen was. 'Do you have a second?'

'Hum...'

'I said do you have a moment?'

'Umm... hold on... yes, what's up?'

Truth be told, Ellen could well have done without the interruption. This book was engaging as heck.

'Is there anything you'd like to talk about?'

'Like?'

'Well, you tell me.'

'Oh. Right. Okay, let me think. Well...'

'You and that hubby of yours!' Rose was growing impatient. Here she was, trying to be empathic and supportive and Ellen didn't even get it.

'Oh that.' The distraction of the case's contents had changed the propriety of her thoughts and emotions considerably. 'How did you know?'

'The same way you feel and sense things.'

'Interesting.'

The dialogue began. Fears were expressed as Ellen spoke of the recent argument she and Fergal shouted their way through.

'I mean it could be a blip. Maybe I'm overreacting.'

'You're not.'

'Really?'

'Umm hum. I know you're unsure of so many things at the moment,' Rose knew there were road-block ahead for the couple. 'But I also know you're being guided by a higher force.'

'You know,' Ellen understood what Rose was getting at. 'I've felt that for the longest time, somewhere at the back of my consciousness. I suppose part of me is too scared to acknowledge it completely.'

'That makes sense. The journey you assumed lay ahead with Fergal, now has a grey cloud looming over its head. So much of our lives are contracted before we take on each physical body over many lifetimes.'

'Often, those contracts are made with the people in our current lives, to help facilitate spiritual growth, difficult as that might be.'

'So, what do I do now?' Ellen was once again feeling deflated and yes, a big bit terrified of what lay ahead.

'You trust in the bigger plan at play.' Rose told her. 'Never let go of your faith.'

Unrelenting faith was a miracle in-itself.

CHAPTER FORTY

Two days later, she found a box of opened condoms in Fergal's jacket pocket. Honest to heaven's above, she wasn't snooping. They fell out as she was adjusting his jacket in the cloak room to fit hers in. The jacket fell to the floor from her clumsy grasp. The box slid out onto the floor.

At first Ellen thought they were mints. Fergal had a habit of carrying them with him, conscious of his smoky breath. It was as she collected the box to put back in place, realisation hit. Her heart followed onto the floor with a thump that was heard by her alone.

In a panic to know what to do next, she shoved them into the jacket, closed the door of the cloakroom quickly and put her back to it. The last thing she wanted was for them to grow legs and come into the hall to say hello or something else.

'You okay?' Matt enquired, passing by on his way to the kitchen for juice and crisps. 'You're breathing is heavy and you look a bit pale.'

'Ummm,' she was far from it and stunned. 'I'm grand thanks. Just fine and dandy.'

'You don't sound it.'

'Well, what can I tell you. I'm okay, really.'

That said, she left the scene in a hurry. Matt continued on his journey, urged on by a rumbling stomach.

Ellen climbed the stairs, two at a time. She'd be better able there to gather her thoughts in the bedroom, without having to provide answers to others she hadn't yet found for herself.

So, the very worst had happened. He'd moved on, making his new beginning physical with someone else. She wasn't sure how many of the condoms were missing from the box but did estimate more than one.

How did she feel? Bemused... maybe. Shocked... definitely. Hurt... more than she cared to admit. Angry... we'll see later. Let down... yes, yes, yes. Incredibly.

Analysing the last occasion, she'd seen Fergal wearing the jacket, came next. That was a good thing though. It gave her mind just cause to lift focus to another direction, for a while at least.

Two nights ago, his new mate Frank called in a taxi to collect him. This was a definite indication of a big, bold night of drinking ahead. There'd be the strong possibility of gambling too. Card playing seemed a reasonable assumption.

Weed would be smoked for sure (Frank was a supplier), perhaps even something a little stronger. She could no longer be sure of her husband's choices, especially on the socialising scene.

With the offending jacket slung over his shoulder, Fergal grabbed his cigarettes and mobile phone from the hall table and left with neither a cheerio or goodbye to anyone. He'd taken to doing that sort of things for days.

Returning the next morning, looking like he'd been run over with a truck, he stank of weed. The jacket, an obvious comrade to his activities, was hung outside for a few hours in the garage and sprayed with essential old spray (Ellen's personal stash, but please do use it without permission) before being returned to the cloakroom.

The house phone rang from downstairs, jolting her out of the maze her mind was going through. It rang and rang, each shrill making her more irritable than the last.

'I'll get it!' Matted called out, bringing great relief her way. 'It might be for me.'

It wasn't. Anna wanted to know if Fergal was home yet. Her kitchen sink had a blockage that wasn't shifting with suction. Ellen heard Matt deal with the question. Fergal was usually home around seven.

Ellen was delighted not to have to chat with her mum. She'd only have to pretend nothing was amiss. Today was not the day for formalities and pretences. It was the day for shocks and pain. Things were hurting so deeply; words may not have been found in time to cover up.

And then she bloody well cried. Yep, the very thing she'd didn't want to do, she did. It was hard to admit, but Anna calling seemed to bring her childlikeness to the forefront. Stuff had happened that was difficult to handle, and she wanted the comfort of her mum.

Snivelling and sniffing, (with a few whispered groans), the floodgates opened, the likes of which the Torc Falls in Kerry wouldn't hold a candle too. Whimpering and wallowing into the past, memories to a chunk of nasty stuff resurrected.

Bullying at school, which was pretty brutal. It still left its psychological scares to that very second (mostly for being a weirdo, talking to dead people). Old boyfriends from bygone years, dumped by them in favour of someone else (yes, okay this happened to practically every being on the planet but still, rejection stung).

And then her dad passing away. One of her most favourite dudes in the world, leaving after a cancer battle that he'd lost. That was pretty devasting. Even more so than the emergency hysterectomy she'd had, a year later. Then the…

'Mum!' Shoot, she'd been found out. 'What's up?'

Why hadn't she even considered James was in his own bedroom, right next to hers? What sort of a clown was she assuming the upstairs was vacant?

He knocked on the door before entering. Ellen smiled at him on account of the falls that were still flowing (uncontrollably apparently), blocking her voice.

Sitting beside her with one arm around her shoulders, he waited. Minutes later, Matt joined them, followed closely by Moby. It was turning into a real family affair and getting a little ridiculous. In a house this size, the four of them were stuck in her bedroom waiting for her wailing to cease.

And thankfully it did, with the sharpness only the front door opening downstairs could dictate. Fergal had entered the building. She may be a vulnerable, weeping mess but she'd be dammed if she'd let him see it.

'I don't want him…'

'I know.' Matt got it. 'I'll keep him away until you're ready.'

James, Matt and Moby left immediately. Ellen heard them greet Fergal inside the kitchen, telling him it was a pizza night tonight and to start the phone order for collection.

If he was suspicious with all the attention coming his way (it had been months since his sons and he exchanged with such light heartiness together), he didn't say. Moby greeted every soul the same way each day. No surprise there… traitor!

Ellen couldn't even bare to look at Fergal, turning her back to him as often as possible. It was great to have the excuse of cooking stir-fried vegetables and noodles (she didn't eat pizza) so as to hide the fact she was otherwise occupied.

By the time her meal was cooked, she and Moby shared the kitchen together to enjoy their own foods respectively (well he scrounged a chunk of hers too). If

Fergal had any inking something wasn't right, he never once voiced it.

At around eight thirty that evening, the condom owner left for Anna's house. Ellen knew he'd be gone for a while and was relieved to see him away. The strain to remain normal was tough.

With the coast clear, she checked both boys were otherwise occupied. Satisfied they were (homework and PlayStation gaming), she opened the cloakroom door, lifting Fergal's jacket out of it completely.

The garage was a mere ten steps outside of the utility room. Once inside of it, the oily smell coming from the heating burner consumed the space. She made a mental note to have it checked out for leaks. But first things first.

The front of the box bragged ten condoms inside of it. She counted the items inside twice and twice it told her there were three missing. Three. Not one, not none, three.

With a heartbeat skipping every forth thump and a head full of so many thoughts at once, it was no small wonder she didn't throw up.

Where and when did this... stuff... take place? Was it with the same person or three different ones? One-night stands, or a longer established affair? Did it really matter? Yes, it really, really did.

And the boys. Her amazing sons. What would all this do to them? It was one thing hearing their parents argue. Quite another knowing they'd likely be parting company. It scared her, never mind their youthful minds.

On Fergal's return home, a few hours later, he found Ellen and Moby in the sun lounge just off the kitchen. One was reading, the other napping.

It was unusual to see Ellen drinking a tall glass of wine, but then he'd no idea it was taken to steady some pretty shaky nerves. Both boys were obviously in their rooms.

'Hi,' Ellen greeted him, noticing how tired he looked for the first time in a long time. 'Did all go okay at mums?'

'Yep. Food blockage again.'

'Ah… Would you like some wine poured?'

'Ummm.' Fergal looked uncomfortable. 'Naw thanks. I'll stick with tea.'

Music played in the background from a mixed compact disc Fergal had treated Ellen to last year. It was one of her favourites. She watched him from the rim of her glass, going about sugaring his tea and devouring a whole custard cream biscuit at once. Her heart broke.

When he went to lift the milk from the fridge, turning his nose up at the pong inside the plastic container (it had gone sour), he chucked it down the sink and opened a fresh one. Ellen felt like crying at what was being taken away (not the milk but the relationship).

'Can we talk?' The effect of the wine added courage.

310

The request came out of the blue and took Fergal by surprise. He stopped mid pour, spilt milk over the bench and turned his head towards her.

'I'm not sure that's a good idea.' Direct and to the point, his words spoke a finality he obviously felt. 'I think we passed that stage a while ago.'

'We were always able to talk in the past.'

'Things change.'

Lifting his cup from the kitchen bench along with a half packet of custard creams, he quickly glanced Ellen's way and then left the room with the hurry of a fearful fella.

Just as Rowan Keating had started to sing *The Long Goodbye*.

CHAPTER FORTY-ONE

Fergal's heart finally started to slow down, minutes after he'd reached the recliner chair in the living room. Having the whole room unoccupied, helped him gain composure quicker. He was glad he'd caught a break.

That was unexpectedly tough in there. Ellen asking him to talk had put him on the spot. He'd handled it well, thankfully this time, without an argument or heated debate to go along side it. He despised those with a vengeance.

Had he done the right thing refusing her offer? Why the doubt? He wasn't normally one to ponder decisions but all this new order of things between them seemed to be resetting different rules each day.

Their marriage was over, finite, final. Of that he was completely sure. All the talking they'd already done was getting them nowhere. These past few months had been about action speaking louder than any words possibly could.

Meeting Frank had been his personal godsend. The man was a legend. He'd kept him right all along his separation road so far, advising him in legal matters (*don't leave the house, stay put for as long as possible*).

Fergal had no notion of leaving the very place he'd piled money into for so long. He'd stay put, keep his independence while there and come up financial triumphs when the house sold.

A solicitor's letter confirming the separation would be next, the ball rolling on it last weekend. Ellen should receive said letter any day now.

He yawned a sleepy, dog-tired exhaustion. He knew this was more from his new social activities than from his work but flippen heck, it was worth it all.

He'd never known such a variety of events in his life before now. What did annoy him occasionally though, was how much he'd been missing out on all these years.

Fair enough and to be fair, he chastised his thinking. His married life hadn't been without good times too. He might have set up a new status quo for himself now but refused to see the past years as all doom and gloom. Heck, he'd two great sons to prove that very point.

He knew Ellen had been crying earlier today when he'd come in from work. She tried to hide it but didn't do a great job of covering up.

He'd assumed she'd received the solicitor's letter and had been shockingly upset over its finality. He could be wrong though. She'd hadn't mentioned a thing about getting it. Maybe that was why she'd wanted to talk tonight. Who knew?

Honestly to heavens above he'd no desire to hurt Ellen, none at all. Yes of course she had her annoying traits; unrealistic notions, a pretty decent controlling nature and wasn't as good a cook as his mother. But hey ho, nobody was perfect, even him.

But he'd had enough of it all. Getting out and about as he'd being doing, had shown him that life could be whatever he wanted it to be. There were things to mentally sort out, but he'd continue down this road and keep looking ahead, not back. Definitely not back.

He could murder a cigarette. The very thing that would help calm him down before bed. Maybe even help sleep come easier than it had done in recent days. There was just too much occupying his mind.

The cold nip outside was putting him off going there. When he finally got his own place, he'd smoke indoors until his heart was content. For now, abiding by the house rules, he'd have to make do. He'd go out the front of the house, to avoid Ellen's gaze at the back of it.

Grabbing his jacket from the cloakroom, he hoped the weed smell had left it from the previous evening. That had been quite the night. High as a kite with visions of having wings. Pity today paid the price. His head was bouncing.

The night sky sparkled while the weaning moon gleamed a shine onto the stars around it, emphasising their glow. The small cud-de-sac sat silently around him, two of the other three houses there without lights on, their occupants either out and about or in bed.

He inhaled deeply, blowing a gust of smoke into the otherwise clear, crisp air. Occasionally, as the smoke reached his lungs, he coughed a phlegmy wheeze but inhaled another draw to compensate any loss of pleasure.

Behind him he heard Ellen leave the kitchen. She wished Moby a good night as he settled into his bed in the hall and then walked upstairs. He didn't turn around once. He knew the routine well. No need to exchange pleasantries. Those times were over.

Good gracious above but it was cold. Fergal shivered and pulled the collar of his jacket tighter around his neck. Then he dug his (non-smoking) hand into the pocket of his jacket, hoping to at least save some of his fingers from frost bite.

His hand grazed the item inside. Curious to what it was, he extracted the condom box.

'Holy Moley.' It was Franks. Placed into Fergal's jacket in a hurry, for fear his girlfriend Gloria would come upon them.

'Say nout,' he cautioned Fergal. 'If she asks, they belong to you.'

'Fair enough,' Fergal would cover for a mate. 'Just don't forget to take them out later on again.'

Relieved he'd come across them before anyone else did, Fergal would return them to Frank tomorrow night when they were next arranged to meet.

He'd enough on his plate without the added agro of being found with condoms on him. Moses above knew what would develop from that. It didn't bare thinking about. Legally, it could well upset the apple cart. He needed to be careful of that.

He'd no notion of romance or another woman for quite a while yet. One thing at one time, thank you very much.

The rest would follow in due course.

CHAPTER FORTY-TWO
CHRISTMAS 2003

'I love Christmas time,' Matt O'Hare admitted wholeheartedly as he joined the rest of his family for their traditional present opening, directly after dinner. 'I feel as fat as a stuffed turkey.'

He rubbed his bulging stomach, ever so proud of the mound of food it had just consumed, while at the same time sure he'd finish off the remains of the trifle residing in the fridge before the night was over. 'So, if someone could just deposit my prezzies on my lap, I'll do the rest myself.'

Apart from the new Porsche Fergal had requested, or the George Clooney clone Ellen had craved, the O'Hare family — right down to Moby and his new doggie blanket — were delighted with their gifts.

'I can't wait to get this PlayStation set up for action,' James admitted, already extracting the leads from its box. 'Can you give me a hand, Dad?'

Fergal was only too pleased to help. He was feeling rather hungover from his socialising with Frank and the boys from the night before. The distraction would give him a focus of sorts, albeit a temporary one.

His deep-rooted insecurity created a false belief that he was being judged for his recent actions. His new 'devil-may-care attitude' was purely surface, and not truly honest with what was going on deeper down.

Down there, he was feeling so guilty he wasn't quite sure what to do with it. Arrogance seemed the best option.

Finding it difficult to look at his wife, never mind thank her for the new phone, CDs and aftershave she'd bought him, the indignant mask he'd created was as good a cover as any.

What Fergal wasn't proud of, however, was the rather passionate kiss he'd given the blonde on the way out of Frank's flat last night. That he could have done without.

The fact she'd been flirting with him all evening, only suggested she'd enjoyed the craic as much as his ego had been satisfied. At his age, he still had what it took to land a 'looker.' Of that, he was most proud.

As father and son lent themselves to the task in hand, Ellen saw her chance to exit. Having spent the entire morning under a falseness of enjoyment and festive spirit, (mainly for both her sons' sakes), she felt far from its truth. The strain was telling considerably.

'I think I'll go rest for a while,' she informed the room. 'It was an early start this morning. Afterwards, we'll visit Conor at Gran's.'

Her younger brother had finally made it home for Christmas, despite his flight's delay and the Christmas coach schedules running a little haywire.

'I won't be going,' Fergal growled loudly with his back to Ellen the whole time. 'I've plans of my own.'

Shocked and annoyed at his pre-arranged plans because it was traditional for the family to meet in Anna's home every Christmas Day evening, Ellen was peeved.

This year of all years Fergal knew it was important everyone attended. Conor had told them of his surprise news ahead and now Fergal wouldn't be part of it.

'You know Conor's home,' she told Fergal crossly, 'I told you weeks ago that he was coming.' The two men had always been good friends.

Fergal ignored her for longer than was necessary, preferring to leave her standing until he was ready to answer. It was a power thing (a false one but none-the-less an ego victory of sorts).

'As I said,' he glanced unapologetically her way. 'I've plans.' As far as he was concerned, she could like it, or she could lump it.

'Whatever you like,' Ellen was damned if she was going to show him how mad she was. If he wanted to act like an arse, she had neither the way or the will, to do anything about it.

Matt looked concerned. He knew there was something amiss between his parents. He'd felt it for the longest while. His concern was deep.

Both boys could feel the chill in the family dynamic. It was hard not to. If they didn't, the shouting match between their parents, echoing from the kitchen around the house at three that morning would surely have done it.

'You okay?' Matt asked, as Ellen picked her footing around Christmas boxes and packaging scattering the floor. 'Do you need a hand with anything?' The Christmas dinner tidy up was extreme and still waiting in the kitchen.

'No thanks, hon,' she reassured her eldest, uneasy son. 'I won't be too long. You enjoy your gifts. I'll be back in two shakes of a lamb's tail.'

Rest was far from Ellen's mind as she entered the bedroom upstairs and promptly burst into tears. Rushing towards the en-suite bathroom, she wanted to bury her sobs in the towel there, lest they be heard downstairs.

The past couple of weeks on the build-up to the festive season had been enormously difficult between Fergal and herself.

They scarcely spoke unless it was out of necessity. His drinking had become a nightly affair, either inside or outside of the house. He'd also dramatically reduced the finances he usually brought into their home.

She'd struggled to keep the bills paid and find the extra needed to give them a decent Christmas. Ellen was currently indebted to her mother for a tidy little sum. She really didn't like doing that but felt forced into its inevitability.

Days ago, a solicitor's letter arrived for her. It declared their marriage to be over, with 'unreckonable differences' given as the route cause.

That little gem caused such a shock, opening the letter unaware of its content, that her heart bounced off the kitchen counter, hit the floor and then played games with the lump lodged in her throat.

What had really put the icing on the cake, however, was Fergal's behaviour in the early hours of that morning.

He'd once again come home drunk as a skunk. Upon arrival, he immediately began roaring abuse towards her. That shoe he'd flicked of his foot, didn't just land with a thump on her ankle unintentionally. It was definitely pre-planned.

While she was trying to keep him quiet for fear of awakening the boys, he'd pushed her against the cooker, when she shushed him. She'd pushed back; after all, she was no pushover. This had only fuelled an already lit fire.

'Piss off,' she remembered the anger in his tone as he gathered footing (his shoe missing from the left one). 'You wouldn't hold a candle to the woman I've just been with tonight.' He glared at her through drunken, bloodshot eyes. 'Ugly bitch!'

Insults were now the new norm. From "I don't love you any more," to "Money Muncher," the list was endless. All forgotten the next day of course (by him, not her), like they never happened.

There were fewer things in life more hurtful than angry words. Sticks and stones could break bones — Ellen sighed its truth — but that row would sting for a long time to come.

Name-calling really did wound, with its psychological impact being both long-lasting and a real game-changer.

Their marriage was not just on the rocks; it was sliding into the sea and floating towards the horizon. There was little she, or Fergal, seemed to want to do to save it from sinking.

Destiny was doing its own job.

CHAPTER FORTY-THREE

As pre-arranged the O'Hare family — minus Fergal and Moby — entered the McDowell home just shortly after five p.m.

It had been one whole hour after Ellen had applied a fresh coat of make-up and plastered an almost permanent smile across her face.

The sounds greeting each of them, echoing from down the hallway, decided that all activity was restricted to the kitchen. Judging by the noise level, it was evident that the whole gang were there.

'Hey,' Anna greeted her grandsons and daughter with a hug and a festive wish. 'Happy Christmas to you all.'

Discretion told her not to enquire about Fergal's absence. Call it motherly intuition but she knew her place and she knew problems were pending. As far as Moby's absence went, she wasn't expecting him anyway.

'Did you like the gift I got you, Gran?' James enquired playfully because he knew she'd hate it. 'I just couldn't resist when I saw them hanging in the shop.'

'I did, James,' Anna played along with his joke, thin-lipped but feeling jovial. 'But honestly son, I'm just not sure those fur-trimmed handcuffs will be put to the use they deserve!'

'We'll see. There's life in the old bones yet.'

Everyone laughed, including Ellen. She'd no idea James had done such a thing.

'Now,' Anna told her two grandsons untruthfully. 'I did buy you both a litre of vodka each and some weed for your troubles,' she waved away Ellen's objections to finish. 'But I ended up giving them to the postman and Harry down at the grocery shop yesterday, so CDs and new PJs it is.'

'Ah shucks.' Matt faked disappointment. 'I was looking forward to getting zozzled.'

Conor entered the room five minutes later. He was followed closely by a very tanned and handsome looking Phillippe. Wearing designer jeans and a well-coordinated, pinstriped blue shirt, brought out the blue in his eyes and the natural blond, sun-bleached streaks in his dark hair.

If Ellen didn't know better, she'd swear this tall, lean man had stepped straight out of a magazine; one she'd definitely have bought, by monthly subscription for her eyes only. He was real model material. Roll over, George Clooney!

Instead of goggling at this striking specimen of a man, Ellen turned and greeted her equally fetching younger brother with a hug and a kiss on the cheek.

'It's so good to see you,' she told Conor honestly because she really meant it. 'I've missed you so much. How have you been?'

Conor turned towards Phillippe with a shyness he'd never displayed before. Ellen was quite happy to rest her eyes on the Frenchman too. It was no hardship and besides, she needed the cheering up.

'My cup runneth over,' Conor smirked shrewdly, at the same time quite obviously crazy with happiness. 'You'll understand when you hear the news.'

Conor introduced Phillippe to Ellen with an undeniable sense of pride. No one but her could possibly have guessed how she'd held onto his hand just that bit longer than was deemed necessary. Phillippe did pass her a strange look but then let it slide.

'So,' Conor took the stand. 'Now that everybody is here,' he announced, 'it is my greatest pleasure and joy to tell you all that Phillippe and I,' he drew Phillippe to him and they locked arms, 'are engaged!'

A collective 'Ohhh!' ushered through the crowd, preceding the many shouts of 'Congratulations, it's about time,' (Kate and Meagan in unison with a giggle said afterwards that they'd synchronised the same words at the same time). Then a request was put forward to 'be the best man' (Donal).

'Catch yourselves on!' Conor took control of the stage for the second time. 'Give us both a chance to get used to the engagement first.'

'Frig sake!' (Gemma). 'Leading us all up the garden path for nothing.'

From the corner of the room, Anna's eyes filled with tears. It was mostly from joy but a little from the internal struggle she'd been feeling since Conor had confided to her last night that he was gay.

She'd known of course, right at the back of her mind, somewhere in between him turning sixteen and not as much as a girlfriend in sight.

Then there was the time she'd "accidentally" came across male magazines under his mattress, cleaning his bedroom. He was around the age of nineteen at the time. If any doubt had lingered with Anna, that had done the trick.

'I hope I haven't shocked you, Mum,' he'd said when they'd been enjoying the chilly night air and star-filled sky outside. 'The last thing I want to do is disappoint you.'

As she reassured him that wasn't possible, they'd hugged an embrace that told her Conor was ecstatically happy and that was all that mattered.

Now as both mother and son caught each other's eye from across the room, Conor winked at her, and she blew him a kiss right back.

'Champagne!' Anna declared, straining against the noise in the room. 'Somebody, grab the flutes from the living room dresser.'

'I'll just have apple juice like a child,' Gemma's head sank towards the floor. 'You all enjoy the celebration. Don't mind me.'

'Apple juice my arse,' Anna was having none of it. 'You know I don't believe anybody should give up anything, including alcohol,' she scolded. 'You just need to learn to want it, not need it.'

Gemma was ecstatic, joining the gang of Champagne drinkers immediately. Things were finally looking up. This could well be the party she was hoping for since the start of the festive season.

The night was pitch dark and the atmosphere damp when Ellen dropped her sons off at home a few hours later. The house was in darkness, proving Fergal had long ago left to fulfil his 'plans.'

Matt and James were keen to play their latest computer games, so Ellen knew they'd be fine doing their own thing. She'd text Joan earlier (their next-door neighbour) to keep an eye on them both.

'I want to take these,' she indicated the unopened gifts in the back of the car, 'to Rose and Maeve before the day ends.'

'Go ahead,' Matt ushered her on, 'but don't expect any trifle left when you get home.'

'I know not to, son. Your reputation precedes you.'

Asking one of them to let Moby into the house from his garage retreat, James was already through the door and calling his name by the time Ellen was taking her leave.

Joan waved from her living room window acknowledging she'd be available for the boys should the need arise. It was all good.

As she entered the cottage, Cecilia Flanagan was just leaving.

'I have John and Sarah coming for super,' she giggled into Ellen's face, leaving damp spittle on her cheeks and crumbs of pastry across her new winter coat. 'I'm doing duck and leek sandwiches with gravy,' she revealed, her mouth-watering juicy spittle at the thought. 'I can't wait!'

Rose truly loved the Tyrone Crystal Angel figure Ellen gifted her.

'I know now why I cleared and washed down the windowsill yesterday,' she admitted, not in the least shamefaced it hadn't been done in years. 'It was to give this lovely figure its place in my home.'

Maeve was delighted with the gift of matching blue gloves, hat and scarf. Ellen had thrown a pair of childish earmuffs (with a fairy princess sown on them), into the gift by way of a joke. Maeve was completely taken by them. In fact, she was tickled pink.

'I'll keep them for good wear,' Maeve rubbed their softness against her cheek. 'I can't stand to get them soiled so soon.'

The conversation, as they ate mince pies and drank creamy coffee, turned towards Cecilia. Apparently, she'd visited Rose and Maeve twice in the one day, forgetting her earlier trip and the Christmas presents with it.

'She's so thoughtful though,' Rose pointed to the table. 'She knitted those table mats and coasters as a gift.' Little was said about the tea cosy in the shape of a banana that barely covered the teapot. It was skimmed over to be peeled for another day.

Maeve giggled at the gift Cecilia had given her.

'I got these,' she produced a pack of four pink toilet rolls. 'They're to go with the new bathroom Fergal's building for us.'

'Lovely,' Ellen smiled at Cecilia's intention. 'I see she's thought of every detail.'

Although Ellen objected because of the frost currently freezing the ground, Rose insisted on seeing her out to the car as she prepared to leave.

'I fancy a breath of cool air,' Rose shrugged away any objections otherwise. 'My lungs are crying out for it.'

The stars shone brightly in the December sky, providing light that brightened their path as they walked. Glistening and sparkling, they looked like diamonds, some in clusters, others alone.

'I always loved the night sky,' Ellen confided, glancing upwards as she spoke and tightening the scarf around her neck against the cold. 'For as long as I can remember.'

'Me too,' Rose agreed. 'It holds so much magic.'

'Enchanting and enthralling all at once.'

Rose clasped Ellen's arm as she made to get into the car.

'I want you to know,' her voice sounded serious, her look mirroring the tone, 'that no matter what is ahead for you and Fergal, I'm here.'

Ellen felt distressed. Something ahead, in the not-too-distant future, was about to change the status quo in her life, Fergal's life and the lives of their two sons.

'I hope I'm strong enough to cope with it,' Ellen's eyes welled at the thought of it all. 'It's pretty scary.'

Rose nodded in agreement.

'Of course, it's scary,' she stroked Ellen's newly coloured, highlighted hair. 'You know change is good,' she reminded her. 'It's what keeps us on our toes.'

The drive home was fraught with an anxiety Ellen would really rather not have felt.

'Please help me get through what lies ahead,' she asked Archangel Michael. 'I trust that what is ahead, is all for everybody's higher good.'

The New Year promised progress. Ellen's eyes shone sparkles as tears ran freely down her already damp cheeks, destroying the mask she'd applied earlier.

She thought of her son's and the impact these changes would have on them. She knew she needed to stay strong to help them through it. She also knew she needed to find trust and faith in the Divine Plan.

Staying positive was key.

CHAPTER FORTY-FOUR

On the first week of the New Year, Ellen collected the post from the hall mat where it lay, eager to see if her certificate had been sent. The large white envelope suggested it had, the stamp postmarked "Trinity College Dublin" fulfilled her wishes.

Studying the online counselling course had finally paid off. All the hard work was reaping rewards.

'Whey hey!' Her surprise knew little bounds when she noticed the overall mark she'd been given for her diploma. 'I must have done something right!'

'Big-head,' James teased, on his way down the stairs and into the living room. 'How will you ever fit it through the door?'

Ellen smiled.'

'I'm done,' she told him humbly. 'My deflated ego needed the boost.'

'Well done, Mum,' James praised. 'You did well.' This achievement felt great. Ellen was just thrilled to bits. It meant she could finally start to practise counselling from the recently converted garage. Hopefully too she could 'earn her bloody keep' as Fergal had suggested she do many times in the past months.

Excited, Ellen wasted no time in making plans for marketing her services later that day. By the time Fergal made an appearance in the late afternoon, she'd already decided to place an ad in the local paper.

'I'm not entirely sure how to word this advert,' she sought Fergal's advice after dinner by way of instigating a half-normal conversation between them. 'I want to offer my counselling services,' she pondered, 'but I know I can't ignore my spiritual abilities either.'

Uninterested, Fergal stood to leave. His plans with a gang of mates, a nightclub in Belfast and alcoholic beverages, screeched sheer excitement. They might even go paintball shooting too.

He'd no time to give Ellen tonight (or any other night to be honest), but especially after the way she'd refused to launder his clothes all week long. He could play those games too.

He'd swear as well, if push came to shove, that she was responsible for piles of his clothes landing in the bottom of the wardrobe, off the hangers, each time he went there.

'Ask Rose,' he suggested gruffly, eager to get going. 'She's just a proper little treasure altogether.' Fergal liked Rose okay, he found her to be both kind and nurturing but felt aggrieved by how much she meant to Ellen.

Glancing her way as he made to depart, Fergal felt a pang of guilt. His wife looked hurt and possibly on the verge of tears. He'd upset her. He may have cut ties with Ellen but he'd no desire to deliberately cause sadness.

Clicking his tongue impatiently he marched across the room to where she sat at the table. Glancing at the piece of paper with the advert attempt, he read it quickly. Standing so close to her (after so long avoiding doing just that) unsettled him considerably.

'Stick to counselling,' he advised sharply. 'That way you won't be labelled a witch.'

'My, my,' Ellen was enraged. 'You really are such an arse. I was only asking.'

'Well,' Fergal challenged, 'you did ask.'

'I'd be proud to be called a witch,' she retorted hotly. 'It actually means wise woman, so you've just handed me a compliment, thanks.'

The slamming of the door, seconds later, came as a result of her words. Ellen stuck her tongue out childishly in his direction

'Arse.' So much for trying to be civil. It would seem those days between them were long gone.

At that moment, she despised the very ground Fergal walked on. She knew this arguing and bickering with him was bringing out the worst side of her. She needed to take better charge of herself.

'Stop giving into impulses,' she scolded herself loudly in the hope it would have a bigger impact. 'You know better than that!'

In the end and after much deliberation, Ellen decided to list her advert under "Spiritual Counselling."

'Are you sure you don't mean Spiritual Healing?' Matt asked on his way past to relieve the fridge of the last of the substitute chicken and curry left over from dinner. 'I'm not sure people will get what that means.'

Ellen felt tired, the kind of tiredness that was draining her every resource.

'I've been back and forth forever,' she lamented. 'I'm so tired from all the thinking. I'm going to take my chances with the Spiritual Counselling.'

'Fair enough,' Matt tore half a wedge of naan bread and grabbed the mango chutney to accompany his feast. 'Don't come running to me if it doesn't work out.'

He was rewarded with a playful nip of his bum on the way over to the oven to reheat his snack.

Surprisingly, there was huge interest in the advert. Answering questions about herself and her services, Ellen even managed to rectify some personal uncertainty as well.

Not completely sure which direction she was opening up too, when provoked, the answers flew. It surprised her and some of those who'd asked too.

'I'm not a fortune teller or connected to any religion or dogma,' she stated firmly. 'I use mediumship to help counsel and other spiritual tools as guided.'

By the end of the first week, she had seven definite appointments lined up for that month and three pencilled in, pending confirmation.

'I feel a little nervous,' she confided to her sons as she prepared to meet her first appointment. 'I've the

Angels and Ascended Masters tortured all morning,' her voice quivered apprehensively. 'Asking for calmness and guidance.'

'You'll do great, Mum,' James encouraged. 'Just keep believing in yourself.'

'Thanks James. It's a lovely new beginning.'

'Finally.' Fergal chirped up from the corner of the room. 'Actual money coming in that won't have me earning it.'

'Nobody owns money,' Ellen was taking the high road. 'It's there for all of us. To see it any differently, or indeed take more than is needed, the message has been missed in favour of ego. You, Fergal, have undervalued the role of a stay-home parent. Please don't put so much power with money.'

'It makes the world go around,' her husband retorted, sneering at her naivety. 'Bills need paying.'

'It makes *your* world go around,' she corrected. 'Not mine.'

'Whatever. Bla, bla, bla.'

Over the following week, clarity developed enormously. Ellen found that contrary to her original belief, the counselling diploma she'd studied acted as a valuable backup to what she just knew she'd always wanted to do. No, no, what she was always *meant* to do.

This was New Age Counselling where problems were explored, and causes found with the help of different vibrational energy sources.

She'd been accessing help all week. From her own wisdom and understanding to pulling cards for clarification, Ellen was overcome at how things had developed in such a short period.

Connecting with the Master, Angelic and Faerie dimensions each day felt so reassuring. It comforted her to know she was not on her own or indeed as in charge as her human ego would make her believe she was.

Her last appointment of the day had involved little more than accessing information on the woman's pets that had passed over and the ones still living on her farm, very much in physical body.

Ellen hadn't felt this excited in so long and she wanted to shout her joy from the rooftops.

'It's going really well,' she told Fergal at the end of a very exhilarating week's work while making up the bed. She was eager to involve him in her optimism and provide a conversation between them that was civil rather than snippy. 'I'm really enjoying the experience.'

Fergal bundled the rest of his clothes from the opened wardrobe into his already full arms and walked towards the spare room. Without announcement, he'd removed himself out of their bedroom.

'Congratulations,' he murmured nastily. 'You're officially a weirdo.'

Now to be fair, him formally moving out of their bedroom should have brought her sadness. This time it did not. All she could think of was how she had the king-size bed to herself.

No more un-timely wake-up in the middle of the night. Drunken sleep was the worst, especially when he threw his arm across her chest, or snored so badly the roof nearly came off.

'I like being different,' she called to his back as he left to go across the hallway. 'We're all unique.'

'Bla, bla, bla. Weirdo.'

Maybe at bedtime tonight she'd count her blessings and watch them multiply. Goodness knows she shed enough tears to fill a bathtub. Now they'd officially become a separated couple, it was time to toughen up.

The niggling fear at the back of her head, over how she'd survive alone, would be ignored in favour of courage.

Let's see how that went.

CHAPTER FORTY-FIVE

As the days turned into weeks and the weeks into February, busy was the word of the moment.

Between starting up her own business and helping Gemma decorate the nursery she'd recently taken charge of, Ellen's time seemed to be running away from her. All attempts to dictate otherwise were not working.

'It doesn't sit well with my Sagittarian desire for freedom,' she complained to Gemma as they rinsed paint rollers under the running tap. 'I have to learn persistence and consistency.' (Gifts the astrological sun sign hadn't been given in abundance).

Gemma continued to flourish since her return home. Weekly attendance at counselling sessions had recently turned to monthly appointments.

'They're delighted with my progress,' she spoke proudly of her achievements. 'I've never felt so good and,' she grinned, 'Donal and I had pina coladas last night after dinner,' — her first drink since Christmas. — 'I didn't even want a second one. How in charge am I?'

'You're just amazing. Well done.'

It seemed that all of Ellen's siblings were doing well. Kate had recently started a new relationship with her boss, Declan McNally. It was early days yet, of course, but she seemed hopeful. She was getting ready to introduce him to her daughters at the weekend.

Conor and Philippe were busy planning their forthcoming wedding celebration, arranged for early spring the following year. It would take place in Ireland with a short service in France (holiday included for whoever could make it... yeah!).

Anna was insisting she walk Conor down the aisle while he was negotiating that it might not be necessary as they weren't having a church wedding.

All was mostly well and made even better with Maeve's offer of baking the wedding cake as her gift to the groom and groom. Rose and Maeve wouldn't make the French trip on account of Rose's reluctance to fly (and refusal to go via sea also). It seemed Rose was secretly a yellow-belly over travel.

With her limbs now aching, it was a great relief when Ellen finally said goodbye to Gemma two hours later. She went straight home. It was late, yet she noticed, as she pulled the car into the driveway, that the living room light was still brightly lit.

The sound of the television echoed into the hallway as Ellen entered, locking the door behind her. Fergal glared at her when she walked into the room but refrained from a welcome. The action movie he was watching blasted an explosion. Ellen could have sworn the ceiling vibrated with its effect.

The many squashed beer cans, lying at the side of his chair, told her he was well oiled and likely had been for a while. She felt relieved to know that Matt and James were in their rooms. She doubted whether they were sleeping given the current noise level but at least they were resting.

'Hey,' she began with hardly the will to want to. 'You're up late.'

At first, Fergal ignored her, choosing to concentrate on the film. This was nothing new for Ellen to experience; he'd been in the habit of leaving the room every time she entered, for weeks now.

Ellen yawned. It was definitely time to hit the sheets. She walked towards the door.

'Night,' she didn't expect an answer. 'See you tomorrow.'

'I want to talk to you,' Fergal's words halted her in her tracks as he jumped off his seat and rushed awkwardly towards Ellen. 'It can't wait.'

Ellen dropped her handbag onto the floor, kicked her shoes off and sat down. If this was another argument brewing, he'd definitely win tonight; she simply hadn't the strength or desire to fight back.

'Okay,' she acknowledged. 'I have to warn you though,' she rubbed her aching feet. 'I'm beat.'

Fergal stood, wobbled slightly and then straightened. He towered above Ellen so as he felt he had the upper hand.

'I'm moving out,' he delivered his message as bluntly and briskly as he could muster. 'Tomorrow.'

'I see,' was all Ellen could manage at such short notice. 'Where to?'

Fergal took a swig out of his beer can, wiped the excess from his mouth onto his shirt sleeve and sneered.

'Not your business,' he wouldn't tell. 'I've had enough of this shit and it's time to go.'

'You and me both,' Ellen agreed, feeling stunned now that it was happening. 'On that we can both agree.' They'd been living separate lives inside the one house.

There wasn't any doubt that things between them were bad. Communication, apart from necessary exchanges, had been non-existent for so long she'd given up counting. The strain on everyone was tremendous and it was showing in each member of the O'Hare family, in different ways.

'It doesn't have to be this way.' Ellen felt suddenly frightened at what lay ahead. 'Everything can be fixed if we really wanted it to.'

Fergal was adamant. It had taken him the best part of the evening to work up the courage to put his plans into action. Nothing, bar a nuclear bomb going off, was going to deter him now.

'I don't love you any more,' he brought all further discussions to a conclusion with those words. 'There isn't any point.'

Once the stunned silence was interrupted with another movie noise, Ellen stood to leave. Those words had hurt more than anything else he'd ever said to her.

'Love is unconditional,' she told Fergal before her obvious exit. 'You will always have mine but you're right Fergal,' she confirmed, 'this can't go on. I won't have you treat me this way any longer.'

'Ditto.'

The climb upstairs was one of the longest and toughest ones Ellen had ever journeyed. The fact that she was walking it alone did little to encourage confidence for the days ahead.

She felt devastated that the world they had built was crumbling brick by brick without either a hammer or dust sheet needed in its descent. She felt powerless to stop it.

Yet she knew that deep down, she really didn't want to.

CHAPTER FORTY-SIX
MARCH 2004

'I think it's time you expanded your practice, Ellen,' Rose smoothed the creases over the tablecloth sprawled across the ironing board, as she finished up the last of the laundry. 'You need to build on your reputation.'

Ellen shot her a look as if she'd suggested they climb Mount Everest in an hour.

'Are you kidding?' she asked earnestly. 'Just where would I get the financial backing to do that, pray tell?'

Since Fergal's departure, just over two weeks ago she was struggling in more ways than one. Knowing, courtesy of a higher power, that he'd still be in touch, did little to reassure her about how she would manage now.

Ellen missed him in so many wordless ways, its pain turned physical across her chest. She was concerned about the boys; how was this affecting them and what should she, could she, do to help?

She'd done hours of research. Apparently, as long as one parent was strong enough to carry a parental separation maturely forward for the children, it didn't much matter which one it was. That was kind of reassuring but still, there were other aspects to consider.

Fergal left the very night of his announcement. He insisted he wouldn't wait until morning as previously planned. Matt and James knew nothing about it until the following morning. They'd been unusually quiet for days afterwards, despite her desire to bring things out into the open.

Mad as a bull with her departed husband for leaving her to deal with his choices, rage regularly reared its head. The dishwasher got roared at for not switching on in time. Moby raced ahead in the park when she bellowed that he be obedient (yes, she was sorry for that afterwards and did apologise). It was all very stressful.

Ellen wondered now if Rose had gone insane. With her sons to think of, the finances to figure out and a million and one other details to consider, Ellen couldn't possibly find space in her mind to think of business premises.

'Where there's a will,' Rose insisted, especially at having seen the look of disbelief on Ellen's face, 'there is always a way. It simply requires one step at one time.'

'Rose,' Ellen's maintained, 'I can't possibly, think of...'

'Enough now,' Rose brought a halt to further refusals, as she deposited the tablecloth into an already full laundry basket. She lifted it under her arm, resting it on her hip.

'I have a few pounds put away,' she added as she walked towards the bedroom to put her morning's work inside. 'We'll have a look in the paper for a suitable abode.'

'You're so bossy,' Ellen was astounded. 'Do you hear yourself?'

'I do and yes I am, but it gets things done.'

'There are other ways you know.'

'Not for me. Now, that's all we'll say for now.'

And so, the pursuit for appropriate accommodation began. Between hunting in the local papers and regularly visiting the two estate agencies in town, both Ellen and Rose kept a tight eye out for any new developments in that area.

'One or two rooms would suit well.' Rose announced to all would-be helpers. 'It doesn't even have to be the ground floor. All suggestions will be considered.'

And then, out of the blue-and-white sky, it appeared on a grey morning.

'It's absolutely perfect,' Rose glanced towards the first-floor office space in the town's Main Street. 'The rent is pretty reasonable for this part of town as well.'

Once again, Ellen had reservations.

'Won't it be noisy?' She glanced at the fruit and vegetable store beneath and the traffic-congested street they sat in. 'I can't imagine it would help my type of work.'

'You'll manage,' Rose wouldn't be deterred. 'Let's go have a look. There's no harm in that.'

That night as Ellen lay in the king-size bed, feeling the usual emptiness without Fergal (but not really missing him... strange) the fear of the added responsibilities she'd suddenly inherited with him gone hit home.

She'd recently had to find a reputable mechanic when her car fell sick. Then there was learning how to measure the home-heating oil to see what was left in the tank. Stinking of its aroma, it took days to leave her nostril hairs!

And then there was the strapping of the bicycle transporter to the car. Along with the two boys, they managed. Five nipped fingers later, she wished her grand idea of the three of them cycling the park had stayed just that (it rained big, half way around).

She wondered why things always seemed that bit more troublesome at night. In the morning light, it was so much easier to gain perspective.

Shoving her current troubles to the back of her mind, Ellen dared to allow herself to feel excited. The office space she and Rose had viewed earlier that day was practically perfect, (apart from the odd car horn piercing through the single-paned window). There were four rooms she could work from and a list of possibilities as to how she could do that.

'We'll put heaters around the place,' Rose knew their budget didn't stretch to the premises' electric heating system. 'It will make it cosy and welcoming.'

And so, it was.

The following week, every free duster, cleaning cloth, eco-friendly cleaning product and spare hand available, cleaned and tidied the new office. From top to bottom and from side to side it sparkled, with neither a cobweb nor dust mite in sight. Ellen's feet hardly had time to touch the ground.

'All the fuss is helping keep me sane,' she told her mother over lunch the following week. 'I'm assuming that's a good thing.' She looked a little uncertain. 'I still can't help feeling so sad.'

Anna sighed.

'I wish I could tell you that will pass,' she soothed her youngest daughter with a pat on the arm and a reach for the butter dish. 'The reality is, like grief, it's always there. Time helps,' she consoled, 'but only to move our lives forward as we carry the memories that make it, with us.'

Fergal had absolutely nothing to do with the new business venture even though Ellen felt he may have at least offered. Realistically, they had seen very little of him since his departure, apart from the odd rushed visit to collect extra clothes or work tools from the garage. He'd made it clear from a very early stage that conversation between them was to be kept to a strict minimum.

'I don't want to discuss it,' he told her sharply when she tried. 'There isn't any point.'

The saving grace, however, (if there was one to be saved), was that his silence hadn't been extended to their sons. He was seeing them regularly if not a little bit more than he had, before leaving. Yet it was in this area that Ellen fretted the most.

'James is quieter,' Ellen felt concerned, 'and Matt's talking of part-time work to help with the finances. His school work is bound to suffer.'

'These are their lessons to learn from too,' Anna reminded Ellen. 'Support them with a hug or give them the chance to chat if needed,' she continued. 'You must detach and let each of the boys handle it the way they see fit. Anyway,' wise words from a wise woman, 'if they see you doing okay, and if you are, that's quite a gift to give any child.'

'I know you're right,' she told Anna, close to more tears. 'Yet it doesn't stop me wanting to kick Fergal's shins or shave his hair off for doing it to them!'

'I understand that completely, but please don't.'

CHAPTER FORTY-SEVEN

Anna, Rose and Kate, along with everyone else present, braced themselves as Gemma struggled to uncork the sparkling wine.

'For the love of woman and country,' Maeve warned fearfully. 'Hold the bottle in the other direction or we'll lose our eyes.'

'Just be glad you're having a glass of it,' Gemma told her aunt sternly. 'There isn't enough to go around us all.' She'd been the one in charge of its purchase so the smallest and cheapest one it was.

'Speech!' The family and friends gathered turned expectantly towards Ellen, glasses filled with a mouthful of crackling bubbles each, demanding she play host. Ellen felt touched and actually told them all so.

'I'm really touched to have you all as part of this new venture,' Ellen told the smiling faces and Rose's in particular. 'I wouldn't be here today without your help. Now,' Ellen warned, taking a sip from her own tall glass and wanting to spit it back out. 'Drink up and get going,' she spluttered from the effect. 'My first client arrives in an hour.'

Matt and James were the last to leave.

'We're very proud of you,' Matt hugged his mother, developing the role of spokesperson for his brother and himself. 'It's taken guts to do what you've done.'

Ellen agreed.

'I may not be blessed with patience,' she admitted to her son's' nodded agreement. 'But I've plenty of courage. Thanks to you both, and the support you've given though. Without us working together, this wouldn't have happened.'

'And Rose's bank balance.'

'Yes, that too.'

'Here,' James handed Ellen a piece of paper, as both boys began their short walk home. They'd plans to order pizza with their father's recently left behind credit card. 'It's the suggestions you asked me for.' The creative Pisces mind rarely failed to deliver. 'One might suit for helping to name this place.'

Ellen read James' suggestions after he'd left and selected her choice from his list. With incense burning and soft Angelic music gliding from the corner of the room, she meditated.

She felt contentment for the first time in a long time. This whole venture felt right like it was meant to be. It was scary of course, but in keeping with what needed to happen.

'Welcome,' she greeted Derek McAllister twenty minutes later, with a smile and gift voucher for a return free-of-charge visit. 'You're the first client to come into

Whispers Spiritual Counselling and Wellness Centre. I hope your visit is all you want it to be.'

The developing journey had just taken a huge leap forward. It felt liberating.

That was that. And so, it was.